Additional praise for

PIECE OF MIND

"A moving story of grief, resilience, and self-actualization. . . . Adelman fully inhabits Lucy's voice, and the resulting tale is as realistic as it is uplifting." —*Publishers Weekly*, starred review

"Lucy's narrative is sensitive, witty, and illuminating; . . . excellently drawn. Her journey and the evolution of her relationships offer a rare glance at the unknowable."

—*Library Journal*, starred review

"*Piece of Mind* is such a beautiful debut, one that will indelibly imprint the reader with Lucy's unique voice and vision. She channels the raw states of grief and joy and bewilderment with such a pure-hearted intensity. Her New York is a flickery frontier, exciting and scary, where she toggles between states of numbness and excruciating sensitivity. Michelle Adelman is so articulate about what we know and cannot say, what we can barely stand to know, and what we bravely face each day as individuals in families, together and alone."

—Karen Russell, author of *Swamplandia!*

"From the first page of *Piece of Mind,* I fell in love with Lucy, its quirky, brave, funny heroine. And that feeling grew as she navigates her changing, often confusing, world. Michelle Adelman has created an unforgettable character and an unforgettable story."

—Ann Hood,
author of *An Italian Wife* and *The Knitting Circle*

PIECE
OF
MIND

PIECE
OF
MIND

A NOVEL

MICHELLE ADELMAN

W. W. NORTON & COMPANY

INDEPENDENT PUBLISHERS SINCE 1923

NEW YORK LONDON

For information about permission to reproduce selections from this
book, write to Permissions, W. W. Norton & Company, Inc.,
500 Fifth Avenue, New York, NY 10110

For information about special discounts for bulk purchases,
please contact W. W. Norton Special Sales at
specialsales@wwnorton.com or 800-233-4830

Manufacturing by Quad Graphics Fairfield
Book design by Fearn Cutler de Vicq
Production manager: Anna Oler

Library of Congress Cataloging-in-Publication Data

Adelman, Michelle.
Piece of mind : a novel / Michelle Adelman.—First edition.
pages cm
ISBN 978-0-393-24570-7 (hardcover)
1. Young women—Family relationships—Fiction. 2. Domestic fiction.
I. Title.
PS3601.D4667P54 2016
813'.6—dc23

2015032331

ISBN 978-0-393-35355-6 pbk.

W. W. Norton & Company, Inc.
500 Fifth Avenue, New York, N.Y. 10110
www.wwnorton.com

W. W. Norton & Company Ltd.
15 Carlisle Street, London W1D 3BS

1 2 3 4 5 6 7 8 9 0

For my sister, Caren

The trees that are slow to grow bear the best fruit.

—MOLIÈRE, *The Imaginary Invalid*

PIECE
OF
MIND

1

I WAS BRAIN INJURED BEFORE IT WAS TRENDY. BEFORE THE football players and the boxers and the soldiers started coming out. Before other families emerged to talk about the devastation, before common people started looking for answers. I wasn't hit by shrapnel or gunfire, by a fist or a flying object. I was knocked unconscious by pavement and a wheel, by a driver who wasn't paying attention. By accident.

I have no memory of before. For me, it all started after.

I was hit by a truck. My neck snapped, my brain shook, and I almost died. I was three. Dad believed I was destined to live; in part because the day it happened, it was Tu B'Shevat, the Jewish festival of the trees, and according to some rabbinic law he read, fruit from a tree isn't supposed to be eaten in the tree's first three years of life. In its fourth year, it goes to God, and after that, anyone can eat it.

I was a couple of weeks from my fourth birthday, so maybe on that day I was a piece of fruit, and my soul was still mine. Maybe for a moment I was one with a tree. At times I thought I almost remembered looking up and melding into branches, if only for a second—long enough to feel the leaves tickle, to hear the whisper of the birds, to be spared.

But then, people sometimes feel things when certain parts of the brain are stimulated—an otherworldly presence, supernatural power, supreme calm. A few years ago, I was in a traumatic brain injury group with a girl who saw Jesus every time she had magnet therapy.

Maybe my savior was a tree.

2

IT WAS THE WEEKEND BEFORE THE START OF SUMMER WHEN things started spiraling. It was hotter than usual, slightly more humid, but other than that, the day began pretty typically.

On Friday morning, Dad and I had coffee. It was almost the same routine as every other day, the two of us sitting at the kitchen table before he went out to run errands, or go to meetings, or whatever else he did for the day, before I was supposed to hunt for a job, or get dropped off at a doctor's office, or, once in a while, go to Manhattan with him. I was supposed to be preparing for an interview, though I couldn't think about doing anything before my coffee fix.

No one could brew it the way he could, with a pinch too much cinnamon, extra strength for impact. It was an aroma I didn't tire of, the perfect temperature to warm the chill. Even on the sunniest days it was drafty in that house, a little dark.

I PROBABLY SHOULD have sat facing him rather than the window, so he wouldn't have had to compete with the diversions outside—those blond, unblemished kids riding their Big

Wheels, the construction going on at the bottom of the cul-de-sac; the two squirrels scampering through the trees; and Nugget, the retriever from across the way, waiting for me on the fringe of our yard, ready to play.

They would all have to wait for Dad to finish talking about miracles. He believed in those things, and in grand schemes. The lottery. Organized religion. Me.

I wasn't sure what I believed in. Comic books. Certain superpowers. A sixth sense for animals and toddlers and some people. Caffeine.

"There's a terrific article on that talk-show host who survived a motorcycle accident," he said, nodding at the *Times* sitting beneath my Batman mug. "Did you catch it?"

"No. Should I read it?"

"Not should, must. The doctors said they never saw anything like it. Nobody thought she had a prayer, but she zipped through the entire recovery process. Unbelievable."

I took a swig and examined a picture of the host sitting on an Adirondack chair on the porch of a stately house. Everything appeared orderly—her makeup, hair, the newly stained deck. I wondered what was in the back of her closet.

"You think she saw white light?"

I thought I might have, even though I couldn't really have remembered—not something so long ago, or so traumatic. Maybe what I remembered was seeing the sun peeking through those branches. Maybe that's what I wanted to remember.

"You'd have to ask her," he said. "In fact—you know what? You should write her a letter."

"Yeah, right."

I spilled a little coffee as I was putting down my cup. There were already so many stains and rings on the table that it hardly mattered.

"Why not?" he said, handing me a napkin. "She'd love to hear from another person who suffers from a brain injury, might even put you on her show. Have you seen her show?"

"Of course I've seen it. I've seen them all."

He looked at me.

"While I'm getting ready for the day, I mean. That's what I watch. Background noise? She's too brainy to pander, but she doesn't understand how to talk to her audience."

"It wouldn't hurt to send her a note. She could launch your career."

"What career?"

I got up abruptly for a refill, but that didn't stop him. He kept going from across the kitchen.

"You have a lot in common," he said.

"As talk-show hosts? I hope you're kidding because there's no way—"

"She runs a wildlife charity."

I turned around. "She does?"

"Sure she does. And she's had a long history of volunteering her time at the zoo."

"I doubt that. I doubt she spends her time getting her hands dirty in between takes."

"Not now. It's how she got her start. Read the piece!"

"I will, but if you think she personally reads her letters, you're dreaming!"

"Fine, so forget the letter. Forget I ever mentioned her." He checked his watch. "Let's get down to business."

When I resumed my place at the table, he handed me an envelope, references he'd written himself, names of old friends signed at the bottom. This was how it worked with each new job prospect, tiny alterations with every new want ad. I was supposed to be working toward teaching, aiding in the classroom. I could do that, technically, on paper. I made it through high school, and even college (in seven years), where I took a lot of art classes and majored in education. I liked art, and I liked kids, so teaching seemed to make sense, even though I never got the credential. I was qualified. If only I had that switch good teachers had, the one that gave them the ability to lead and delegate; to move forward, in straight lines; to stay on task; to be prepared with extra handouts; to know just when to hug the kid who was having an off day.

I was that kid. I was the one who moved sideways, lagged behind, forgot my buddy in the partner system and lost the group.

The one time I subbed (for the one principal who was willing to give me a chance), I lost the roll-call sheet within the first hour. And one of the students during lunch. And the job by the end of the week.

It was probably because I didn't have executive functions—which, among other basic skills, relate to organizing, prioritizing, reasoning, disciplining, goal setting, time managing, decision making, and impulse control. In a file somewhere there's a report from the neuropsychologist who evaluated me. *My executive function is severely impaired due to frontal-lobe injury.*

When I pictured the inside of my head, I didn't see a lot of gray.

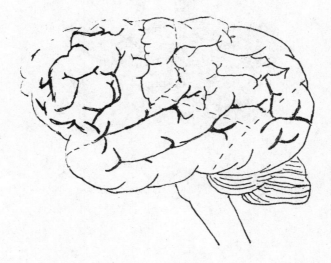

This is a normal brain.

When I pictured my brain, I saw a pinball machine lit up with pockets of potential; if you hit certain levers in particular spots, you could unlock special doors and this flood of creativity, or conversation, or crying might pour out. The rest of the board was filled with dead zones, where the lights were dimmed—where all of the functions I didn't have, all of the could-have-beens, lay dormant.

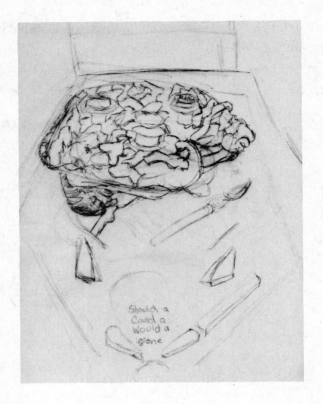

This is my brain.

"So," Dad said. "Are you ready for the interview?"

It was another teaching position. I took a breath, and then a sip.

There were parts of this job that seemed tailored to my skills. Because I did understand the keys to coloring outside the lines, grasped why the graham-cracker-apple-juice ritual mattered, and needed and loved reading those storybooks as much as any child could. The pictures came first. I got that.

Arts and crafts I could do well. I knew how to make a mess with clay and paints and sand. If I could have found a job that allowed me to play all day, that would have been perfect. If the hours were flexible enough. And I didn't have to be there all the time. If I never had to clean up.

"I was trying to find my special interview outfit this morning when I realized Harry had one of my shoes," I said. "Sometimes I wonder if he has a dog complex. You think I should buy him some cat toys, so he doesn't get confused?"

I motioned to take a sip of coffee. "Is there more in the pot?" I got up and brought it over. "You want more?"

"In a minute." He'd only taken a couple of sips. "So you have the shoe now?"

"Yeah."

"And when exactly is the interview?"

"I guess I'm supposed to call."

"But you haven't yet?"

"No, because it's really far away. And besides . . ."

"Besides what?"

"I'll never get it anyway," I mumbled.

"What?" When he was annoyed, he claimed he couldn't hear me. "What are you saying?"

"Can we change the subject? I'm done with this."

"You're done with this? Then what are we doing here?"

I wasn't sure, actually. So many times I wanted to ask him if we could start over, to tell him to stop marking up the classifieds with hopeless red stars and circles, to help me find a new path that didn't involve the switch, that maybe didn't involve a job either.

But then we would have had to consider an alternative—a route that accepted my limitations, one that was different from his, and everyone else's we knew—and we couldn't do that then because admitting defeat meant giving in to disability. It was okay being known as someone who was a little different, or who marched to the beat of her own drum, or who had been through a lot, as long as she had other things going for her too ("clever," "talented," "funny," "and so on," according to Dad.)

"Challenging," sure, maybe even "challenged," but never disabled.

The job search had been an integral piece of our morning ritual for two years, ever since I had finished my coursework. It was a complex exchange full of limited expectation, consistent disappointment, generalized coddling, and overall dysfunction. But it was comfortable.

Not that I could have articulated any of that to him then.

"I don't know why we keep doing this," I said.

He peered into my empty mug. "Take the last of it."

After he poured the remains, he peeked at his wrist again and said he had to go. Some kind of sales call, he said. For what, exactly, I wasn't sure. The focus of our talks was never on him.

"I'm putting this first on today's list: I want you to call that woman to see if you can set something up. Ask her when, at her convenience, she might be able to squeeze in fifteen or twenty minutes to talk to you—"

"I know what to say," I said, because I wasn't planning on calling, and because: Do you realize how old I am?

I was what, twenty-seven? I didn't want to remind either of us of that, and not of his age either—forever oldish, it seemed. I turned away whenever he winced going up or down stairs, when he ran out of breath.

He kissed the crown of my head on his way out, and I watched his car fade beyond the driveway.

3

When Dad left, I scanned the refrigerator, the regular spot where the schedule was posted, underneath the same dirty magnet we couldn't bear to part with (a faded image of Wonder Woman that Mom had picked up years earlier), and I took it in:

1. Call woman for interview!

Of course he included an exclamation mark, and of course it was first on the list, because it was the last thing I wanted to do.

Maybe later. Maybe after I did some research on that talk-show host. I wanted to read that article he had left for me. It would be interesting to see if she really had a brain injury, or if it was only a concussion. I could watch her show and see if I could make a diagnosis. That seemed like the right thing to do. At least then I could give Dad a more detailed evaluation of her performance.

If I was going to watch TV, though, I would have to see what else was on, which meant I wouldn't be able to turn away—no matter how ridiculous the talk-show topic, or how poorly animated the daytime cartoon, and it was already getting late.

Maybe if I was going to watch, I could stick to educational programming, like Animal Planet, to learn more about animals' natural movements and impulses, to better understand their bone and muscle structure.

This would help me practice some of my animal whispering and sketching skills on Harry, or Nugget, who was still waiting for me to play outside. But before I could play, I'd have to shower. What number was that on the list? Four? I wasn't there yet.

2. Take pills.

Done. Obviously.

There was the Imitrex and Inderal for my massive migraines, and the Effexor to address my depression. I'd tried all of the SSRIs at different times, in different doses, until I found a cocktail that worked. Severe depression didn't necessarily run in the family, but it did tend to run in brain-injury groups. So not only was my head dented, but it was also chemically imbalanced, which presented a whole new set of issues—moodiness, irritability, lack of motivation, feelings of helplessness, extreme fatigue, lack of focus—issues that sometimes overlapped with symptoms of the injury, and had, in the past, warranted separate trips to the hospital, including a couple of stints in psychiatric wards (the last time was a full decade ago), and a general dependency on drugs.

The pills had helped stabilize my moods, even if each one had a side effect that thinned my hair and slowed my metabolism, which meant more drugs to combat those issues, which meant more dizziness, and nausea and headaches from missed doses, which meant more coffee to combat the headaches and sluggishness. Sometimes it seemed the side effects were indistinguishable from the injury.

Still, the pills offered me some consistency, which was preferable to clinical despair, and better than the hospital or too much time on therapists' couches, so I didn't have much trouble swallowing them. I had been steady long enough for my doctor to phone in the refills with a quick physical check-in a couple of times a year, and I only had to see a talk therapist on an as-needed basis.

But in the end there was no prescription drug, or behavioral therapist, or cognitive psychologist, or support group that could transform me into someone else. Because each brain is variable, and mysterious, and there are no quick fixes. At least that's what the doctors said.

3. Feed Harry.

Already done.

By all accounts Harry looked about average, as far as orange tabbies go, not too old or young, though he had to be at least ten now, not too overweight or too slight. He wasn't one of those adorable cats who somehow remained kittenlike into adulthood, but he wasn't unattractive. Some cats were plagued with disproportionate eyes or ears, or tails. Harry was just fine the way he was, with his worn coat and mild arrogance. I appreciated that he never pretended to be anything else.

Feeding him was the first thing I did most days. He'd sometimes mew, if he was starving, but mostly he just ate when he felt like it, which made things easy. I refilled his water bowl.

4. Shower and dress.

Clearly. Later.

Luckily, I never had any problem with these basic skills, which is why I never needed a home nurse or any real kind of help, why I was perfectly capable of being alone for long stretches of time.

So of course I needed to shower, but maybe I could go back to sleep first, just for a little while. I was beginning to feel sluggish. Or maybe another cup of coffee could do it, since I had held off for this long. . . . That would give me time to finish that comic book I'd found in the basement the other day, or the rest of the newspaper Dad left out. And actually, it was time for lunch, almost. Soon enough.

So I'd come back to number 4.

5. Find clothes for potential interview in the future.

Fine. I could play along with the charade as well as he could.

I went to my room and examined the mess. Clothes were everywhere—spilling from the closet; exploding out of the chests of drawers; on the floor, mingled with cat hair and dust; on the bed, where I would sometimes put them after I picked them up from the floor. There were a few things that were hanging, but they were smooshed and musty and moth-eaten and probably needed to be cleaned.

I tried to fold a few shirts, a pair of pants, attempted to begin to organize my closet. But folding well required fine motor skills, and I didn't have them. My hands were weak. I wasn't able to make a tight fist or maneuver my fingers in precise movements (except sometimes with a charcoal pencil or paintbrush), so I did the best I could with broad, sweeping motions. Mostly what happened was my folds became clumps. Again, and again. This made me want to rip the clothes apart, to throw them at the ground and at the bed, to leave them everywhere, which made them especially hard to find when I needed them.

There was a black skirt in the back of my closet I could probably use. And there was a blue shirt hanging next to it. It was only slightly stained on the sleeve, just a splash of coffee I could cover up—there were no light colors in my wardrobe; I knew better—but this shirt was too wrinkled for an interview.

The iron was in the linen closet, but we didn't have an ironing board, or a lot of other household items since Mom had died—the losses seemed to accumulate without our knowledge somehow, a new item disappearing whenever we needed it— so I figured I could just put it on the floor and work from there. It would only take a minute. But the iron got so hot so fast that it left a mark on the carpet, and when I moved the iron to the shirt, it singed a spot, and when I tried to move it away, I hit the edge of the metal with my palm, leaving yet another mark.

Now it was basically afternoon, and I still didn't have any clothes to wear or any idea of what I would say to this woman if and when I called. I could review my résumé if I could find it. I'd have to make sure I had a clean copy. That would take a while.

I could tell her about how much my art meant to me, how much I enjoyed connecting with kids over crayons and cookies, especially one-on-one. Groups were intimidating. Could I say that? Probably not. And I probably shouldn't mention that it would take me hours to get there, that the idea of doing that commute every day was exhausting. It was a bad idea to tell her how unpolished I appeared, no matter how much time I spent before a mirror, and that I couldn't find an outfit for an interview anyway, and that it was silly to imagine getting up early enough to try when it was already whatever time it was and I was still wearing my pajamas.

6. Do some research for more jobs.

Seriously? See numbers 1 and 5.

7. Think about cleaning your room. *Really!*

He always underlined that part, and always included it on the list, and I always had the same response. I'd underline *think*.

I had been told many times, mostly by Dad, that my room was hazardous. I could see how cluttered it was, from an objective perspective; he even took pictures once to make sure I understood.

"*Grey Gardens*," he said, waving photos in my face.

"How would you know?" I said. "You walked out after five minutes of that movie."

"I saw enough," he said.

He couldn't see how I could forget to close a box of cereal, a bag of chips, to put the top back on a tub of peanut butter. How I could let the toothpaste in the bathroom sit as it crusted over in the sink, and spill over the tube. How I could leave that hair in the drain, and never bother to notice the grime in the shower, or the mildew and the residue between the tiles, the water on the floor.

Reams of papers were scattered everywhere. Used art supplies and plastic tchotchkes were crammed into corners of my room because I couldn't bear to part with anything.

By the end of the day, the mess I made had spread from piles into masses, and by the end of the week, my room was a colossal accumulation of socks, magazine ads, broken pencils, action figures, and stuffed animals all collected to form my own private menagerie. No one else would be able to bear it, but this room belonged to me.

Every cleaning crew Dad had ever sent over refused to work unless I could first get my room into "manageable" shape, a concept I didn't understand. So eventually Dad gave up, and I closed my door.

I did sometimes think of what a normal person's list might have said, if I was another version of myself:

8. Pick up dry cleaning, or **9. Buy milk**, but I couldn't do errands because we didn't live within walking distance of shops, and I couldn't drive.

I had tried learning once, when I insisted it was important to have a license as a central rite of passage. But I didn't have a sense of direction; I usually went the wrong way, and I couldn't tell the difference between left and right. *See my hand? Look what letter it's forming.* It was an L, but I didn't see it.

Dad took me out driving once. We barely survived it.

So I didn't know what side of the street I was supposed to be on, I said, once Dad had stopped yelling. *So what?*

I guess for most people a sense of direction was instinctive, but I had to think about where I was going, and then I still wasn't sure, and you didn't have time to think when you were on the road with other drivers. So I never got behind the wheel again. It bothered me when I was sixteen and still had to get a ride from my father, and again in my twenties when I had to depend on my teenage brother, Nate.

But I couldn't help it. My brain was complicated. I couldn't blame everything on the parietal lobe, for example, even though that was the part that supposedly had something to do with direction (along with the hippocampus), because the parietal lobe also played a role in reading, writing, and drawing objects, and those were some of my best skills. Those were the tasks that didn't need to go on the list. And yet the parietal lobe also had something to do with math, which I couldn't do either. Dad basically cheated me through high school until I could meet the minimum graduation requirements, which is why I needed to go to a college that didn't count the math portion of the SAT, which is why there was never any math on the list.

Number 10 might have said *Cook dinner.* I tried cooking simple things like spaghetti or scrambled eggs or boxed brownies every once in a while, but Dad didn't approve. I tended to forget details, like turning off the oven. There were a few incidents involving burns (I almost always forgot to use a mitt) and explosions (tinfoil in the microwave) and small fires (small towels and napkins too close to the burner). Luckily, none of them were very serious, unless you counted half a scorched cupboard (that was what fire extinguishers were for), or half a scorched hand (aloe was useful), but they were enough eventually to steer me away from the kitchen.

Dad stocked the snack cabinet with plenty of cereal, peanut butter, and snack packs. He kept the refrigerator full of string cheese, hummus, apples, and carrot sticks. There was no danger of ever going hungry.

In the evening, most of the time we ate something he could heat up quickly, like frozen dinners or instant rice dishes, or pizza that he could pick up from somewhere else.

THE REST OF THAT DAY went fast. After a shower, I watched a documentary on the growth of the ivory black market and the devastation of elephants in Africa, made more coffee, read the rest of the newspaper, and found a random string for Harry to play with. It probably originated in one of my shirts. He didn't always go for the string, but this day he did, and that meant a little exercise for both of us.

Once we were sufficiently tired, we sat together by the windowsill and watched the outside. When I spotted a squirrel focused on an acorn, I grabbed my sketchbook. He was holding the nut in his tiny hands, gnawing on it piece by piece.

I'd originally discovered a penchant for drawing animals in seventh grade when I met Russell the pit bull, the dog who patrolled the house at the bottom of our street. Allegedly, he once bit a little girl's hand when she was giving him a treat, but I never believed that. He was a victim of breed profiling. And besides, no one came close enough for him to bite, except for me, the day he posed.

Russell, a guard dog known for his rigid posture and guttural growling, was always on high alert, but for the twenty or so minutes I stayed with him, he let down his guard. He stopped howling when he saw I wasn't going to break his electronic fence, and he even let his tongue hang out as I began to draw him. In my finished picture, I imagined him as the commander of an army, a leader torn by the honor of his obligation and a sympathetic will.

"Isn't that something," Dad said when he saw any of my drawings, but that time he added, "really."

As I studied the squirrel, I started to get inside his head, imagining his determination pulsing though my pencil. But just as I began to find some rhythm on the page, Harry leapt up from a dream and startled me.

When I turned around, the squirrel was gone and Dad was home.

4

Dad arrived carrying bags of Chinese food. First we lit the Shabbat candles because it was Friday and that ritual still mattered to him, the idea of bringing light into dark and separating the workweek from the weekend.

In the old days, when Nate was small and Mom was around, we'd have a proper meal with challah and wine, and an endless debate about the prospects for peace in the Middle East. Sometimes Mom and Dad would rehash the odd news stories they'd seen on TV or heard on the radio—they'd always heard the same stories, even when they listened to different stations or watched different channels—so they filled each other in and took turns correcting each other.

Most of the time they seemed to somehow balance each other—she with her pragmatic optimism, he with his quixotic romanticism—both of them with these bursting hearts. But on Friday nights, their dynamic tended to swing to one of the extremes: from joyful bliss to blowout. It was never clear at first which way things would turn.

One Shabbat in particular I remember, Dad brought home extra appetizers and extra sparkling wine and extra cake. He handed Mom an oversized bouquet with purple flowers and curled ribbon from the florist, and he kissed her, a real kiss, as he entered.

"Ew," I said. I was probably twelve then.

Nate was too little to notice, only six or so.

Dad created a spread and filled our glasses as he proposed a toast "to new beginnings." For a few minutes, it was so much fun, all of this novelty, all of us laughing and joking. I even got to taste the wine. But then the whole thing started to feel a little strange. It wasn't normal to have this many appetizers in our house. And we didn't usually make toasts before the prayers.

Nate said he felt sick to his stomach pretty soon after Dad raised his glass. Maybe he had an inkling something was off.

Dad smiled and took a sip of his scotch. "You ready for the news?"

"Yes!" we all said.

"I'm leaving my job."

Mom's face was white, almost instantly.

"Everything is going to be fantastic! I'm telling you," he said. "I've got plenty of leads for other things, much better things. Believe me."

"You're leaving or you left?" she said.

He didn't say anything for a second.

"With no discussion?"

"What's to discuss? This is a good thing!" he said. "I promise you it is. We're celebrating here."

She looked around the table and took Nate out of the room without another word.

She didn't talk to Dad for the rest of that evening.

Later that night, I found her sitting awake on the stairwell, staring out into nothing. Biting her nails.

It startled me to see her there. For as long as I can remember, I've had to get up a minimum of two times in the middle of the night—for water or the bathroom, or just to walk around—but it was almost always just me in those moments.

"Are you okay?" I said.

I'd never seen her like that. She worried, of course. I knew she worried. But not outwardly in that way, so I could feel it so concretely. Most of the time she was so joyful, so ready to laugh at herself, that you just wanted to absorb her energy by being near her. Everyone did.

I sat next to her, and she pulled me close.

"You want to know the secret of marriage?" she said.

"You think I'll ever get married?"

"I think you'll do whatever your heart desires," she said. "Just remember, the quality you love the most in someone is the same one that will drive you craziest."

"That's the secret?" I said.

"It's a good one to remember."

"Are we going to be okay?" I said.

"Of course, peanut." She took a deep breath and gave my hand a squeeze. "This too."

It was her favorite line: *This too shall pass.* It was cheesy and cliché, something her grandmother used to say, but it worked enough that night to make both of us feel better.

The roughest patch did pass eventually. After a couple of months, Dad found more work. He always went to some kind of office, first recruiting and then consulting before getting a job in sales.

But what does your dad do? Marni Masterson asked me once during lunch.

"He works in business," I said.

As what?

"A businessman."

It was all I ever knew. He didn't like talking about work, so I didn't press for more.

When Dad mentioned the office, it always seemed his mind was elsewhere—plotting, maybe, or daydreaming about the big windfall, the creation of his own company.

He never found another foundation position as good as that one he gave up.

The Friday-night fight became its own ritual, as Mom began to notice Dad's penny stocks, and then miracle weight-loss drugs, and pricey supplements with too many claims for healing taking up too much space in the medicine cabinet.

"It can't all be true," Mom said.

"But what if it is?" Dad said.

And then, one Friday night Mom didn't come home.

As hard as she tried, she couldn't plan for everything.

It was a car accident on a random day in November. There had been intermittent freezing rain. Road conditions were unexpectedly slick. The police report said something about a deer and a patch of black ice. She had been unable to avoid hitting either.

All of it seemed wrong. She couldn't kill a spider, let alone a doe. And it wasn't cold enough for ice.

For a while, I half believed some force was going to pluck her from her grave and return her to us. In the afterlife, the gatekeepers, or whoever was in charge, could have only apologized. *We didn't mean to do this so soon,* they might have said. *Two accidents is too many for one family. If we'd known how much you were leaving behind . . .*

But that was years ago. I was fourteen when she died.

Since Nate had left for college, we'd lit the Shabbat candles, said the Lehadlik Ner to welcome in the weekend, and then retreated to the living room to eat in front of the TV.

DAD POURED his scotch and grew progressively more vocal as we watched *Jeopardy!*. He dominated in any questions related to history, geography, religion, and science, but I always beat him to the buzzer in the arts, animals, and pop-culture categories.

He sat in his recliner with his legs up, Harry on his lap. He pretended he didn't like Harry, but he never kicked him off his chair, and they fell asleep together most late nights watching the news.

After Final Jeopardy, we cracked open our fortune cookies. *Doors will be opening for you,* Dad's said.

"You see?" he said with a big grin. "You never know what life will bring."

I rolled my eyes. "You're taking your fortune cookie to heart?"

"Why shouldn't I?" he said. "The cookie knows. Did you call that woman today about the interview?"

"I will," I said.

He sighed. "What does yours say?"

You have a yearning for perfection.

"Hah!" he said. "Yearning!"

"The cookie knows," I said. "That's what you just said."

"Well, nobody's perfect."

There was a lightness in his tone. He didn't mean anything by it and yet—

"I can be a perfectionist," I said. "You don't think I'm capable of perfection?"

He put down his cookie and gave me a more serious look.

"Of course you're capable, sweetheart," he said, lowering the volume on the TV. "You're capable of anything."

I wanted the conversation to end.

"Tomorrow's Saturday," he said after a while. "What do you say we feed the ducks?"

"What ducks?"

"At the Nature Center."

I couldn't remember the last time we had gone there.

"You can bring your sketchbook," he said. "And the doors will open for both of us."

5

On Saturday morning we were set for our adventure—after I had time to find and gather all of my things and figure out how to pack. Then after some cartoons and reading a section of the *Times*.

Dad eyed the stale bread on the counter.

"You ready?" he said finally.

I wasn't ready to get nipped by an angry duck (I had once been pinched so hard my leg was red for days), but the bread was gathering mold anyway, and there was something in his tone . . . Maybe it was because it was the start of the summer and he had an itch to get outside, or maybe it was because he was feeling nostalgic and he needed to revisit a place he hadn't been in a while. As regular members of the Nature Center, we used to go every Sunday, even when it rained. Or maybe it was the cookie.

"I could be," I said.

"Terrific," he said. "Maybe we should bring them a box of quack-ers."

I groaned, though there was something comforting in his corniness.

There weren't just ducks at the Nature Center. There was a whole farm full of animals—cows, goats, sheep, pigs, chickens, rabbits—all providing ample opportunity to draw, so I stuck my book inside my giant tote filled with dried pens and markers, and torn pieces of paper stained with crayon and coffee, loose change and collected buttons. As long as there was space in the bag for the book and a fresh pencil, the rest could stay.

Dad packed a picnic basket. Actually it wasn't a basket. It was a plastic bag. He held on to the "good ones," the sturdiest kind for these occasions. He loaded it up with cheese sticks, trail mix, apple slices, and sandwiches.

"It's too much," I said.

"Nonsense," he said.

"We'll never eat it all."

"We could get stuck, and you could get hungry."

It was useless to argue with him, and besides, within the first fifteen minutes of the car ride, I ate a third of the snacks.

"You're supposed to save some of it for lunch," he said.

"I'm car sick," I said.

I only ate it because he packed it. I was actually a little nauseous—I always was in his car—but I turned up the radio. We listened to the same newsflash every ten minutes, as though we were waiting for some kind of revelation to emerge from the static.

When we got there, it took us ten minutes to walk from one end of the parking lot to the duck pond. And then Dad realized we'd left the bread in the backseat. We'd do the feeding on the way out, he said, when he could park closer.

We needed to park closer because of his knee. He'd been a slow walker since I was small. I remember him playing tennis at one point, sometime around first grade maybe, but over the years his gait had degenerated into a lip-biting limp. We needed a handicapped sticker for his car, but he wouldn't admit anything was that serious.

"I just need to stretch it out," he said.

He'd been looking a little paler lately, slower even than usual. I knew he hobbled through the streets of New York, never complaining about any pain. He never took a day off work, never called in sick, never felt the need to see a doctor.

"Why would I do that?" he'd say. "I'm healthy as a horse."

Why are you limping? people said when they saw him after not seeing him for a while. And he'd laugh, but not really. He'd look away quickly and make a noise with his throat.

"Just a little stiff," he'd say.

I wished I could have driven, so I could have dropped him off at the front entrance, but he never would have let me drop him off at the front, and he never would have let me drive.

"Do you need help?" I said as I watched him struggle to make his way out of the car. It was too low to the ground.

"Don't be ridiculous," he said. "I'm fine."

"Fine," I said.

It wasn't like I was in a rush. I couldn't move very fast either.

When I walked, my feet shuffled, another effect of the injury. I stumbled, often, and I was unevenly balanced. My reflexes and coordination didn't work. I couldn't play a video game, or throw a ball, and I couldn't understand how to toss a Frisbee, but I could walk fine. It's just that I moved in a slanted line, so I sometimes bumped into the person walking next to me, which usually meant Dad.

"Sorry," I said, every twenty or so steps, but he'd just smile.

It's not like it hurt him. He was moving too slowly to get hurt.

We were a pair, the two of us, taking hours to get through any museum or park.

WE WENT to the museum first, a historic-looking building dating back to Colonial times. I picked up pamphlets on making apple cider and maple syrup, on constellations observable on common night hikes through the trails, and an advertisement for a special talk on African hedgehogs. There was a great picture of a hedgehog on the cover—beady, angry eyes, as though someone had lifted him from his natural habitat to pose for a stupid promotion, and he could see right through it. When I looked into those eyes, I could sense his frustration.

"Don't you already have that pamphlet?" Dad said, peeking over my shoulder.

"A hedgehog? No, I definitely don't own any hedgehog pictures."

"Did you see this one?"

"What?"

He slapped a pamphlet against his hand: WE NEED YOU! INQUIRE ABOUT WAYS TO HELP.

"You want to donate money?"

"No, not money. You! You could offer service and time! You could ask about volunteering."

"Why would they want me? I don't know anything about nature."

"Of course you do! Who's a more qualified volunteer than you are?"

"Anyone! But fine. I'll take the pamphlet. Let's just go."

He bought me a handmade candy straw in the gift shop, and we resolved to see some animals.

There were the usual cows, sheep, and piglets at the farm, but they all seemed to be hiding from the sun, huddled in little houses and shady spots behind stacks of hay. They appeared determined to sleep the day away. I understood the impulse, even if I missed the chance to interact with them, so we moved on.

The otter pond was always a favorite stop, as few creatures were more endearing than otters with dark, wide noses and watery eyes. Their fuzzy heads made them indistinguishable from the stuffed animals modeled after them. Dad and I could agree on that, but we had missed the feeding, so they were mostly in the tanks beneath the surface of the water. I took out my sketchbook and thought about drawing.

"There's nothing to see here," I said after a while.

"What do you mean? You can see them under the water."

"Those are rocks."

"Oh."

"But we can stay here if you want."

"No, no," he said. "We still have to see the ducks. Let's get otter here."

I had almost forgotten about the ducks. I volunteered to get the bread because I didn't mind the idea of a little extra walk, and I thought maybe I could grab a handful of the trail mix in the bag while I was there.

He didn't argue. He watched me shuffle the whole way.

On the way back, when I was almost there, I fell. I could have tripped on a crack in the gravel, or a misplaced pebble. Or my feet.

I fell a lot. I couldn't always piece together when the blisters had formed, or the green spots, or bumps, or cuts. I had once plunged through the floor of the museum house here, though I had seen the sign that said HOLE and had told myself to walk around it, because it wasn't enough to tell myself things. My body acted on its own sometimes, no matter how hard I attempted to retrain it.

The guard saw me and jogged over to help.

"I'm fine," I said, thinking everyone was staring. In fact, there were only a few people around, and they didn't seem amused so much as concerned.

That was the thing about people. They were willing to provide me with their helping hands when I had fallen on the ground. That was the only plus side of the physical effects. If people couldn't see my mind churning out distraction after distraction, squandering my concentration, they didn't seem to understand why I couldn't pay attention, or calculate the tip on a bill, or finish a task. But if they could witness the way my left foot dragged behind my right; and my clumsiness, because I couldn't stand straight; and my falling, they could feel some compassion for my differences.

Over time, bruises, cuts, burns and scratches seemed to hurt less. I liked to believe I'd evolved almost enough to resist the pain, as if I'd developed an extra layer to shield against real hazards. I'd adapted, like that lyrebird in the Amazon who could mimic the call of the chainsaw, or the gecko who could blend into artificial colors, the earthworm who could grow back its behind. They'd all found ways to move beyond humiliation. I could too.

"Really," I said.

Still, Dad limped over, as fast as he could, and yet slowly enough for me to have enough time to realize I had ripped another pair of pants.

"Are you sure you're okay?" he said.

"Yes," I said. "But look."

The bread was scattered across the ground. I had been trying to pick up the pieces when a couple of squirrels approached. One of them, a black one, stopped to gaze at me for a second.

"I didn't hit my head, did I?" I said.

I watched Dad look down to assess the situation. He didn't have his box of Band-Aids or peroxide to offer. He seemed a little short of breath.

"Actually the bleeding isn't bad," he said. "Your head looks fine."

When I sat up, I noticed the squirrels were gone. All I could see was hot asphalt, dirt, and rocks for what seemed like miles ahead. I could feel the sweat and dirt mingling along my cheeks, and the urge to shower was suddenly overwhelming.

"Can we go home now?" I said.

"You don't want to feed the ducks?"

"I'd really like to leave," I said. "If that's okay."

"Of course that's okay," he said. "You're the one who likes the ducks."

"Me? I'm not the one who—"

"What?" he said.

"Nothing," I said. "I'm ready to go."

Both of us were probably too old for the ducks.

ON THE WAY HOME, we made one quick stop.

"Just a minute," he said as he pulled into the corner store.

He kept the radio on for me, and when he returned, he tossed two packs of gum at me.

I could see he was holding a few lottery tickets.

"Did you win?"

"Three dollars!"

I wondered how many he had bought that week, but he didn't keep track.

"I have no idea," he said, backing out of the parking lot without looking. He almost hit a bike, and then a chipmunk.

I closed my eyes.

"What do you want for dinner?" he said.

"Didn't we just eat?" I said. "All those sandwiches?"

"Did you finish all of it?" he said.

"Not everything," I said. "But I had enough."

When we got home, I retreated to my room to read, and Dad returned to the living room, where he could put his feet up and drink his scotch in the glow of the Yankees game.

6

Rarely did Dad arrive after dark; almost never did he not call to check in two or more times before he made it back. But on Monday night, I didn't hear from him.

I checked the schedule. *Dad home 6ish.* It was six thirty. There were no notices on the wall calendar—no invites or special events hanging from Superman's magnetic cape, or Spider-Man's sticky web, so I sat by the window with Harry to look out for him during commercial breaks. I checked the kitchen clock, over and over again, because I didn't have a watch. They'd all gone missing—washing mishaps, strap malfunctions, scrapes—so I was always late, but now he was, too. Seven, and then seven thirty, and where was he? When was I going to eat? Was I even hungry? It was hard to tell.

I scanned the television for alerts of accidents on the tracks or holdups on the trains, unexpected weather patterns. There was no news.

When I returned to the window, I saw there was no traffic either. So I watched Nugget, my favorite neighbor. He was sitting in the last strip of sun on his porch, taking in the dusky breeze. I knew that if I could concentrate on the folds in his fur and the half-shut eyes, I could channel all of my energy away from Dad. My most powerful distraction: a sketchbook and an animal, a connection no television show could compete with.

I opened a blank page for Nugget and imagined him as an all-powerful retriever, the kind who could fetch people as well as bones, who could sniff out bodies from the rubble and run to the city to bring home lost fathers. I began to draw with supreme concentration, images of a new kind of superdog filling my head, and my hand, and my canvas. The Yellow Redeemer was born.

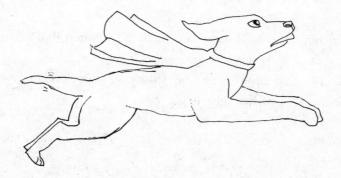

Just as I began the process of shading, the phone rang. "Dad?"

It was Nate. He had just finished his junior year at Columbia. He only called on birthdays and special occasions.

"Did you want to talk to Dad? He's not here."

"I know," he said.

"How do you know?" I knew something was wrong. I could feel it in the tingly vibration beneath my skin.

"Are you with him?"

"I'm not sure how to say this, Lucy, so I'm just going to say it." He hardly ever used my full name. It was always Luce, or Hey.

"Are you sitting down?"

There was no place to sit. In the kitchen, you had to stand when you got the phone.

"I'm fine," I said.

He took a breath.

"He's not okay, is he?" I said.

He didn't have to answer. I knew by his pause that he wasn't, and by the fact that he was never late.

It was a heart attack. He was gone before he'd reached the hospital.

Neither of us said anything for what seemed like a long while.

"I'll be home soon," Nate said. "Just stay where you are."

There was nowhere else to go.

7

TECHNICALLY, I WAS THE OLDER SIBLING. BEFORE MOM DIED, I was the babysitter on the few nights they went out without us. I was the one who taught Nate how to draw the perfect Snoopy, a U and P with a nose; the one who explained to him why most of Disney was crap. Though we could appreciate the doors the studio opened for the collective imagination, we could not get behind the saccharine endings, or the flat characters, or the dated standards of beauty and gender roles, especially in the earlier stuff. I was the one who made Nate realize that Batman was better than Superman—because he was known for his intellect, and he didn't rely on supernatural powers to win. Because Batman was real, and dark, and the darker the better, especially when accompanied by touches of humor. The more complex, the more interesting, the more it was worth investing in. I was also the one who told Nate how to embrace camp— from the Justice League to the Legion of Doom, in pet monkeys and Wonder Twins, and in the marvel of the Super Friends. We could watch without talking then, communicate in glances that only we understood. He had things to tell me.

Did you see him escape that death trap? Nate would say with his eyes.

"Like magic," I'd say out loud, and he would beam because he knew I understood him.

Sometimes he wanted me to pause so he could use the bathroom, or it was time for a special treat, or he was in the mood to read a book. I could almost always anticipate his needs based on the expression.

"Is this a good one?" he'd ask as he pointed to a comic book on the shelf or a movie on the rack.

"You've never seen this? You have to see how great it is!" I'd answer. Or, sometimes, "It's one of the dumbest things ever. You have to see it to understand how dumb it is!"

Either way, he'd sit beside me on the floor, legs crossed, ready to listen. When I laughed, he laughed too, and when I stopped laughing (which was hard once I got going), I'd look at him, this flawless little boy, and think I only wanted to make him laugh again.

It was around the time Nate was elevenish and I was seventeenish, a few years after Mom died, that things began to change. Dad told us to order pizza one night because he had missed his train, and Nate decided he'd rather have mac and cheese, so he made it himself—enough for both of us. He knew how to use the stove and how to measure out the butter and milk; he even added tuna for a casserole effect, like Mom used to.

He started bagging his own lunches after that, and asking for certain brands of clothes, and different haircuts.

Then there was that morning when I fell down the last three steps and caught him looking at me. As he reached down to help me, I noticed something different in his eyes—concern, sure, but also distance. Like he knew he would never do something like that himself, like he also knew he'd probably have to help me again. Like he realized in that moment how different we were.

Nate didn't have an awkward phase. He was unburdened by acne, inertia, chronic fatigue, loneliness, excuses, conditionals. He had a sparkling smile, was exceedingly responsible, and possessed a natural air of authority. By the time he eclipsed puberty, he started to appear older than me too. People always said that, that he seemed older than he was.

And what a handsome face, they'd say. Rugged good looks.

When Dad died, it didn't matter that Nate was born six years after I was, or that he was only twenty-one. We both knew he was in charge.

WAITING FOR HIM to arrive that night, I was afraid to move, worried that the slightest twitch would make the situation real. So I sat on the floor with Harry, clenching every limb, trying not to notice Dad wasn't in the next room at his desk, or fixing a drink at the bar, that he wasn't about to waltz in with surprise ice-cream sundaes, because, as he put it, ice cream in itself was cause for celebration.

When I heard Nate approach, the thoughts began to spin: What would he say? What should I say? How would this work? Was there a particular greeting we were supposed to exchange?

As I stumbled up from the floor, I watched him walk to the door. He was moving slowly, weighted down by a heavy backpack. Even with the heat and the sweat, his hair was short and neat, his T-shirt clean.

Sometimes I almost saw myself in him, in a funhouse-mirror kind of way. I was softer and rounder, my face, my body. His eyes were a little bigger, deeper brown, with a better shape to his brows, a defined jawline, perfect calves. He was taller, stronger, more toned. I had less hair, frizzy and scattered, and a redder complexion—marked by many more scars.

Yet I clung to a certain potential. A few years earlier I had wandered into a department store searching for a bathroom and ended up getting coaxed into a makeover from a Clinique counterwoman who had said "there was hope." Brushes, powders, liners, and shiners—I charged it all to the emergency credit card, figuring if I could just do what she did every day . . . but I couldn't. Applying makeup was a routine that involved discipline, planning, and coordination. I didn't have those qualities. I never seemed to have enough light to see what I was doing, either, couldn't stand long enough before the mirror to use mascara, got overheated in the bathroom from the steam, was always running so late I was lucky if I managed a coat of lipstick. So I stowed the supplies under the sink in the free vinyl bag, just in case, until the bag collected mold amidst a pile of curlers I'd never found the occasion to use. But I always remembered the woman who had said there was something there, in my face. That something might have been genetic.

Nate was eight when Mom died. At the funeral, he was a miniature version of himself, a tailored suit and tie, matching shoes. The women fawned over him at the ceremony, the men shook his hand, and he stood bravely through it all, never asking for extra attention.

When Nate was eight, it was already clear who he was: attractive, poised, comfortable. Some people seemed to have success written on them from birth, in their smiles and DNA.

I wondered if we would have been more similar had my brain developed the way it was supposed to, had I never had the accident, or the side effects to treat the effects of the accident, if he represented a male version of who I could have been.

Once he put down his things, we found ourselves in prime hugging position. It seemed like the thing to do, though we weren't natural huggers; neither of us knew how much pressure to apply.

He went in for a kiss on the cheek, but I wasn't anticipating that, so we missed each other, and then he pulled away.

"You look older," I said. I hadn't seen him since his winter break. "You look taller too."

"Still six feet," he said, making his way toward the living room. "Even."

He sank into Dad's recliner, which was dented from years of watching *Jeopardy!*, baseball games, History Channel documentaries, local news, and terrible late-night movies. Nate seemed too slight to occupy the space.

"It would have been nice if he'd warned us in some way," I said. "Like in a dream? As a cow or stalk of wheat. Maybe he did, and we don't remember. Or we ignored the signs. Do you believe in that? Or that he's here now, watching us?"

I wanted to believe that. To know he was guarding our spirits and our minds, our sleep.

Nate closed his eyes. "I don't know."

"Don't you think we should talk about this?" I said.

He got up and began searching the bar.

"It's kind of a big deal, isn't it? With Mom, you were so small, but this—it hits us both, doesn't it? I know it hasn't had time to hit yet, really, for me anyway, but you think things will work out?"

He poured himself a scotch.

"You drink that?"

"Today I do." He winced as he took his first sip. "How about you?"

I thought about it, to honor Dad, but it only reminded me of his absence, how much he would've liked to pour that drink himself. And besides, I wasn't really supposed to drink on my meds, or kill any more brain cells. I needed the strength of the cells I had. But I couldn't miss my chance.

I took Nate's glass and swallowed what remained all at once.

"Take it easy," Nate said. "It's not meant to be pounded."

"Oh well," I said, wiping the bitter spots from the corners of my mouth and my collar.

"Dad did a lot of stuff for me, so I just kind of don't want to end up on the street, if that's okay," I continued. "Because I think I would be if he didn't make sure I wasn't, and I know it's not your job to assure me that won't happen, but—"

"Luce, this just happened." He took a giant breath and poured himself another swig. "I literally walked in two minutes ago. Can we wait on this conversation?"

"Okay," I said, but my thoughts didn't work that way, in planned chunks. If it wasn't a pinball machine, it was like a solar system in my head, a swirling darkness filled with little constellations of ideas, loosely connected by random strings. I heard Dad explain it that way to a family friend once, as if he had been inside my brain with me.

"What did he look like?" I said.

"What do you mean?"

"You saw him, right? To identify the body?"

He looked at me and took another sip.

"You know what?" he said. "I'm glad you asked about that."

"Was it awful?"

"No, it wasn't. His face was all washed out, but it was almost like—the way his mouth was curved, it was like he was almost happy. Like he was okay with the whole thing. Like maybe he was going somewhere he was okay with."

"You believe that?" I said.

"I don't know, but I think he did." He raised his glass and took another sip. "I hope he did."

I TRIED TO stay out of Nate's way in the days that followed. When it came time to plan the funeral, he led all of the arrangements, got in touch with whomever we were supposed to contact, knew what he was supposed to say and how to say it, drove Dad's car wherever we were supposed to go. We had to pick a box for him, and a plot. We had to call people and identify pallbearers. We had to meet with the rabbi.

We said "we," but it was all him. I was suspended in some kind of fugue—sleep, dreams, nightmares—all the same shadowy haze. If I slept enough, I wouldn't have to think.

I probably would have slept through the funeral if Nate hadn't woken me.

He gave me only forty-five minutes to get ready. If Dad

were there, he would have given me a couple of hours, so he could have assigned me a special role, maybe a prayer he liked or a poem he found, and so he could help me remove the lint from the nice outfit he would've taken me shopping for the day before.

But as it was, that morning I had to sift through the pile of potential interview clothes on the floor to find something that could work; at least I knew the blue shirt was out. I couldn't remember if I had combed my hair. I didn't have the energy to scrub the toothpaste or Harry's fur off my top, couldn't find hose, couldn't make my legs any less bruised or gleaming white or bristly, couldn't force my shoes to fit my feet any better.

In the end, I settled on the wrinkled skirt and a dark sweater riddled with moth holes. No one else seemed to notice.

THE FUNERAL HAPPENED so quickly that I barely registered it had happened at all.

After the rabbi spoke, said some nice things about Dad's generosity of spirit and mind, his broad smile and kindness, his soul and fullness of life, I noticed a lot of people were teary and red-faced. Who were those people? I didn't recognize most of them. And yet there they were, touching my shoulders and covering my hands in theirs, kissing me on the cheek and whispering softly about mourners in Zion and Jerusalem, like their whispers could reach inside me and soothe the pain. Their pain was real. I could see that. Even Nate, who decided he didn't want to say a few words in the end, seemed shaken.

I recognized that I should have been that way too, but I

wasn't then. It was as if my emotions were guarded by a special coating, protected from reality.

It was probably because I kept waiting for Dad to come back, for him to bring around the car himself after the funeral so we wouldn't have to walk in our nice shoes, to unlock the doors for us manually, because he never got used to the gadgets, and then lower the radio so that he could suggest a stop at the local diner for homemade cinnamon doughnuts.

If Dad were there, he would have praised the two of us: for our poise and maturity, for planning such a terrific commemoration, for our unparalleled teamwork—we could go on the road with such well-oiled coordination, doing what who knew, but something. The Dynamic Duo, he would say. At it again!

If he were there, he would have wanted to celebrate our eloquence and dignity, to reward us for our efforts. He was always so proud.

No, we would have told him. *This day is yours, not ours.*

Nonsense, he would have said. *This affects all of us.*

8

AFTER THE CEREMONY, WHEN EVERYONE WENT BACK TO THE house, I escaped upstairs with Harry and went through Mom's old perfume drawer, the bottles that had never been thrown away, the place I went to mist particles of her in the air. There were moments when I could feel her suspended in the scent she wore on the day she died—hints of warm vanilla and lavender.

When it happened, she was young, in her forties, and full of life. That's what people always commented on: her gusto. Rather than walk, she did this little jog, with her head down and her arms in a tight swing—from the car to the post office, to the grocery store, to the bank and back—as if to squeeze out as much time as she could from each chore. People like that were supposed to live forever, or at least until their nineties.

So why then? What was the difference between an accident and a miracle, coincidence and fate? A second earlier or later in someone's thought process, a left turn versus a right, a decision to seek help immediately or wait until the pain subsided, a doctor who could work magic and one who was having an off day? Brain injured versus brain dead.

How was it fair that one family would have to distinguish between different "accidents"?

How could two siblings who were still growing up have to suffer through the loss of both parents?

There weren't easy answers, of course, which was probably why I could still detect her, why there were days when I could sense her hovering. It wasn't like I could hold a conversation with her, but I knew she was there, that she knew when I needed her.

She came back because she had to. I bet she fought hard for that right. *You can't do this*, she might have said. *You can't make me some martyr without my permission. This isn't about me. This is about them.*

Nate said Dad looked like he was at peace in death, but I couldn't imagine Mom was.

So she stayed. She stayed in whatever form she was allowed, the only way she could. She stayed without saying a word.

In the first couple of years after she died, she appeared with some frequency, every couple of months it seemed, maybe even more than that in the first year. I saw her full face, expertly dressed (always in her relaxed jeans and a pale-blue sweater), in her signature red lipstick, unmistakably Mom. But it was only for glimpses, hurried shots of knowing glances. I was the only one who could see her.

The first time I thought I caught her, we were at the Central Park Zoo. Dad had taken us there as a special treat, to help distract us after the shock of Mom's death had passed. Nate, at eight, loved the fact that there were wild animals in the middle of the park, but he kept asking to explore all of the hidden pathways outside of the zoo: the waterfalls and bridges, and the carousel he'd seen in picture books. I could've stayed inside the zoo all day staring at the different animals, especially Gus, the polar bear.

There were three bears then: Gus, Lily (who passed away in 2004), and Ida (who died in 2011). Ida was historically most prized and praised, for working the crowd better than any other animal, and for winning the specially arranged challenges—hidden peanut-butter treats and treasures buried in caves—two steps ahead of Gus. I had read books and any articles I could get my hands on to learn all about their diets, their histories, and their personal struggles.

I had also seen videos of polar bears playing in the wild, like giant dogs frolicking in the snow, and I was entranced by their ability to swim so gracefully. Inuit folktales posited that the bears were actually humans cloaked in bear suits. That seemed like a reasonable theory when they stood upright. They were a different kind of breed. They weren't as aggressive as other bears, and they tended to live their lives in isolation. Mothers abandoned their cubs around the age of two so they could learn to fend for themselves, though siblings sometimes stuck together.

Gus, with his giant white mountains of fur and enormous gleaming eyes circling through the water, was always the bear I was most excited to see.

The moment I saw him with Nate and Dad I felt a strange, tingling sensation, like I wasn't quite in my body, like maybe I was dreaming.

"I've been here before," I said to Dad.

"Of course you have! Your mother took you here. Don't you remember?"

"Of course I remember," I said.

It was 1994 when Mom took us that first time. I was nine, the same age as Gus, and Gus's neuroses were at their height. For hours on end he would swim the same lap, flipping from the same rock, emerging at the same time before beginning again. Some blamed his behavior on his captivity. Maybe he longed for freedom, maybe he was bored, or maybe it was simply his nature. For me, there was something endearing about his repetition, his inability, or maybe his unwillingness, to stop.

I couldn't keep my eyes off of him. When Mom asked if I was ready to go, I said no. I wanted to stay to watch.

You could catch him from two angles: one inside, near the bottom of the tank, where you could see his whole body if he stopped at the window, and one outside, looking over the landscape of rocks and his playground.

Mom wanted to leave. It was getting chilly, and Nate was fussy, but she said okay, we could watch from inside, because she could see how much it meant to me.

She let me stand in front of the tank window for hours.

Eventually, the zoo hired specialists to curb Gus's routine. He was given his own spa, new toys, and a redesign of his space. The key, they said, was to keep his mind and body active, and all of the therapy apparently worked. But over the years, you could catch him occasionally lapsing into old habits, as though he were reminding us of the true self ingrained beneath his fur.

The day I met Gus again with Dad and Nate, Gus was calm—a little older, maybe a little wiser. As we watched him from behind the glass, I didn't expect all of it to feel so familiar, to feel like she was still there with me—in the murmur of the wind, under my skin. I could feel her, even if I couldn't see her.

I knew Mom was watching with us.

After that, Mom and Gus and the zoo were forever connected for me.

THE SECOND TIME Mom appeared, it felt more tangible. It was in the midst of a fight I was having with Dad. He was going on about my sloppy homework and the mess in my room and the example I was setting for Nate. We were all in crappy moods all of the time, and I was in the worst mood of all when I saw her dart across my line of vision.

It was as if time stopped for a fraction of a second, and I could perceive this impulse pressing against my shoulder, beneath my bones, holding me in place. I immediately blurted out her name, "Mom."

"Are you okay?" Dad said, concerned maybe that I was having an aneurism or suffering from early dementia.

"Sure," I said. "I was just daydreaming."

But I wasn't dreaming. I could smell her, the lavender and vanilla, and I could feel her—the cool breeze on the back of my neck and the soothing presence. It was a sense of tranquility better than any sedative.

After that visit, I tried to search for her, but it didn't work that way. She only came when I wasn't expecting it, yet always subtly, when I needed her.

As I got older, she appeared less often. In fact, it had been years, and the last time, I wasn't sure it was her at all. I couldn't really see her in the same way, and I had never been able to speak to her. Still, I knew she was around.

Maybe she had a choice at some point: eternal joy in heaven, or whatever the Jewish equivalent of heaven was, or staying back. Just so she could watch. So she could say *I'm here.* Because she knew there was comfort in that. Presence. Sometimes that was all you needed.

I wished I could have felt her then.

Mom's approach was so much different from Dad's. Sure, we argued a lot because a brain injury is not an excuse for bitchiness, she liked telling me, and she could be bitchy too. But she also made me laugh, and forced me to open up, and to think: Why did I storm out of the restaurant? Why was I allowing my self-worth to be determined by a future driver's exam? What did I really want to do if I didn't go to college? She was patient enough to wait for my answers, which arrived sometimes hours, or days, later.

She listened without condescending, told me when I was "full of shit," and when I needed to "listen to myself," and never failed to produce her mantra: "This too shall pass."

Of course, I probably rolled my eyes, and then Dad would swoop in, as if on cue to explain it, because he loved explaining things even if he'd already told the story a million times, especially if he'd had a few scotches.

This was the story: King Solomon asked one of his advisers to produce a ring that would have the power to make people feel sad when they were happy, and happy when they were sad.

The adviser looked everywhere for this ring that Solomon

assured him existed. He had six months to find it. The day before his deadline, he went to see a merchant, desperate with his problem. The merchant took a ring and engraved it with the initials for the Hebrew words *Gam zeh ya'avo*. This too shall pass.

The adviser was thrilled. But when he brought the ring back to Solomon, the king was crushed. With those words, he realized all of the power, money, and success in the world were fleeting. All of his greatness too would pass.

Nothing was forever. Not the good or the bad. That was the power of the ring, the magic of awareness.

The telling of the story provided the necessary time for the words to sink in. Dad was right to make sure we knew what it meant. But it wouldn't have worked without Mom's nonchalant setup. He must have known that because after she died, he never brought it up.

After she died, I understood that life could be snatched up and stolen when you were least anticipating it. But I had ruled out the possibility that it could happen again. I had assumed Dad would be around at least as long as I was.

I STAYED IN Mom and Dad's room for a while after the funeral, going through creeky drawers, hoping to find something important. When I checked the area by Dad's dresser, I almost expected to find him scooping up the loose change, old receipts, and Megabucks stubs, and stuffing them in his back pocket. *This too*, he might say if he were there, because now was finally the appropriate time to say it. But he wasn't there, and I couldn't stay in his room without thinking of what was missing, so I went into mine and collapsed in the darkness, knowing no one would dare to brave the mess inside.

As I lay on my bed listening to the buzz of visitors in the dining room below, I closed my eyes and imagined he'd be back when I woke up, that all of this was another convoluted misunderstanding.

I slept with a pen so I could take notes, just in case either parent appeared in my dreams.

But in the morning the only marks were splattered on the sheets, mistaken leaks from the ink.

9

MARTY WAS DAD'S ATTORNEY AND ONE OF HIS OLDEST friends, and he'd flown in from Florida, where he was prematurely living in some retirement community. I refused to acknowledge him at first. We hadn't seen or heard from him in years. When we were little, he'd send us oatmeal cookies and Season's Greetings cards featuring Pomeranians donning reindeer antlers. When he came by after the funeral, he brought two loaves of banana bread and a box of chocolate lace cookies. He was a good man, but I knew that he was also the official bearer of my fate, and I wasn't ready for that.

"How're you kids holding up?" he said, raising his glassy eyes. He was wearing a polyester blend and a mustache, a grayer version of the man I'd seen preserved in an old photo album.

While I chugged coffee, Marty helped himself and Nate to the scotch from Dad's bar. Neither of us answered him.

"The best time for this kind of thing doesn't exist," Marty said, finding a seat on the couch. "But I have to tell you, that being said, the timing couldn't have been worse."

He took a sip.

"Because of me?" I said.

"No, not because of you, sweetheart," he said. He looked at Nate. "It just so happens that your dad took out a massive home-equity loan to get out of some other debt, probably to help pay back some loans, some outstanding credit card bills that had spiraled beyond his control. It happens all the time, this sort of escalation. I'm sure he would've been able to fix things if he had the chance, but—"

But, he told us, there were too many buts. There were years of accumulated losses, compound interest. He had gambled on bad investments, and in the effort to get rich fast, he had gotten poor fast. It was never what he intended, but it was the way things had worked out. No savings, no safe-deposit box, no adequate preparation.

Dad packed snacks for long days and road trips because he knew we'd get hungry even when we said we wouldn't; spare blankets for our chills, even though we'd started out being too hot; pillows so we could rest, even when we promised we wouldn't get tired; assumptions that we could count on him even when we thought we didn't need to. And yet.

Dad was a dreamer, as Mom used to say, so he probably believed he would win the jackpot, or that his investment in a long shot would somehow pay off.

"What about life insurance?" Nate said.

"Afraid not," Marty said. "He cashed it out to cover losses, a temporary fix."

"Didn't he have a pension from his first job?" Nate said.

"Long gone," Marty said.

I understood. I knew this was who he was, deep down.

But it seemed unfair that I was the only one who let mistakes spill out on my skin and my clothes, through my bruises and stains.

"Why didn't he tell us?" I said.

"What's to tell?" Marty said. "He didn't want you to worry."

Marty looked at Nate again. "You're not responsible for his debts. That you need to know. But the estate, the house in other words, there's nothing for you monetarily speaking. It all goes to the collectors."

Dad would've asked us to see the silver lining. But it was so hard without him there to point it out.

Nate scrutinized the bread as though it contained some secret message. That made me want it.

"Are you going to eat that?" I said.

"No," he said, pushing it toward me.

He began gnawing at his fingernails. "I'll get a job."

Marty nodded. "You'll have to."

"And I'll have to leave school," he said.

"For a short time, maybe. But they're understanding about these things," Marty said.

"I'll have to give up that internship with my professor, and I guess I'll have to forget about the band."

"Temporarily," Marty said.

"I can work," I said.

"That's sweet," Marty said. "But not necessary."

He explained that keeping my insurance plan and qualifying for disability meant verifying I was incapable of any kind of serious work anyway, which was something Dad and I had previously discussed in my effort to get him to lay off the idea of going on interviews and job searches. If I was going to get a job, it had to be part-time, and it had to be so low-paying that it was almost volunteer. Marty was the one who first mentioned this idea of going on disability in the first place. After Mom died, he wanted something sustainable for the future, a way for me to keep my insurance and a little extra income regardless of what job Dad was or wasn't working at the time. So at least that part had been taken care of.

"Then why do you care about me working?" I asked once.

"Why do I care?" he said. "Why don't you care?"

For Dad, it wasn't about money. It was about normalcy, or about the ruse of creating normalcy. I got that. But it was also about purpose. If I was going to be a volunteer, I could be the most important volunteer in the country, or the world, someone who could save the children, or the animals for that matter. Or I could become a prolific penniless artist, or a world-class teacher, maybe even a talk-show host. "Why not a talk-show host?" he'd said. I was funny enough, he'd told me. Funny and smart enough to be anything. And if I made enough money as a talk-show host, then I could pay for medicine out of pocket, and then who cared about the insurance anyway? That was the way he talked sometimes—in fantasies.

The problem was I hadn't figured out what my fantasy was, and in the meantime, we hadn't determined a realistic alternative.

"I have to go now," I said, banging my knee on the buffet on my way out of the room. Harry, as if on cue, leapt out from beneath the table and followed me upstairs.

I limped to Dad's dresser and held one of his Pick 6 tickets, examining the numbers. If only I could feel him somehow. I squeezed the stub for a minute, but there was no life inside.

———

BY THE TIME I ventured downstairs the next day, Nate was already scanning want ads and making phone calls. He moved the boxes of cookies and fruit baskets and all those fruit bouquets that looked like flowers from the table to the counter to spread his laptop, printouts, and notebook pages across the surface. Dad's copy of the *Times* lay beside the stack of sympathy cards, untouched in its blue wrapper, preserved like a prayer book.

"What happened to shiva?" I said. "Are we done?"

"We had a solid day," Nate said, hardly looking up. "Everyone paid their respects."

Some distant cousins and a stream of people who said they were old friends had showed, a couple of Nate's close buddies. The rabbi.

"But didn't the rabbi say it was about giving ourselves time to mourn?"

"We don't have that luxury right now," he said.

"Does that make us bad Jews?"

"No," he said. "That makes us responsible."

He must have called every person he knew, in some kind of special order, through a method of checks and balances, using a series of arrows indicating which people came from which other people. There was a particular way he answered his phone: *This is Nate*, in a deeper tone than usual. He changed his voicemail, and cursed at machines after he hung up, and in between phone sessions, he zipped out of the house to go running.

He looked different depending on the hour, as though he could pass for sixteen early in the day, if I squinted and focused on his faded tee and frayed shorts, and thirty later at night, if I concentrated on the tight hairs springing from his collar. I could almost detect the creases creeping around his eyes, the darkness beneath them deepening.

Wasn't it only last year that he spent the whole summer sunbathing, sprawled out on the roof? No job beyond some random house painting he said he was contracted to do, no plans beyond his beer, his guitar, and his friend's basement.

"You're tanning?" I said to him on one of those days.

"Just getting some sun."

"Isn't that how you get cancer?"

"Vitamin D," he said. "It's natural." He spent a few minutes admiring his forearms, holding them out against my whiteness. "Look how dark I'm getting."

I lay with him for a minute, if that, before the heat became unbearable. "You like this?"

"It's the best part of summer," he said.

I supposed that now Nate was getting his vitamins through his running, baking on the pavement while the roof remained bare.

"Is there any way I should be helping?" I said to him after I watched him zip through two phone messages—no stutters or pauses.

"I've got this," he said. "It's under control."

It didn't feel that way to me. There were no tasks, no lists to follow, or to pretend to follow.

I didn't leave the house, fearing I wouldn't be able to get

back in. If I lost my key, there'd be no one with a spare. If I lost my way, there'd be no one to tell me where to go. It hurt to get up, and it hurt to sit down. Everything felt heavy. Mostly I stayed in bed, absorbing sheet creases in my face, staring at the cracks in the ceiling. It would probably collapse soon, fall on my head and press against my skull. I could almost feel the strain against each strand of hair, the pressure pulling in all directions, the dull throbbing and pinching. When the roof caved in, I'd have nothing to hold on to.

10

AFTER GIVING US A COUPLE OF DAYS, MARTY RETURNED ARMED with a dozen bagels and a pound of lox. We sat at the dining-room table, where it was impossible not to notice the empty seats.

I savored the saltiness of the fish, comfort sliding down my throat.

"How're you doing, honey?" Marty said. "You hanging in there?"

"I'm here." I touched my head. It ached.

"Any leads on jobs yet, Nate?" he said.

He sighed. "I should be able to start next week."

I stopped chewing for a second.

"Already, huh?" I said.

"Looks like it," he said.

"That's great," I said. "You always get what you want."

"You think this is what I want?" He looked at me. "It's not what I want."

He cut his serving into tiny pieces, until we could hear the scrape of metal against plate.

"Believe me, I'd much rather be sitting here planning my courses for next semester."

"You'll be able to do those things later," Marty said.

"I know," Nate said. "It doesn't matter now. None of it does."

"How much will you make?" I said.

"Enough," he said. "I hope."

"Enough is very little at your age," Marty said. "What will you be doing?"

"Well, considering this economy, and my lack of experience and degree . . ."

"You're not going to sell your body, are you?" I said.

He smiled at me. "Luckily, one of my buddies has a cousin who has a restaurant. I told him I'd work any and all hours doing whatever he needed. They're desperate, so it's good timing."

"Good for you," Marty said.

I surveyed Nate's plate. He hadn't made a dent in his fruit salad. He caught my glance at the strawberry, and for a second we connected.

"Take it," he said, bumping it beside my bagel.

But he kept looking at me.

"What? I have something on my face?"

"Anyone need more coffee?" Marty said, heading for the kitchen without waiting for an answer.

"Listen," Nate said when he was gone. "We've been thinking about how to handle all of this."

"Who's we? Where was I?"

"You were here," he said. "Marty and I were talking when you were asleep. You were kind of out of it after the funeral."

"I still am."

"Understandably. But the thing is, if you don't have a job—"

"I thought I wasn't supposed to have one, for the insurance?"

"Right, but if I make what I make on a great day, living in the city—"

"I get disability checks. It's just a little bit, but Marty knows how all of that works. He can show you. And I'll get more now because of Dad and his Social Security. Marty said that. It won't be a lot more, but still. I can support myself."

Marty returned then. "We wanted to talk to you about that," he said. "Part of the reason I'm here."

He pulled out a brochure and handed it to me, a sunny display of smiling faces from every major ethnic group. There were printed schedules and routines, meal option plans, a room with computers in it.

"What is this, a retirement home?"

"It's for people who need a hand," Marty said. "And it's only forty minutes north of the freeway."

"A hand?" I said.

It was a home for disabled people who were handicapped, or otherwise severely incompetent.

"What the hell?" I pointed the fork at Nate and lost control of my voice. "You want to stick me in here?"

It wasn't the home that bothered me so much as the concept. "Disabled" conjured images of wheelchairs, palsy, spittle, thick glasses. I wore contact lenses.

My brain worked well enough to let me think and reason and understand things, and as freely as I could acknowledge why I had no job and why I lived at home, whenever I spent time with other disabled people, I felt disconnected.

I didn't like the idea of repeating my time in the special class with Lewis Lessen, the pale boy who threw up once a day, just because I didn't get math. I clung to the goal of getting back to the regular track, even if I understood that I would never be regular. As much as they teased me when my clothes didn't match, or when I tripped over their feet or back-packs, as often as they excluded me from their parties and their lunch tables, as many times as they actually pasted signs on my back without me knowing, and once deposited hun-dreds of pieces of paper in my hair affixed with gum, I didn't want to be special.

I preferred spending time with people like Nate and Dad, even though I didn't really fit into their world either.

Dad got that. That's why the job search had seemed so important to him. That's what I realized after the fact. Even if I didn't perfectly blend in, at least with my family I thought I always had a place at the table.

Until that moment.

"Are these people brain dead or retarded?" I said.

"Lucy," Marty said.

"What, I'm not supposed to call them retarded? You're right. I'm the one who yells at other people for doing that. Sorry. I probably do belong in that home."

"A," Nate said, "we never said that."

He slowed his speech enough to speak calmly and ratio-nally. I wished I could do that.

"And B, it's not a home. It's a community with solid facilities. They'll make sure you get your meds every day so you never have to go back to the hospital, and you're never in danger. It's peace of mind."

"Right," I said.

I didn't want a community. I wanted a family.

"It'll be easier on you I guess, on me too really."

I started to get up.

"Hang on a minute, sweetheart." Marty touched my arm. "We just want to consider all of our options in case."

I moved away from him. "In case what, I get more disabled?"

"Come on, Luce," Nate said. "This isn't all about you."

"I never said it was!"

"Okay," he said. He took a breath. "You're obviously not in a state to discuss this right now."

"I'm fine," I said.

"Listen, you have to understand that Dad did certain things for you that I can't necessarily take on."

"Like what?"

"You want a list?" He used his fingers to count. "One, he shuttled you around in the car. Two, your daily schedule. Three, your shopping. Four, your prescriptions. Five, your meals. Six, doctors. Seven—"

"I get it," I said.

He took a second. "We weren't prepared for this, obviously, and we just want you to maintain the level of care you've always had."

"You're right," I said. "You should worry about your own life."

"You're not listening to what I'm saying," he said.

I looked to Marty, searching for some element of Dad's parental perspective that would set things straight. But Marty didn't have any kids, and he hardly knew us, let alone how to handle us.

"Guys, it's a lot to digest," he said. "Enjoy the bagels, think it over, and I'll check in later. Nothing has to be decided now."

WHEN MARTY LEFT, I went straight to my room.

I imagined the people at that disabled home were nice, even with half a brain. They might have played checkers at night, and Candy Land, Monopoly without the houses. People there would think I was a genius because I'd have things to say. But I didn't like the idea of talking to myself.

I had joined a brain injury group once, thanks to Dad, to learn real-world skills and to become a part of a community. But the people in that group weren't like me. They all had different scales and variations of hurt. A couple of them had actually been lobotomized, and while I didn't blame them for that, I worried that somehow their missing brain cells would start infecting mine. I knew it didn't make sense, but that was how it felt, so I distanced myself until they accused me of elitism. Then I got defensive.

"I'm sorry if I'm not stupid enough to want to join your club," I'd said.

I didn't mean that they were stupid, necessarily, but that's how it came out. I said I was sorry, and really I was—"It's the filter!" I'd cried—but I was still kicked out for losing control, for what they claimed was one too many times. I felt badly that I had made anyone else feel bad, assuming they were smart enough to realize that I had been insulting, but overall, I wasn't terribly disappointed.

It was a little different those times I was in the hospital for the depression, in the psych ward. When we took group walks to the coffee shop or around the block, everyone stared at us like we were *Cuckoo's Nest* come alive, half-comatose and cracked, just because we didn't brush our hair or button our shirts correctly, because we had bigger things to worry about. But in the hospital, there was always an out, the goal of release—after two weeks, or four weeks, or once, even eight weeks. Back on the meds, back on routine, back to reality meant back to life outside of an institution.

Plus, I always had this feeling that madness was one with genius, with the best art, with deep understanding and connection to the world. Anyone who had any kind of a soul saw a therapist at some point, had a bout with hopelessness, got a little anxious sometimes. But a brain injury was something else. Because even those who were injured were all injured in different ways, and even if you could alter the brain's composition with pills, you couldn't necessarily repair broken cells. You could remove them, but you couldn't replace them.

Thinking about all of this made my head hurt. All I wanted was to go back in time. Back to before all of this.

I shut my eyes until I saw stars, tightened my fists, clung to Harry, and tried to summon Dad by visualizing him materializing in the humidifier. I would have taken him in any form then—vapor, ghost, insect—some kind of signal to let me know things were going to work out, that he was behind it in a weird kind of way.

"Are you okay?" Nate said. I had forgotten to shut the door. "What are you doing?"

It was the same tone Dad had used that time I told him I saw Mom peeking through the window one Sunday morning: mildly alarmed. He wasn't ready to hear the truth. He never was, so I told him it wasn't really her. It was just a squirrel that looked like her for a second.

"I'm fine," I said, but Nate didn't leave. "Did you want something else?"

He picked up an old copy of *The Fantastic Four* sitting on my dresser. It was between four mugs, a broken birdcall clock, and a melted pack of Trident.

"You can keep it if you want," I said. "The comic? Actually, it's probably yours anyway. You used to love that one."

"I did," he said.

He began thumbing through it before raising his gaze just enough to meet my eyes.

"You remember that?" he said.

"You were obsessed. I made Dad drive us to every store on your birthday—what was that, six or seven? So we could buy up all the different issues. And I tried to make the emblem on the cake out of that gel frosting, which ended up smudging and looking blobby, but at least the colors were right."

He finished going through it, and then nodded like somehow he'd found the answer in what he'd skimmed.

"I loved that cake," he said.

I watched him take in the space, the clutter, the mess. He

looked tired finally, as though he could sleep right there, his head sandwiched between two piles of magazines. It made sense; he had been running nonstop since he'd been home, but it was the first time I'd seen him reveal any weakness.

"That was really cool of you," he said.

"Yeah, well, birthdays are a big deal when you're little," I said. "Mom always said that."

"She did," he said.

"Every birthday."

"By the way," he said. He picked up a jar of Nutella, examined it, and then put it back. "Nice place you've got here."

"I wasn't expecting company. Did you want a spoon?"

"It's so gross it almost seems intentional," he said.

"Thanks?" I said.

He didn't say anything for a minute, but he didn't leave either.

"Nate?"

He exhaled, deeply.

"Maybe," he said.

"Maybe what?"

"Maybe you should come with me."

"To live?"

"We're not sure the insurance would cover that other place anyway. And the thing is, obviously we wouldn't force you to go somewhere you don't want to go."

"But I don't want to force you to live with me," I said.

I tried to make eye contact, but he was absorbed in the comic. It didn't seem like he was reading so much as staring.

"Right?" I said. "I mean, what do you think?"

"What do I think." He repeated the question like it was an epiphany, closing the book and sliding his fingers across the cover. "I think it's fucked up that Dad left us without a will."

"Maybe that was for a reason. Like he wanted us to talk, so we could figure it out for ourselves."

Dad always stuck me on the phone when Nate called, and made us eat at the same time when he visited, and compelled us to see the same movies and exhibits even if we couldn't agree because he believed if you forced the situation enough, it would begin to develop naturally. But what happened if you pushed too hard?

"The Dynamic Duo," Nate said. "He always wanted that."

"I'm surprised you remember him saying that," I said. "That was only when you were young, when I held your hand."

Nate searched for a second for a place to sit, but there was only the bed, so he leaned against the dresser.

"I'll do what you want," I said. "It's okay if that home is what you want."

He looked at me then. "What do you want?"

"What do you mean? In general? I don't know. It's good for me to be around normal people, I think. People with goals and dreams. People like you."

"Everyone has those," he said. "Don't they? Don't you?"

"Well, it's not like I want to be a doctor or a CEO or something. I know that's not possible."

"Obviously," he said, focusing his attention on my sketchbook on the floor. "But didn't you ever think about what you'd like to be when you grew up? A famous artist?"

"Not really. Maybe once. When I was in fifth grade, and my

teacher said I was really good and might even have a future. I dreamt about having a gallery show. But not since then. Not since I studied art with people who were really good at art. Then it just became a hobby."

"But don't you ever fantasize about the future?"

"I don't really think ahead. I mean, not like I see myself dead. I just always see myself this way—in this house. Maybe that's why I still feel like Dad's coming back, like he never left."

"But he did leave." He skimmed the comic again. "So what do you want now?"

I noticed Harry was hiding under the bed, and then I thought of Nugget and how it might feel to have him follow me around, to have an animal sense when I really needed him, more a companion than a pet, a playful youngster over a temperamental old man.

"A dog?" I said.

"Forget it," he said. "Anything else?"

"A normal life, I guess."

"What do you mean, normal? You have to be more specific."

"I'm not sure what you want me to say, Nate. What do you want?"

He took a deep breath and then seemed to take inventory of the room again.

"What I want," he said. "What I really want is to stop wasting time. What I want is to stop worrying about what's going to happen so we can get going. What I want is for us to get the hell out of here as soon as possible because this place is probably covered in mold, and I'm guessing each minute we stay here is a minute stolen from our life expectancy."

"Now you sound like Dad," I said.

"Start packing," he said, tossing an old T-shirt at me.

It landed on my head.

"You were supposed to catch that," he said.

"Are you sure?"

"Yes," Nate said. "Your reflexes should be better than that."

"You know I have no coordination," I said. "I meant about packing."

"I'm positive," he said, checking his back for dirt. "Let's move."

11

Nate's job would start as soon as he could get back to the city, which meant as soon as I could gather my things.

I knew this, and yet I spent hours walking in circles around my room, creating a path by stuffing things along the way into Hefty bags.

Nate peeked inside one. "Garbage?"

"It seemed like the best way to pool my things, since I don't have any luggage."

"Great," he said. "We can make a stop at the dump on the way out."

"It's not garbage." My voice was rising. "My stuff is in there!"

"Relax."

"No, you relax."

He sighed and began to head out, but at the door, he turned around. "No, you know what? Enough relaxing. It's time for planning. Here's what we're going to do: I'm going to pick up three boxes, and when I get back, you're going to fill them. But whatever doesn't fit in those boxes doesn't come with us, so you'll have to choose carefully."

"Why do you decide how many boxes?"

"Because it's my apartment. And it's hardly big enough for one person, let alone two. There's zero room for storage."

"Oh," I said.

I'd forgotten we'd be living somewhere else. Not just my room transplanted into a different home, but a new environment entirely.

"One box would have been fair, but I'm trying to be generous because you have so much crap in here. While I'm out, by the way, you should start going through it."

"I said okay."

"I'm leaving now."

"For the boxes," I said. "I got it," though I didn't really, because I had no concept of where to start. I had never had to pack to go anywhere for more than a week. And even then, we always had to stop at the drugstore first because I left my toothpaste or contact-lens solution, or shoes once.

As I began sorting through the pile that was closest to me, I found an old sketchpad and a box of crayons. I hadn't seen them in years, so rather than let them go to waste, I sat on the floor, fixed my attention on Harry sleeping against a separate heap of clothes, and filled in pages until Nate returned.

WHEN HE CAME BACK, it was clear that no progress had been made, but he didn't initially acknowledge that. He placed the boxes on the ground, reaching his hands out the window to feel for air. His collar was stained with sweat.

"Let's start small," he said. "Do you need that card?"

It was an old playing card featuring a small kitten curled up to a dog. "We might be able to use it if there was no tear. You think we could fix it?"

"No, I don't," he said. "Have you thrown away a single thing?"

"I'm trying," I said. "You can search the trash."

There were some pencil sharpener shavings, two old birthday cards, used tissues.

"Let's keep going," he said, using his shoulder to wipe the sweat from his face. "We don't have time to mess around."

"Okay," I said. "You don't have to be so serious, you know. You don't have to be an asshole about this."

He looked at me. "This isn't personal, Luce."

"Well, we're not going through your stuff."

"My stuff is all gone." His face was red.

"Fine," I said. "You can throw away the card. Just do it with respect, okay?"

"Okay," he said, and he took it into the other room.

But then he began taking my consent for granted.

"Those pictures are hard to find," I said, when he went for the old stack of glossy Wildlife Federation cards I had been saving to learn more about elephant and marine turtle anatomy. And then he threw away my favorite issue of *Dog Fancy*, which I liked going back to for inspiration in the animals' expressions.

"I need those, Nate," I said. "Those are models for my work."

"There's not enough inspiration in the twenty other issues we saved?"

"Twenty? More like two."

"Two too many."

When I couldn't stand it anymore, I tuned him out and entered into my own private zone—until he accidentally kicked Harry.

"Nate!"

"I'm sorry," he said, crouching on his heels to reach for Harry beneath the bed. "I didn't see him."

Harry scratched.

"Shit!"

"He's sorry," I said. "He's not used to outsiders. When you don't know many people, it's kind of hard to get them to come over."

He shook his head at me. "Aren't you supposed to get him declawed?"

"Haven't I done enough to constrict him?"

He huffed out of my room to find a Band-Aid, and he didn't bother coming back.

HOURS LATER, after I overfilled each one of my boxes, I caught him in the bathroom standing before the mirror examining his scalp.

"What are you doing?" I said. "Checking for lice?"

"I'm losing it," he said. "Just like Dad. Might as well shave it now."

"You're crazy. Your hair's still twice as thick as mine."

He ran his hand over the top. "It's all going downhill from here."

"You're joking, right?" I took in his profile—strong nose, cut jaw, thick eyelashes. This was his prime. "You can't see what's there."

"Nope," he said, taking in his reflection for another few seconds. "I can see too much."

He rolled up his sleeve and strapped on his music. "I'm going out for a run."

"In this heat?"

"Best time to do it."

———

NATE RAN FOR a long time.

After an hour and fifteen minutes, I pictured him lying in a gutter, bloodied and disoriented. In the suburbs, the streets weren't well lit. He might not have remembered that.

After two hours, I considered going out to search for him. He could've had heat stroke or passed out. He didn't have a water bottle. But if I left, I didn't want to risk him coming home to an empty house and worrying about me, and I didn't want to change out of my pajamas anyway, so I decided if he wasn't back by the late show, I'd panic, and at that point I could consider involving the police. But I really hoped it wouldn't come to that.

Because it was easier to imagine he was out fighting crime, donning black tights and apprehending criminals, or visiting Dad in a secret hideaway he had built to fake his death and escape his debts, or even just running for an unnaturally long time.

I took out my sketchpad and tried to create a SuperNate. I would've done better if he were a dog, but the likeness didn't matter as much as the concept. If he could run for this long, the Man Who Could See Too Much could pump up his heart enough to protect us against any harm.

I WAS HALF ASLEEP by the time I realized Nate was home—
sitting on the recliner, drinking a beer he must have found in
the basement refrigerator, gazing into the TV. He was sitting in
front of one of those fruit bouquets someone had sent, picking
at grapes.

For a moment, I forgot he had been gone. "You're home?"

"Yep."

He was watching Cartoon Network. *Justice League* was on.
"Which one is this?"

He was distracted. "I'm not sure."

"Maybe you should try to sleep?" I said.

He took a sip. "This is better than trying to sleep."

"I thought you could sleep through anything."

When he was little, he dozed on lines and in waiting rooms, train stations, and airports. In high school, he slept until noon on weekends, and until dinner on holidays.

"Not anymore," he said.

"You know seals only sleep one and a half minutes at a time? Half a brain at a time. Sheep sleep half-awake too, so they're ready to run if they need to. Do you need a sleeping pill?"

"Do you have one?"

"Maybe."

I got up and started rifling through old pillboxes.

"No, wait, I found some really old Valium once, to counteract the Ritalin I tried for focus. But I guess Dad threw that out," I said. "I do have some extra speed, because it doesn't work for me anymore anyway, you know, after I built up a resistance. But you obviously don't need that, and you're not looking for antidepressants. . . . Did I take that today? Yes, I did. Friday, right? I emptied out the Friday box. I'm good on pills, by the way. Dad stocked up last week. I have enough for at least two months. That's weird, huh? Do you think he knew?"

Nate turned down the TV. He was munching on pineapple and strumming his guitar. He didn't seem aware that I could hear him.

"How about Benadryl?" I said. "Dad used Benadryl sometimes."

He always kept his medicine in the bathroom, I told him, the bottom drawer I guessed. I could find it for him, but he said no, he would get it.

After he got up, I waited for him to come out. I waited for the shower to turn off and for the toilet to stop running. I listened to him opening and closing the medicine cabinet, and opening and closing the door under the sink. I waited, but he stayed in there.

I fell asleep waiting, watching the yellow light creep through the cracks.

I DIDN'T SEE Nate until much later that night when I got up for some water.

He was sitting on his bed sifting through papers beneath a tiny reading lamp, the same one he'd used to read his comics. There were open cans of energy drink on his dresser.

"You're working?"

"Making a budget."

I wanted to see what kind of numbers he was studying, but as I moved toward him, I knocked a few papers off the bed.

"What are you doing awake?" he said, reaching down to get them before I could.

"I get up a lot. I'm always thirsty. And I guess I miss him."

"Who?"

"Dad."

He closed his book.

"I mean, I know it just happened, and it's natural to be a little down. I'm fine."

"Are you sure?" he said. "We haven't really talked about it."

"No, I'm okay. I was just telling you why I was up, because you asked. Not because I want to bother you with it. I don't. Unless—are you okay?"

He took off his glasses to rub his eyes, and I noticed his hand was a little jittery.

"Sure," he said.

"There's a lot of taurine in those drinks," I said. "And caffeine. Tons of it."

"That's the idea," he said.

"Don't you have to be careful with that, especially if you're taking sleeping stuff?"

"Nah, I'm used to pulling all-nighters."

"Well, are you hungry? Sometimes it's hard for me to sleep when I'm hungry, so I was going to see what was in the pantry, in case you wanted me to check for you."

"No," he said, resuming his work. "I'm good."

"Actually, I bet there are still some snacks down there," I said. "From before. Dad always bought too many. I know there's still a lot of fruit, with the sympathy cards. And some casseroles. Lasagna maybe. People keep dropping stuff off. It's nice how they want to help us by feeding us, even if they don't know us or talk to us. Does it say they should do that in the Torah, you think? Something about feeding mourners to fulfill the obligation? That sounds like a mitzvah. Not that I'm hungry, really. I was just trying to connect, like over ice cream and cookies. That's what sisters do, isn't it?"

"Sure," he said, raising his eyes for a second. "I miss him too."

12

MARTY OFFERED TO DRIVE US TO NATE'S ON THE WAY BACK to the airport. It was essentially on the way anyway, he said, and we had too much stuff to take the train. Plus, we were a sad sight, the three of us. Nate probably looked okay, but he was dragging from fatigue, and I couldn't handle my garbage bag full of stuff, let alone a shower, and Harry, who was bouncing in his carrier against my leg, confined in a foreign environment. We weren't built for the train.

The rental was economy size, and it was extra-compact, with a tiny trunk, so the rule was that we could only bring what we could carry, and I had too much. Nate strapped on his backpack and managed my three stacked boxes with minimal grumbling, but I couldn't contain my bag. Things were falling out everywhere in the driveway, and on the walk to the car, I had to stop, again and again, to retrieve the dribbling cards, and pictures and coins. The fourth time it happened, Nate took the bundle from me. I was worried he was going to throw it all away, but instead he glared and hauled it over his shoulder, squeezing it into the back.

"Thanks," I said.

I'd thrown up on every road trip we'd ever taken, which is why we stopped driving distances over an hour once I was old enough to read, and once we realized reading only made things worse. This ride would hit right at the cusp of my limit, but I could handle it with the window open and Harry at my feet, as long as I had the front seat.

I could see Nate through the rearview mirror, pressed against the door in the back, his baseball cap pulled over his eyes so he could pretend to sleep while boxes pushed into his ribs.

"Sorry," I said, over the hum of the radio.

He'd closed his eyes. He might not have heard me.

NATE'S NEIGHBORHOOD was Washington Heights, or if you're a broker, Hudson Heights, he told Marty.

When we got out of the car I could feel the streets steaming. It was much hotter than it was at home, even though it was so close. I missed the shade, and the breeze, things I didn't realize I was missing until I caught the whiff of garbage mixed with body odor. By the time we started unloading our stuff, my hair was matted against my head, and the sweat was trickling down my shirt.

"You okay?" Nate said.

"I think so," I said.

He rested his elbow on the rusty railing of a decaying building. "This is it."

"Here?"

It was a dark brick prewar building, cracked all along the

edges, a ripped green awning, and a front door that wasn't closed all the way. I wondered if Dad had seen it. He must have when Nate moved in, though he had only been there for a month. Nate had told us over the holidays that his good friend and former roommate Byron could score both of them their own places for less than what the university was charging them to share. Nate had told us Byron wanted his own place because he was on track to graduate early and was already entrenched in the family's real-estate business. It was silly not to take advantage, he had said.

Dad agreed, but now the apartment didn't seem very inviting, or secure, or anything like home.

Inside the lobby, an open space with a row of broken mailboxes and a radiator, it was even dirtier. Not messy, how I kept things, but unsettled. The paint was chipping all over the floor, the tile on the floor was broken, and the ceiling seemed ready to cave. Spiderwebs and thick dust lined the windows.

His apartment was on the ground floor, and the first one you saw through the door.

"Is it safe?" I said.

"Sure," he said. "This is just how it is."

I wasn't sure if that meant everybody was unsafe, or if this unsafe was actually safe, but as long as he was there, I guessed it didn't matter.

The apartment was small. An alcove studio is what they called it, but it was more like an open room with a closet, a kitchen, and a bathroom. There was a thick wall separating a zone of the space to house a bed—almost enough to make it a one-bedroom, Nate said. It was pretty big for city standards, he added, but not compared to our house.

A black trunk acted as the coffee/dining table. On top of it sat decorative pipes, cigarette butts, and magazines featuring women in bikinis. In the center of the room was a fuzzy orange couch Nate said that he had found on the corner of the street. The couch was old. I didn't really care about that, but I did wonder what was lurking in the yarn, the trace of stale beer, the Febreze to cover it all up. It seemed to belong to someone else.

"It pulls out," Nate said. "It's comfortable. I've slept on it before. Though . . . I guess, I mean, if you needed to, you could take my bed."

"Me? No. I've slept on couches before. I used to fall asleep on the one at home all the time."

"We can keep your stuff in my area," he said.

His bed was held up by concrete blocks, so there was a bit of empty space beneath it, but definitely not enough space—anywhere.

"We'll make it work," he said.

Nate transformed the couch into a bed and left the throw pillows in the remaining shared zone as a seating area.

I watched Harry take a slow lap before settling into the sofa. His stripes matched the upholstery almost perfectly, like he was a part of it.

The adjustment wasn't as easy for me. I got up at least four different times that first night, and on each occasion, I wandered, unsure of where I was. I searched for signs of my old room—my paint splattered chest of drawers, the one-eyed giraffe I'd had since I was little, the fractured ceiling. Here there were new, unfamiliar cracks. Bigger ones.

———

IN THE MORNING, Nate's alarm woke me through the wall. A long beep followed by a staccato, followed by silence, and then another set. Snooze, I guessed. Then the radio. I heard the weather forecast a couple of times, and the traffic report, and Nate's grunting during push-ups.

After a while, he hovered over my couch until I acknowledged him.

"I'm off," he said. "There's a subway map on the fridge, and some cereal in the cabinet. We're close to the 1 and A trains."

"Wait, you're going?" I threw on pants so I could meet him face-to-face. "When are you coming back?"

"Late I hope," he said, making his way toward the door. "I need every second they're willing to take me. But your keys are on the counter. Get to know the neighborhood. You might want to check out the Starbucks an avenue over. They're having an open house this week."

"I'm supposed to get a job?"

"Well, theoretically, you could get something to keep yourself busy for a few hours a week, right? It wouldn't hurt for us to have a little extra money."

"I don't think I could work a job every day."

"Right."

"I mean, I wish I could, but that was the thing with Dad, the fight we had? But maybe part-time at a place like that would be okay, if their coffee didn't make me sick. Actually, I'd probably drink it anyway, because I wouldn't be able to resist, but the bitterness would never leave me."

"Fine."

He had his hand on the knob.

"Besides, don't they specifically hire people with developmental disabilities? I mean for that place, you either have to be super-competent, or super-disabled, don't you? Do you think I'm disabled enough?"

He was halfway out the door. "Just use today to settle in."

"Wait," I said. This was going to be the first day I was on my own since Dad. "I'll walk you out, to watch you do the lock? I should do that, in case I need it later."

It seemed simple enough, a little extra twist to the left, or was that the right? He had done it so quickly that how to turn it escaped me by the time he made it down the hall.

I DECIDED IT wasn't worth the risk to try to leave the apartment. I was terrified something would happen to me. Not that I'd get mugged or shot, or that Harry would get out somehow. But that I'd lose the key, or lose myself and not know how to get back.

I didn't want to break anything either—the oven, or the TV; I couldn't make sense of the remote control.

In the shower, I wasn't able to work the drain, so I left a mess of hair and a pool of water, and when I got on my knees to try to fix things, I banged my head against the bottom of the spigot. Sharp, shooting pain, but no blood.

I crouched down on the tile, rubbed my scalp, and thought about passing out. I wouldn't have minded passing out then.

I wanted to call Dad; I almost thought about trying, but that only made the hurt worse.

So I didn't move, but as my head began to throb, I began to sail outside of myself. The colors around me seemed tainted. It was as if the apartment were surrounded by the film of a soap bubble, and I knew as soon as I caught a whiff of vanilla that it was Mom. There was a hint of white space, a soft glow, a slight vibration. She was there. I was sure of it.

I had been hoping to find Dad that week, but in a way it made sense that he had moved on. All of his life, he was obedient to religious authority, so why would the afterlife be any different? If God, or some other spiritual figure, told him it was time, he would accept that as his moment to depart.

He took his Judaism seriously. He asked for forgiveness on every Rosh Hashanah, and fasted on Yom Kippur.

On Rosh Hashanah they will be written
And on the fast of Yom Kippur they will be sealed
How many will pass on and how many will be created
Who will live and who will die
Who in his time and who not in his time

He never talked about the concept of a hereafter, not even in the context of Mom, those times I'd said I'd seen her. He had always changed the subject in an effort to distract me, though I wondered if he ever saw her too. Maybe he did believe in a spirit world, but he just couldn't access it the way Mom could. Maybe he was missing that extra layer of sensory perception that would allow him to float between two realms. Maybe Mom was different.

Mom was the one who talked about believing in other-worldly energy, reincarnation, spirits. This one morning when

I was little, I remember seeing her staring out her window, vacant. When I asked her what she was looking at, she told me she had just seen her sister, the aunt who had died a couple of years earlier. Where, I wanted to know, but she didn't answer, and then she asked me what I wanted for breakfast, and that was it. Unless maybe that wasn't it. Maybe her sister was always there. Maybe Mom was too.

It was Mom whom I had seen before, Mom whose visage was associated with the sweet fragrance, Mom whom I already knew would've been the one to cut some deal to skirt the rules, to figure out some way back whenever she wanted.

"Come on," she'd say to the angel at the gate, her new best friend. "Let me go. I won't tell a soul."

Maybe you could see if you believed. *If you'll believe in me, I'll believe in you, said the unicorn to Alice.* Maybe that was all you needed.

Sometimes, when the brain was jiggered, you could swear the most outlandish hallucinations were real. I knew that, of course, and I knew too that smacking my head against the spigot had established another nasty bump on my head.

But this vision was not because of that. This was something else.

Mom was back because she knew I needed her then. Not that I didn't need Dad, but Mom and I had already established this relationship, and with Dad gone, I really needed her.

She flashed before me dressed in her signature jeans and cashmere sweater and then disappeared. But it was enough to soothe my nerves, enough to reassure me, somehow, that things would get easier.

13

THE REST OF THAT DAY, I WAITED FOR NATE. I READ HIS BIKINI
magazines and ate cereal. I played with his guitar until I got
bored and feared I'd break the strings. Harry hid when I tried
to sing. I sifted through one of my boxes and spread my things
across the floor. But there were no shelves or drawers, no place
to put anything, even if I were a good organizer. I couldn't do
anything without asking Nate first, so I just left things alone
and waited.

It had to be close to ten when he startled me at the front
door.

"Hey," he said, opening the fridge.

"How was your day?" I said.

"Long."

"You were at the restaurant this whole time?"

"Yep." He grabbed a beer and began to guzzle. "Turns out
the manager needs a shit ton of help, so I volunteered for everything. If I do enough, I should be able to move up the ranks."

"That's great," I said. "Right?"

"It's something," he said. "Hell of a lot different from a
school day."

He put the bottle in the sink, and with the clanging Harry ran into the closet.

"What's his deal?" Nate said.

"He doesn't know you, or this place. It has to be weird for him."

I watched him drink more beer.

"I'm kind of hungry," I said. "Are you? I ate your cereal."

"All of it?"

"Sorry. I'll buy you more."

"Forget it," he said. "I'll make some sandwiches."

"Okay," I said. "I can help."

Peanut butter I could do, tuna if the salad were made, but I didn't quite get how to make grilled cheese. He slapped the cheddar and bread on the burner so quickly that I didn't have a chance to grasp it.

"Can I do anything?" I said. "I mean I'd like to help if I can, in some way."

"Just take a seat," he said.

We settled into the cushions on the floor and zoned out for a while in silence before he returned to the agenda.

"How'd unpacking go?" he said.

"I started, but I wasn't sure where I should put things."

"Maybe this weekend," he said, exhaling.

"Great," I said. "Maybe she'll come back when we're together."

"Who?"

"Mom. I think I saw her today. Has she been here before?"

He stopped chewing and inspected me.

"What?"

He began talking in softer tones, like I was going to break if he pushed too hard. "What do you mean you saw her? You mean you found an old picture of her, or you spotted someone in the neighborhood who looked like her?"

"Forget it," I said, turning away.

I brought my plate into the kitchen.

"Luce, what are you saying?"

"It's not a big deal," I said. "Maybe we could watch some TV."

He was shaking his head.

"What's the problem?" I said.

"Oh, I don't know, the fact that you're seeing dead people? Are you losing it?"

"No."

"Because if you need to see a therapist, you need to let me know."

"I will."

"Seriously. If this is the beginning of some kind of manic episode, we have to address it and get you in to see someone. We have been going through some big shit lately. It's understandable that it would be hard to deal with. Of course, it would be really cool if you could hold it together, but if you can't—"

"Forget it!" I said. "She's gone now. She was never here."

"You mean Mom," he said. "Are you sure?"

"I'm sure it was nothing, okay?"

"Luce, listen," he said. "I don't want to be an asshole. I mean if you're actually seeing ghosts—"

At least he was laughing a little then, and I was too, because it was an absurd conversation we were having. You had to see it to believe it, and there was no convincing someone who couldn't see.

"Can we move on now?" I said, grabbing Harry for moral support.

"Good idea," he said. "Did you check out Starbucks?"

"Was I supposed to do that? I thought I wasn't."

"Because you don't like the coffee."

"Because it would be hard for me to work there."

"Right."

"You don't get it," I said. "Can you imagine if you didn't have executive functions? You can't do jobs without them. I'm not sure how to talk to you either. I think that's related. How is this supposed to go? Us conversing as adults, as people who are supposed to know what we're talking about—big things. Do you know what you're talking about?"

"I'm still trying to figure out what you're talking about." He finished his second beer. "Just so we're both on the same page here: Are you telling me that you're incapable of work? Not that you don't want to, or that you're too tired to, but that you can't do it?"

"Not incapable, just—it's not how I want to be."

He sighed again, heavily, rinsed the dishes, and grabbed another beer.

"You're drinking more?"

"Yes." He took a long pull, burped, and looked at me. "You want one?"

"No thanks."

I watched his gaze gravitate toward the far end of the room.

"Did you touch my guitar?"

The case was slightly open, and it wasn't exactly where he had left it. How had he noticed that?

"Did I? Sorry. I must not have locked it the right way."

He ran over to inspect it. "Did you mess with the strings?"

"No, I don't know how. Think you could teach me sometime?"

He looked at me. "You're interested in guitar?"

"Sure," I said. "I don't think my fingers can move that way, but I could try. Right?"

"You could try." He took a second. "What about temping?"

"What about it?"

"A lot of it is like monkey work. Stuffing envelopes, answering phones, making copies. It's what I would've done if I didn't get the restaurant gig. You don't have to think at all."

"Monkeys think. Some can paint, and they know sign language. And math."

"You wouldn't have to do any math."

"Wait, you're serious? How would I get there?"

"I'll drop you off at the agency on my way to work."

"Tomorrow?"

"Why not? Getting out will shield you from the dead."

"I guess that's good that you're joking now, that you don't think I'm crazy."

"I didn't say that," he said. "Look, neither of us is expecting you to get a job. But what if you just gave it a shot, for the hell of it? Just to see. Unless, of course, you had other plans."

14

WHEN THE NEXT DAY CAME, I GOT UP THE SECOND NATE TOLD me to, was ready quickly on his command, and followed him to the subway. Sometimes, if I was nervous enough and the occasion rare enough, it could work that smoothly.

But not for long.

The subway station was packed. I'd only been on one of them a few times before, with Dad, always on off hours, never having to carry anything else. I didn't remember it so crowded, so many people squeezing down the stairs at once. Was anyone moving?

I began to sweat, the heat rushing to my face while I pictured myself being smacked to the ground, trampled on.

"How will all these people fit?" I said. "There's no room. Isn't that a law of physics or something?"

"There's always room," he said.

At the turnstile, he handed me a card and showed me how to swipe, but he went through so quickly I missed it. I tried using the wrong side. Then I had it upside down. Then the screen said "too fast." Then it didn't say anything. I was caught, holding everyone up behind me. "Nate?"

"Like this," he said, trying to show me with a hand gesture from across the way, but I still couldn't do it.

"Come on!" some guy said.

"You come on!" I said.

"Can I do that for you?" he said.

I considered it, but I couldn't tell if he was sincere, so I stepped out of line. "Nate?"

He pushed through the door to come back around to help.

I focused on his easy glide.

"That's what I did," I said.

"Okay," he said. "Now, walk through."

I assumed that would be it and the train would be in front of us, but to get down to the platform, we had to make our way onto a massive escalator. It was steep. I concentrated on my feet for balance.

The train was arriving as we were descending, but we managed to cram ourselves into the last car. There was no place for us to sit, so we leaned near the door. I wasn't a practiced leaner. I kept swaying over, losing my footing, falling into Nate.

"Sorry," I said.

"Me too," he said as I stepped on his toe.

Dad had been on a train like this one every day of his adult life, to get to whatever meetings he needed to attend. I couldn't see him doing this in recent years, handling his bum knee in this kind of traffic. But he would've loved riding with us then, all of us acting like adults on our way to work. I imagined he was watching us from some secret spot we couldn't find, beaming at the image of the two of us squashed together.

Neither of us spoke until the final approach toward our stop.

"Watch the gap when the doors open," Nate said. "We can't afford any more accidents."

AFTER HE LED ME to the office, Nate wished me luck on the welcome mat before rushing off. He handed me his old phone and told me to call if I needed anything.

"You can do this," he said.

I nodded, though I was pretty sure I couldn't. After he left, I stood outside the glass doors for a while on my own, watching the waiting room through the entryway. My feet were sore from the funeral shoes; they were too narrow, and stiff, and I didn't want to sit in there. Not on a hard, armless chair with people who matched the décor—black and white lines and angles, leather satchels and shiny hair.

But as much as I felt compelled to walk away, as many times as I'd done it before, I couldn't do it then. I had to try for Nate. That was our agreement. And for Dad, who would've been so proud to see me there after I'd blown off that last interview—in matching shoes, at a reasonable hour. Maybe I could manage to fool these people long enough to hire me.

In the waiting room, I zeroed in on a chubby guy with bifocals and marked him as the least intimidating seat neighbor. His shirt wasn't tucked in, his hair was poofy, wet from sweat at the roots, and there was an empty space next to him.

I realized how sticky I was myself as soon as I sat down and felt the back of my shirt pressing against me. Everyone besides me and Poofy seemed like a friend of Nate's—crisp, clean, and pressed—blessed with Supercool powers, ease in the way they shifted legs, crossed feet, placed hands on other hands for emphasis. They all seemed to be members of a secret club.

When they weren't conferring, they were writing things down, reviewing papers, studying things. I took an art class once where we didn't have a textbook. Instead the professor showed slides. He made startled sounds sometimes or cried if the image moved him enough. Still, moments before the final exam, everyone was flipping through pages, reading and scribbling. What are you studying? I said. They didn't answer. I realized then that during the slide presentations they had all been taking notes. I passed the exam because I took every-thing pass/fail, and because I understood those slides intui-tively. Art, I didn't have to study. People, I did.

What are you writing? I almost called out to the rest of the people in the waiting room. I took out a piece of paper and thought about sketching the Supercool Friends, but then I noticed Poofy's résumé and realized I needed to find my own from my tote, not that there was much on it. Dad had helped me create it. It listed my education and some volunteer expe-riences I had exaggerated (the afternoon at the Humane Soci-ety, a couple of evenings at the soup kitchen, that one time I'd visited the old-age home). I had packed it the night before on Nate's advice, but it was buried at the bottom of my bag, so to get to it, I had to extract everything else—a few fliers I'd picked up for lost pets, my sketchbook, pennies covered in something syrupy, crayons. It was crumpled on the bottom, a coffee spot in the corner. I tried to de-crease it as I waited for my turn. And then I looked up and saw it was time.

The woman who called me into her office, a woman with an unusually small head and unusually large curls, barely scanned my wrinkled résumé, or me as I contemplated her mane. If she gave me just a cut of that hair from the bottom, a few locks she wasn't using, and I were somehow able to stick them onto my head, I would be brimming with styling possibilities. I could be someone else.

She shook my hand and gave me a disapproving once over. Before I had time to check myself to see if it was a specific stain or detail she was noticing rather than an overall impression, she began the interview.

"Do you know Word?" she said. "Excel? PowerPoint?"

No, I didn't.

"Can you type?"

One finger at a time.

"How are you with filing?"

I pictured myself hiding folders, stashing them behind drawers, underneath storage bins, in the crevices between the cabinets, through the garbage chute. My head banging against hard corners over and over again.

"I'm not very good at organizing," I said. I wasn't good at lying either.

"I see." She looked at me. "And what were you expecting to find here? Because you know this is office work, correct?"

"Yeah, I guess I was just . . . my brother said you—" What was I expecting? "I don't know."

"I see." She returned her attention to her computer. "Well, I'm sorry, but it doesn't seem your qualifications lend themselves to our services."

It should have been a relief; I wouldn't have to sit in an

office for the rest of the day, or the week. It wasn't a surprise. But it was her tone—the condescending callousness, the judgmental speech patterns—that stung the most.

Because somehow I had let myself think, if only for a second, that this woman with the mane might have said something else. That she might have said: *Office work might not be for you, but there is this one thing I have that just might be a fit . . .*

There was that school principal in an interview for a permanent sub position a few years earlier who'd said that she liked me based on grounds she couldn't put her finger on. She said I was a "stitch" when I told her how much I liked graham crackers, and she mentioned a positive aura around me that gave her a "warm" feeling. Halfway through the interview, she gave me this look as if she were seeing some quality in me that nobody else had seen, a look that made me believe that I could actually be somebody.

It turned out that getting up every day at the same time, early enough to meet the kids at the door, was something I couldn't do in the end. I also had trouble sticking to a set curriculum. I kept losing the lesson plans, and my train of thought when I was trying to explain things to the students, and the students themselves when I took them out for recess. If I was in charge of just one or two kids, that might have worked out, but this was a class of twenty-five. At the end of the week, the principal didn't have to tell me I wasn't welcome back. I knew before the conversation began. I was just glad she didn't yell at me or tell me how disappointed she was. Ultimately, when she told me she was sorry, she said it like she meant it.

It was that fleeting moment of hope she had given me that I was searching for in the temp office. The woman with the hair had taken it away.

"Fuck." I thought I had said it under my breath.

"Excuse me?"

"I have to go now," I said, scraping my knee against the underside of the table.

I rushed out, head down, as the burn began to set in.

I HAD TO get away as quickly as possible. Nate had pointed to Central Park on the way over. I should have paid more attention when he did that because I knew it had the zoo, and the zoo was filled with real animals—not Harry-like animals. At his core, Harry, with his white, socklike paws, was an old man who was afraid to leave the house. I often pictured him in a bathrobe and slippers. He wouldn't last a day in a zoo.

But I had fond memories of this zoo. Memories of both Mom and Dad, memories of escaping into a different domain, memories of Gus. I needed to go back. I didn't think. I just started going, first in the direction not facing the sun because it was really hot. Then the other way when that seemed wrong, but then I wasn't sure which way that was, only that I had been walking for too long, and the blisters between my toes were growing.

I called Nate from the phone he gave me.

He didn't pick up. So he was busy, or else purposely not answering, and I didn't want to bother him with a message that would come out broken and dramatic, so I called back.

Again. And again. Four times, until finally—

"Lucy?"

"Oh, hi," I said. "Is it you?"

"What's wrong?" he said. "Are you okay?"

"Can you tell me how to get to the zoo?"

"Where are you?"

"In front of a building."

"That's not helpful. Are you still at the agency? What happened?"

He was annoyed. This was why I didn't want to call.

"Don't worry about it," I said.

"Don't hang up. Are you all right?"

"No." I couldn't hold it in anymore. I didn't want to cry or scream, but, "I don't know what to do!"

He sighed.

"Do you see a bodega anywhere?" he said.

"One of those little shops? There's one here."

"Great. Now, go inside and buy a water with the twenty I stuck in the front pocket of your bag. Then ask the person at the counter for directions. You'll be fine. Call me back if you need to, but only if it's an emergency."

I was hesitant to ask for directions because I didn't want to hear that I was slow, or that I didn't seem dressed for the zoo, or that it wasn't anyone else's job to direct me.

"Do you know where the park is?" I said finally.

The man at the register didn't look at me. He pointed directly behind me.

"That? I was walking beside it the whole time?"

He didn't answer.

"Is there a zoo in there?" I said.

"Central Park Zoo," he said.

"Where is it? I mean, where's the entrance, for the tickets?"

He pointed behind me again.

After a mistaken loop around the entrance, I made it to the gate. Seeing it there in all of its glory, was, I imagined, like stumbling onto the Fortress of Solitude. Here was the place that could guide me toward inner peace. I had found it, on my own—sort of—and I knew everything would be okay.

I WENT FIRST to the penguin house, where I stood in the corner beside the A/C vent. It was the coldest room in the zoo. I waited for the freezing air to dry my sweat as I took in the scene, pressing against the railing to get as close as possible. I watched the penguins totter from rock to rock, alternating between clusters of socialization and bursts of swimming. They would stand regally for moments at a time, with their flippers back and beaks pointed high, before plunging into the tank and starting over. It seemed like they were content to have their fish fed to them, their partners and friends predetermined. Did they know it was all ice and mirrors? Did they care?

When I was sufficiently cool, I found the Polar Circle, home of Gus. First, I looked for him from the outside. I stood before the bridge and scanned the rocks for a sign. As soon as I caught a glimpse of him diving into the water, I went below to get a better view.

I kept my eyes on him from the window—his energy, his motion, the whir of his coat—and I focused. He caught my gaze, and he paused. For a split second, it was as if his whole demeanor changed mid-lap. It wasn't a real grin, but his leathery gums crept upward so that I could spot an enormous tooth. He looked straight at me.

My mind relaxed enough to lock out the noise. I grabbed my sketchbook and began to draw, following the charcoal as it glided across the page. It was as if I began flowing into his head, he into mine. I didn't have to think, or reflect, or work. I just followed his lead until he began to emerge on the page as clearly as any portrait I'd done.

When I was finished drawing, I had no desire to leave, so I just sat and watched. I could have watched for days.

"You know they're not actually white," a woman said. Her voice was deep but cheerful.

I turned to face her. Her hair was long and wavy, in a way that seemed to match her figure. She looked like she was in her thirties or forties, though I wasn't sure because she wasn't wearing any makeup or accessories beyond a digital watch. I appreciated that she didn't seem to have time for trifles.

"Pigment-free, I know," I said. "It's just the reflection of the light."

Her name was Sally. It was printed on her name tag, on her zoo shirt, which matched her khaki shorts that were pulled up to her chest. She seemed surprised that I knew what I was talking about.

"We're closing soon," she said. "We need to start heading to the exit."

I nodded my thanks to her, and then she peeked at my drawing.

"Well, that's very good!" she said, smiling and squinting at me like I was a child.

"No," I said. "I mean, it's not much, but—you work here?"

"Going on fifteen years."

"Wow."

"As a matter of fact, I started as a volunteer," she said. "Now I lead the whole squad."

A volunteer? Really? How do you do that? I could've asked a hundred questions, but Sally was already headed to her next stop, and I didn't want to pester her.

As I was leaving, I kept picturing the wide smile that stretched across Dad's cheeks, the eager eyes. *See?* he was saying. *Doors opening.*

IT SHOULD HAVE TAKEN about forty-five minutes to find my way back to Nate's, but that night it took me two hours. First, I had to roam around for a while to find Columbus Circle. I still didn't get the difference between East and West in the park, and I wasn't sure anyone else did either. It seemed like people were pointing me in the wrong direction each time I asked. Then I wasn't sure exactly what I was looking for: a literal circle? A metaphorical intersection? An upscale mall was the easiest way to mark it. But then I went downtown instead of uptown, and then accidentally got on the red line instead of the blue line, and then the local instead of the express. I got yelled at by two women for blocking the door, squeezed out of an elevator, and, alongside a group of snotty teenagers, serenaded by a mariachi band. I'd nearly cried twice, almost tried to get out of a moving train once, and had to sit down on the floor on the final stretch because I thought I was going to faint.

But whenever I was tempted to scream, I closed my eyes and imagined myself swimming with Gus, the penguins at my side. I examined the sketches I drew and in my mind returned to the zoo.

I wasn't sure what time it was when I made it to the apartment. It took me a while to unlock the door—I kept relocking it—but I was comforted by the sight of Harry's gleaming eyes greeting me in the darkness.

As I crashed on my sofa, I realized that I'd seen more people that day, more people since I'd moved to the city—hundreds, maybe thousands—than I'd seen in whole years at home. Here, I realized, I might have the chance to lose myself in an entirely different way. Not that I would necessarily want to— that prospect was terrifying—but for the first time, I could see the appeal of that freedom. There were so many trains here, so many streets, so many different options for moving in different directions.

Maybe for a second, that didn't seem too daunting. Maybe for a moment, it even seemed to open possibilities. Why couldn't I be someone here? Maybe I could be someone who worked at the zoo.

I passed out fully clothed and didn't move again until morning.

15

Living with Dad, my routine had consisted of a couple of naps a day, and maybe one activity every other day—a drive to a store, for example, or an appointment with a therapist or headache specialist. Occasionally, there was a trip to a museum or park. But nothing could compare to my day at the zoo. My muscles ached in places I wasn't sure I had muscles—in my feet, and at the bottom of my spine. My shoulder too was strained from carrying my bag all day, shooting pain into my neck.

Nate found me in my pajamas as he prepped for his morning commute. "You just rolling out of bed?"

"I might go back to sleep. I have a pretty bad headache."

The pressure was pounding against my eyes and sinuses.

"I don't think temping is right. For me. But I'd like to find something else to help, like getting a job at the zoo. I could do that I think. Maybe not every day, but—do you think I could make money that way? Like an intro job? Maybe a trainer in training if I went there enough? There was this lady who mentioned volunteering—"

"Did you take your medicine?" he said.

"Yeah, I'll be fine in a couple hours."

"The migraine pill?"

"I just need to eat something. And sleep. It happens a lot."

I began rubbing my temples, which probably only made things worse.

"What happened at the temp agency?"

"Nothing, really. Temping is for people who have lots of hair, who have notes to review. There was nothing for me there."

"Did they say that?"

"Basically."

"Well, that sucks."

"Yeah, it did," I said. "I'm sorry it didn't work."

"Me too," he said. "I guess I'll have to try to pick up more hours."

"Is that even possible?"

He didn't answer.

"At the zoo, I did a really good sketch of Gus, the polar bear. You want to see?"

"I don't have time." He was fixing his collar and smoothing the bottom of his shirt, trying to get rid of the wrinkles. He didn't own an iron. From the side, with a squint, he was still a kid playing dress-up. "I have to go."

"Maybe I could work with Gus. I mean, what if I could somehow look into working there? Dad mentioned that once too, with the talk-show host. So what if that's a real thing?"

"You tried to tell me."

He was gathering his things and pushing them into his bag when he met my eyes for a second.

"About Gus?" I said. "I did, right?"

"You can't have a regular job. You're right. I guess I just had to see it to understand."

My throat was knotting up. It was the tone.

"Do me a favor, all right? Don't just stay here all day. Try to do something productive."

I wasn't sure what that meant. Making soap? Knitting scarves?

"I'm not the same as you. I just wanted you to know that, so that if I can't—"

"I'm late." He grabbed his keys and checked his watch. "But we need to go over some ground rules before I leave."

"Do we have any more coffee?" I said.

He poured me a mug and then proceeded to deliver a lecture that might have been appropriate for a kindergartener.

Here are the keys. Never leave home without them. Here is the phone. Never leave home without it. Charge it every night. Here is where I charge my phone. This is how you call collect. Remember 911. There's also 311. This is my number. Memorize it. Here is where we live. Here is a subway map. Here is a street map. Here is a twenty-dollar bill I want you to fold into the pocket of your wallet. Here is how you know when something is worth calling me. This is the household cleaner. Here is the soap and water. This is how you clean as you go.

I nodded through all of it, but it was too much all at once. It was stifling.

Once he left, I knew that I needed to get out.

I WANTED TO go back to the zoo, but I didn't want to pay for admission again; I wanted to try to conserve the money Nate had just given me, and to save my valuable time with Gus, so I started walking. He had said the Starbucks was in a nicer area, away from the clumps of people milling around stoops. About ten minutes in, I was lost, but I found a different coffee shop off a side street that smelled so tempting I couldn't help myself from drawing closer—and closer still, until I saw a sign. Help Wanted.

Just when you thought all hope had vanished, you could look up and see something like this: Me behind the counter distributing independently operated java to the masses, a regular location for a fixed wage, smelling of beans, imbibing caffeine. Maybe this was what fate was. Coffee, I could do.

"What's your take on the day's special?" I said to the man at the register. He was compact, and very pale, almost translucent. His hair was nearly white, and his eyes, magnified by wire glasses, almost entirely clear, marked only by the slightest tinge of green. I wondered how he'd look stained with mocha.

"It's very popular," he said.

"And how does it compare with the other blends?"

"Umm . . . I'm not sure exactly."

"Is it more of a dark or medium roast? Does it have that earthy, Indonesian feel or is it a lighter, brighter flavor? How would you characterize the acidity? Is it closer to a Sumatran, Kenyan, or Costa Rican flavor?"

"Wow, you must really know your coffee." He rubbed the fuzz at the back of his head. "I'm probably not the best person to ask."

"Don't you work here? You looked like you did, because you were behind the counter, but I guess you don't. I'm sorry."

"No, I do."

I waited for him to say more, but he didn't. He just observed me, as though he were about to say something else.

"Right," I finally said. "Do you know anything about the Help Wanted sign on the window?"

"What? The sign! I meant to take that down." He scurried to the window to rip it away. "My father thought—we thought we needed someone who—did he send you?"

"Who?"

"No one." He stood up straight and pushed back his narrow shoulders. "There is no position at this time."

"Oh." The glimmer of light went black. Again. "I get it."

"I'm sure that if we had a position, we would have considered you."

"It's okay." I took a heavy breath. "I can't do jobs anyway. I don't have any experience, and I'm a hazard. I'm missing that switch people need for work. I don't know what I was thinking."

He didn't respond.

"But I'll still have coffee, I guess, since I'm here, if that's okay. The Ethiopian?"

When he handed me the cup, I pulled out my crumpled bills, but he refused them.

"First-time-customer special."

"That's okay," I said. "I wouldn't want you to get in trouble."

"I'm in charge of the counter at this location."

"Really?"

"Yes."

"I mean, great. Not like you don't seem like you could be in charge. See how I do that? Mess up the connection? Now I'll go. Thanks—for the coffee. It looks good."

I eyed the newspapers hanging on giant wooden sticks in the front of the shop and collected as many as I could hold. About half of them fell by the time I got to an empty table in the back, but there weren't many people, so I didn't hit anyone. The man at the front came around the register to help me.

"Sorry," I said.

"It's okay."

He smiled a little awkwardly, in a way that didn't make me feel self-conscious enough to leave.

It seemed every ad in the Classifieds was seeking experience, or skill or organization. There wasn't anything about the zoo, and there weren't any calls for all-purpose playmates to dogs or to children who could take care of themselves, so I stopped searching and began to look around.

The walls were beige and decorated with frames of artificial sunsets, cottages in the country, shoddy brushwork, and clumsy composition. They seemed especially tacky contrasted against the dark-cherry paneling in the back. I took out my sketchbook and began drawing a modified version of a waterfall.

"My mother did the one in the middle."

I hadn't noticed the man from the counter standing behind me. He was carrying a fresh pot of coffee and offered me a refill. His voice was as wispy as his frame.

"She did? That's—wow."

His cheeks turned pink.

"I'm Frank."

"Frank. My dad always told me to say the name after you hear it to remember. Three times. Frank. And then use it in a sentence. You should try the coffee, Frank," I said. "It's really good."

"Thanks, but I can't. It hurts my stomach." He paused, as if in deep thought. "I like tea sometimes."

"Tea's supposed to be good for you."

He stared at me, not in a repelled kind of way, more like he was fascinated.

"What was your name?" he said.

"Oh. I should have said that first. It's Lucy. And I should say your name again too, Frank. Right?"

He nodded and waited another second, making sure I wasn't going to say anything else, before pouring and walking away.

Then he walked back.

"I think I've seen you before," he said.

"I don't think so," I said. "I just moved here."

"Oh." His face was flushing again. "I thought I saw you in a group meeting, a while ago."

"What group? When?"

"I didn't meet you. I heard about you, and I saw you once, before they told you to leave."

"The brain injury group?"

"Yes."

"You were in that? That was humiliating. I mean, for me it was." I searched his face. "You don't look familiar."

"I was there after you," he said. "My first day was your last."

I hated thinking about that place. I took a big sip.

"Did you have brain surgery too?" he said.

"No, I was hit by a truck."

"That must have hurt," he said.

"Yeah, I'm sure it did. I don't remember. I was only three."

"I used to get seizures. All the time. Now I don't, but things are sometimes fuzzy."

"Oh," I said. I couldn't think of what else to say.

I wanted more coffee, but there wasn't any left in my cup.

"Would you like another pour?" he said.

"No, that's okay," I said. "I should probably stop there."

I got up to leave.

"You didn't like the group," he said. "I'm sorry I brought it up."

"It's okay."

"I was just happy to see you here."

"That's nice," I said. "I guess I wasn't expecting to talk about brain injuries today. That's all. It's not the first thing I bring up."

He nodded and returned to the counter.

I thought about saying goodbye to Frank on my way out. It was nice of him to give me coffee, but he seemed busy with a few people at the register, including a towering woman carrying a pug.

"You have to leave your dog outside," Frank said to her. "It's policy."

"What?" I said. I had said it in my head, but it had come out audibly, loudly apparently.

Frank turned to face me, and I searched his eyes. They weren't red or puffy.

"Are you allergic to dogs?" I said.

"No, but my father made this clear: pets don't have a place in an eating and drinking establishment."

"You know, speciesism is a serious problem in this country."

His whole face was pink now. "I'm not sure I'm—following you."

"I'm sorry," I said. "I don't even work here, so—why should I care? I shouldn't. The customers can speak for themselves. Well, the dogs can't speak for themselves, but—I'm sorry. I was on my way out."

Halfway to the door I caught sight of the pug through the window. I could see his expression drop as the woman walked back in, and I thought of how rough it must be, so reliant on someone else for every need. I tried to count the folds in his face, worry lines from all of the anxiety, how many fell around his mouth, beyond his snaggled tooth, the strip of tongue pushing past his pout. I parked myself on the windowsill and opened a blank page of my sketchbook.

Rough circles, then a face, a sad, sagging tail. I began to draw as I settled into his expression, his watery eyes. A single tear could break down the barriers of speciesism.

I entered into my zone. My fingers began to burn, the pencil moving faster than I could control it. I was filling pages in minutes, somehow flipping faster than my normal coordination allowed, when I heard a voice.

"Is that mine?" the dog's owner said.

"What, this?" I got up from the window ledge to face her. "It's just a sketch. I mean it's sort of him, but it's pretty generic at this stage."

"I love it," she said. "And you are?"

"Lucy," Frank said.

He had again covertly positioned himself behind me.

"Charming," she said.

I followed her out, trying to keep pace. I wanted to know what she liked about it specifically, but her legs were too long, my breath too short, and I lost her as soon as she curved around the block.

Still, I wasn't too disappointed. When I turned around to face the shop, I realized I had found another place I might be able to return to, which meant this had been a productive day, a day when I had done things. Real things. Nate would have to approve.

16

WHEN NATE GOT HOME THAT NIGHT, IT WAS EARLIER THAN the night before so I was still awake, but he hadn't given me fair warning.

"I'm cleaning up now," I said, mouth full of pretzels. "Do you want one? I mean not from the floor, but—"

"Luce," he said slowly, as though he'd been up for days, "I really need you to pitch in."

He opened the refrigerator to pull out the requisite beer. "Have you noticed how little substantial food we have?"

"I got oatmeal."

He looked at me. "Really?"

"The unsweetened kind, because it's healthier, and it was on sale. And milk. That's a staple, right?"

"It is."

"Plus, there are more pretzels."

"I guess I'm not hungry."

"Did you have a rough day or something? Because mine was pretty decent."

He got down on the floor to pick up a couple of flyers and

a magazine I was flipping through earlier while searching for the remote control.

"This is from two years ago," he said. "How did it get here?"

"After you left, I went to this coffee shop, and I met these people, and I searched for jobs."

He stood up. "Did you find one?"

"Well, not exactly, but—"

"It doesn't belong on the floor," he said, moving back to the kitchen.

"Sorry," I said, but he couldn't hear me over the water running past the dishes.

I followed him and raised my voice. I watched him pop a pill, Advil or Excedrin, I guessed.

"Do you have a headache?" I said. "Can I help?"

He turned off the faucet. "Did you say something?"

I wanted to tell him all about my day, about Frank and the pug. It was the type of day Dad would've eaten up, but I could see it wasn't the right time.

"I'll clean up the magazines."

SOMETIME IN the middle of the night, long after I'd gone to bed, I woke up, stumbled toward the kitchen, and found Nate on a cushion gazing into nothingness. His mail sat unopened on his lap; a couple of beer bottles surrounded him; an ashtray filled with short cigarettes sat beside him. Were those joints? He didn't look like himself. He looked like another Nate—disheveled, lackadaisical, unaware.

He drank milk straight from a bowl of cereal.

"Are those Lucky Charms?" I said. "Where'd you get those?"

"Get what?" He wiped his mouth. "Guess you caught me. They had them in the dining hall."

"You still go there?"

"I wish. I used to bring in a giant container every day, fill it with cereal, and stuff it into my gym bag when no one was looking. I just remembered I still had the container I filled before I left. You want some?"

"No," I said, examining his stash. "It's yours."

But the marshmallows were so bright and enticing, the oats so hearty and friendly. The perfect accompaniment to Saturday-morning cartoons. I could taste them.

"I mean, maybe just a handful if you have any left. . . ."

He poured a pile into my hands, and I popped the pieces straight into my mouth.

"Like candy," I said.

"The ideal balance of sweetness," he said.

"Yeah, but isn't it late for cereal? Why are you up?"

"It's never too late for cereal," he said.

I grabbed more.

He moved the container away from me. His eyes were bloodshot, and he smelled like herbs.

"They're addictive," I said. "You ate this every day?"

"Oh man, all the time. Nothing better to satisfy the cravings. There were so many late nights, so much reading and studying all the time."

"Sounds hard."

"Sometimes, but it was worth it. It was like you would sit in this giant space in the library surrounded by all of these great minds, hundreds of years of great minds before you, and just take in knowledge. Like you could feel your brain expanding with all these new insights at every turn, all these smart people making you think. Like their only job was to make you think. Then we'd take these study breaks in the lounge where we'd eat cereal and argue over cartoons or have paper-airplane contests, and it was all bullshit, and it was all perfect. That's how it was on the best nights. When my only job was to study."

"You'll go back."

He hesitated before answering. "One day."

"What was your major again? Philosophy?"

"That was last year."

"Do you still want to be a doctor?"

"Maybe. But I was heading in a different direction this year. Political science."

"Law school?"

"Or policy."

"Save the world," I said. "You could totally do that."

He fished out a bag of pot from the inside of his backpack and began rolling joints like a professional, his fingers two-stepping. How much had he already had?

"You want some?" he said.

"I don't know," I said. "You do this a lot?"

"I wouldn't say a lot," he said, holding it out to me. "Only at night. You ever try it?"

"Isn't it bad for you?"

"Healthier than pharmaceuticals." He took a drag and released some smoke in my face. "More natural than those pills you take."

How much more harm could I do?

I tried to inhale the way he did.

"Now, hold it there," he said. "Don't let go."

I didn't, until the coughing gripped me. Then I waited to feel something other than the deep burn in my throat, for the colors to change and the room to shift, for my perception to alter into enlightenment. Wasn't that how it was supposed to go?

"I don't feel anything."

"It takes time." He took another drag. "It might not work at all this round."

"So what am I supposed to do now?"

"Relax," he said, holding it out to me again. "Try again if you want."

I did, and I coughed again, and still, nothing. "It doesn't work."

"More for me then," he said. "I wish I had this more often."

"Drugs?"

"Time," he whispered. "It's the time that counts. Time to sit back and slow down. You know what I'm saying? I don't have time for anything these days."

He inhaled.

"What would you do?" I said.

He exhaled.

"Play my guitar. All day." He closed his eyes and smiled, as if imagining himself in another world, maybe even another body. "Eat Lucky Charms."

"You'd probably get really fat."

"Then no one would recognize me."

"You'd like that?" I said.

He looked at me, hard for a second, and then away. "You really think you saw her?"

"Who?"

"Mom," he said.

"Yeah, but I was probably dreaming or something."

"Tell me about it," he said.

"I had just hit my head on the faucet when I drifted off—I think, unless I was awake and it really was her. It could have been a concussion."

"So weird," he said, taking another drag.

"I know. You already told me you think I need help."

"No, I mean you probably do, but you'd think you'd see Dad."

"I know," I said. "I was thinking that too, at first. But I've seen Mom before."

"Seriously?"

"At home. A few times, actually. Who knows for sure. It wasn't like her, her. It was like the mist of her, the essence. But I'm pretty sure it was her."

"Not Dad?"

"I don't think Dad had that side of him, the spiritual side. I think maybe that's why he was more religious than the rest of us. Because he was searching for that thing Mom already had. I think I have it too. The sense, or whatever you call it. Do you have it?"

He put down the joint. "I don't know."

"I think you might," I said. "I think we both do. You remember the pinky story."

Once, when I was in school, I lost my fingertip in the slam

of auditorium doors, and Mom said that she knew something was wrong the moment it happened because Nate doubled over in his highchair with some mysterious pain in his hand. He was hysterically crying until she got the call about me, and by the time she hung up, he was fine. She believed he could feel me. She believed we were linked.

"I was two," he said. "Who knows if that was true."

"And remember when you fell off your bike and I knew? Dad didn't take me seriously at first, but I called out that you were in trouble, that we had to go find you. Then we opened the screen door, and there you were, in the middle of the cul-de-sac, just sitting there holding your ankle. Dad looked at me then. How did you know, he said? I just knew, I said. I could feel you."

"Yeah, I guess I do remember that."

"What if she never left?" I said. "I mean, it makes sense in a way that she'd want to stick around, for us. That's how she was."

He didn't respond, but I could tell he was listening.

"If Dad had died first, she would have known we'd be taken care of. She would've planned for that and gone in peace, right? But Dad took it all as it came, whatever seemed right at the time."

He stared ahead for another minute before speaking again. "Huh."

"What?"

"That does kind of make sense. I'm not sure it will tomorrow, but . . . huh."

"I've had a lot of time to think."

"You think she'll come back?" he said.

"I wouldn't be surprised."

"Right," he said. "But you are pretty nuts."

I threw a marshmallow horseshoe at him.

He hit me with a rainbow.

"It's late," he said. "You should sleep."

My mouth was dry. "I think I wanted water."

I tried to get up directly from my crossed-leg position, but I wobbled back down. He let me use his shoulder to balance myself.

"Did you want some too?" I said. "Didn't you want to play some music before you went to bed?"

He didn't answer, but I poured him a glass anyway. This was the first time he seemed calm enough to talk. I had to seize the moment.

I rushed to fill our glasses in the kitchen, but by the time I made it back to the living room, half of the water had sloshed to the floor, and the lights were out.

17

Except for the zoo, which had become my favorite destination to fantasize about, I didn't often itch to go places. But the next day, I was hankering for the coffee from that shop. I remembered how to get back there, which seemed like a big deal in itself, and because I'd managed to get up when Nate did it was almost like I was going to a job. I made sure to wear a clean shirt, and to blow dry my hair so it would seem fuller after the shower.

Frank noticed me before I had a chance to examine the chalkboard.

"Hi," he said.

"I was hoping to try the house roast today."

"I'm sorry if I was racist before." He seemed nervous. "I didn't understand—I still don't really understand, but I don't always get things the first time, and—"

"'Speciesist' is what I said. But it was a nasty thing to say. It was blurty, and not true, necessarily. I don't even know you. I'm sorry. I do that sometimes. And I'm sorry I drew the pug because now other pugs might try to come back. I guess you hope they won't, so you don't have to deal with that again. But it doesn't matter. I like your coffee."

His face was the color of Bazooka. "Your drawing was good."

"The pug? No, there's nothing there yet."

He didn't protest.

"But thanks," I said.

This coffee wasn't as tasty as the Ethiopian, but it was decent, and my spot in the back was open, so I decided to wait there and keep an eye out for any displaced dogs.

That pug and his owner never did return, but after settling into my seat and getting halfway through my cup of coffee, I noticed someone else. Actually, she noticed me.

"Miss?" she called out in a weathered voice. She was a tiny old woman sitting at the adjacent table.

"Do you draw animals?" she said.

"Are you talking to me?"

"Yes. The name is Enid."

She extended a small, polished hand. I was scared to take it for fear of breaking it, but I didn't want to offend her, so I was extra-careful.

"I don't do it officially or anything," I said. "It's just for fun, in a comic-book kind of way. When the inspiration strikes and I connect with them."

"I saw you connect with that flat-face dog yesterday," she said.

"Yeah, he was sweet."

She reminded me of a miniature dollhouse, a full white mane and manicured nails and earrings all shrunk down to scale. I wondered if there were old-people stores that catered to dwindling bones, negative inseams, a special coupon attached to her copy of *AARP*. Could you get that magazine if you never retired from anything?

"My favorite companion was a spaniel mix. My own little mutt. I saved her from one of those shelters. Belle was her name," she said, gazing up at the ceiling. "She's gone now."

"I'm sorry."

"Don't be. She lived sixteen glorious years. Can you draw her?"

I didn't draw on demand, especially not for animals I'd never met, but I liked this Enid. She talked to me like I had value.

"Do you have a picture?" I said.

"Pictures are for people who can't remember. I can describe her in perfect detail." She tapped my pad with her red pointer. "Her paws were my favorite part. You could start with those."

"Now? Actually, it works better for me when I'm stirred in some way. It's much harder to go from nothing. It's more of a process. I usually start with the head, not the paws. It's not about the details with me. It's more about the story—behind the eyes."

"You'll make an exception for Belle," she said. "Everybody did. They were like chocolate-chunk cookies. You wanted to eat them up, pads and all."

She closed her eyes. "Golden hair with flecks of black along the nose and eyes, like a mask. She'd put her paw on my lap and say, 'How do you do today, Enid?' sweet as could be, before sneaking off to raid the snack cabinet. When I told her to get off the furniture, she'd gather all of her weight in one spot, like a little wrestler, and cock her head as if to say, 'Why bother?'"

"Can you see her yet?" she said.

I liked communicating with the animals myself, when they could send me their live vibrations, and I could meet their eyes and descend beneath their coats, so I could feel their moods and emotions, but I guessed I could try it this way once.

"That's it," Enid said, as I began with rough circles.

She looked toward the ceiling again. "She loved the water. Her favorite route to walk was along the Hudson. Every morning, we'd start at Fort Tryon and cut down along the bike path at One Hundred and Eighty-First. Then we'd go as far as we could go. Riverside Park, the Upper West Side. Once we made it all the way to Fourteenth. She always pulled me toward the river."

Enid took a moment and looked at me. "The day I scattered her ashes was the day she finally got to go in."

Jews didn't cremate. They buried in pine boxes. Was Enid Jewish? If I wasn't going to get into her dog's head, I'd have to get into hers, so I could get to the dog through her.

"What do you think happens when you die?" I said. "Do you believe in ghosts? Do you believe dogs can become ghosts?"

She didn't answer for a minute. I wondered if she'd heard me. I thought about repeating or rephrasing when she looked at me again.

"Why should it matter what I believe?" she said. "You're the artist."

"It's just something I've been trying to figure out lately. Fate too. Any thoughts on that?"

She shrugged. "I know better than to rule anything out."

I nodded.

"But I also know I can't expect *anyone*, or *anything*, to make my decisions, justify my choices, or excuse my mistakes."

"What about accidents?" I said.

"What about them?"

"Are they just accidents?"

"I'm hardly an authority on these things," she said.

"But you seem wise," I said.

She laughed. "I am not young enough to know everything."

"I've heard that before. I think it was on my teacher's bulletin board in high school. I can still see it, the black lettering. Oscar Wilde?"

"Oscar Wilde probably said something like it, but no." She was proud of herself. "It's from a play by J. M. Barrie. *The Admirable Crichton.*

I looked into her eyes. They were a very deep hazel. "Are you an actress?"

"Only in my dreams," she said. "Look, people think there's some kind of cosmic significance for everything that happens. But in my experience the universe doesn't stop. It doesn't make exceptions. It just goes, and it's up to us whether we want to go with it."

"So you're not religious."

"I don't like labels," she said. "I like looking at the world in a way that gives me motivation to keep going. And at my age, I take whatever motivation I can get. Would you guess I'm eighty-five years old?"

I might have. Old was old in my mind, I almost said, but I didn't.

"There are days when I wake up and forget how old I

am. I think, I could climb a goddamned mountain. I think, I remember when I was twenty-four like it was last week. And thirty-nine. And fifty-two. But then I realize I don't have time to waste thinking about the past. So instead of feeling depressed or sorry for myself, or giving in to some half-baked expectation, I get out of bed and get dressed and go somewhere. Every morning."

"You come here?"

"Not always here. But somewhere. That's all that matters."

"It's a good rule," I said. "You have more energy than I do."

"There's no excuse for that," she said.

"Well, there sort of is."

She seemed concerned.

"Executive functions?" I said. "I have issues with those."

"Who doesn't?"

"I was hit by a truck."

"Recently?"

"I was three. But the damage is still there."

"Everyone's damaged," she said. "Though three is an early start. I'll give you that. Three is when we start coming into our own."

"I guess so." I had heard other people say that to Mom and Dad, how I was so ahead of other people in the early milestones, how it was such a shame I had to start over. I didn't like to think of that.

"Do you work?" she said.

"I'm trying to work some things out."

She took a moment to take me in, the whole of me, and put her hand on the table next to mine.

"Then you have time to draw Belle."

She got up and headed to the door.

"Wait," I said. "Will I see you again?"

"How else will you get the job done?"

I had a decent enough sketch to begin with, so I started to follow Enid to the door. But when I was standing on the mat, Frank called out.

"Lucy," he said.

He didn't wait for me to turn around.

"Are you coming back tomorrow?"

"Sure." I moved to face him. "I'll have to finish that drawing here, so that Enid, when she comes back, I can . . . Will that be a job? I wonder if Nate would count that. It's something."

"Nate?" Frank said. "Is he your boyfriend?"

"What? No, he's my brother. I live with him now, which is hard. Because I don't work. But he takes care of us, which is weird because he's younger. But it's more financial than any-thing else. Well, basically that's what it is."

Frank was staring at me.

"Too much blurting?" I said.

"Do you think that you might want dinner one day?" Frank said.

"What?"

"I feel like we have a lot in common."

I wasn't sure how to respond.

"Or it could be lunch. If that's better for you."

"No. I mean, yes. I like dinner."

AFTER I LEFT, I considered the meaning of our exchange: Did he want to have dinner as a date or as a friend? A friend would be good. I didn't have many of those. That time in the brain injury group, I hit it off with a girl who had short-term memory problems, but I had to remind her who I was and what our plans were at every turn. Following up required more maintenance than I could handle. I'm sorry, I said, but I need so much of my own.

Robby, whom I met in an art class one day in college, was the only one who ever made friendship seem easy. He thought it was funny when I lost my balance and stumbled into his easel. Other people laughed, a couple scowled; I braced myself for a scolding after I made him lose control of his brush. But he thanked me for giving him another excuse to throw away the piece he was working on.

Robby didn't ask why I needed an extra few weeks, and then an extra year, and then another one, to never finish the work. We all have our demons, he said.

Then he moved to California with his partner. Every once in a while he would check in, but he had his own life, and after he left, I didn't want to bother him.

I supposed it wasn't ridiculous to think that Frank was interested in something else.

I didn't know if I liked him that way, though he wasn't unattractive. And he was nice too, nice enough to think it was nice to have a possibility. Why not? I hadn't thought of men very often, or sex—because of the injury, or the drugs to treat the injury, or the lack of exposure. I didn't really crave those things, or long for them. But when it came down to it, I didn't mind the concept.

In fact, I'd almost had two boyfriends in my life.

Jason was more of a friend. In high school, he started talking to me in gym class because he had asthma, and both of us were relegated to the sidelines, and there wasn't much else to do while the class was running around the track. He pushed the hair that covered my face behind my ears so that, he said, he could gauge my reactions to his jokes, which were not very funny, but which I laughed at anyway. I figured it was the least I could do, since no one else had really bothered to acknowledge me, not in a positive way in any case.

He called me once, to tell me he wasn't going to make it to school the next day.

And one time, in the parking lot, while we were waiting for rides and no one was paying attention, he kissed me. It didn't last for more than a second, and it was just that one time, but when I replayed the scene, sometimes it felt like more.

Then there was Smitty. We met at a volunteering fair Dad made me go to one summer to help bring meaning to my life. We both agreed it was a good idea, but there were no positions for me at that fair, and I had to stay the whole week anyway, and it was a long week, with lots of booths. Smitty kept bumping into me.

Neither of us fit in there—he was in his fifties, with a gold tooth and a lisp. I never asked him what he was looking for. I just assumed he recognized an ally in me the way I had in him. In the afternoons, he asked me if I wanted to have coffee across the street, which he always paid for, but as far as I knew, this was what friends did.

On the last day, though, he leaned in for something else, and I turned away. It took me by surprise, but maybe if I had known it was coming, I would have been better prepared to deal with it, and maybe then I would have at least had the chance to see him again.

When I was a little girl, and I played house with another little girl across the street because our moms were friends, I thought about whether I would ever get to have a house myself. When she cut out little pictures of dresses and talked about who she would marry, I fantasized about having one of those big weddings too. But even in those visions, I wasn't sure. It was hard to see past my shoes. I realized they'd have to be flat so I wouldn't fall, the dress stain-resistant, the man someone who could see past all of that, the man who could see past all of that someone I could see past. It took a while to rule it out entirely.

18

ON THE NIGHT OF OUR MEETING, I WASN'T SUPPOSED TO SEE Frank until eight, so I took a nap at five, slept past the alarm to six thirty, and then scrambled to get ready. I still had to shower and pick a dress, but when I tried to shave my legs, I wasn't careful, and though it didn't hurt really, blood spurted everywhere—on the hardwood, and on the sofa cushions as I was racing to find paper towels. I thought maybe I could cover things up with a blanket, if I could find one—later.

I didn't have time to cover up the stains on the dress, but it was dark, so I hoped no one would notice. I couldn't find any Band-Aids either, so I attached some toilet paper and moved on. Maybe if I could make myself pretty enough, he wouldn't focus on my legs.

I tried some old mascara from that vinyl bag, but I ended up poking myself in the eye, until it was red, and whatever was left ended up streaking my face—across my nose, around my lids like a meerkat, and all over the sink. It was waterproof, so it didn't rub out entirely. But it was better than nothing, I guessed, with the lipstick and the blush. When I was done, the sink ended up as a painted canvas. I would've taken a picture if

I had had a camera, but I didn't; I knew Nate wouldn't appreciate it, but I couldn't try to clean then because I was already late.

Hurrying led to me falling, which I never seemed to remember until after the fact. I secured myself by grabbing onto the lamp by the couch, but tumbled hard enough to tip over the lamp, which then smashed. I wasn't supposed to run; I knew that, but in my head, it seemed so effortless. I admired people who could brush themselves off after stumbling and bounce back up. I didn't bounce.

As I reached down to pick up the broken pieces of the lamp, I caught a reflection of myself in the mirror. My hair was a mess even for me, and I was so tired that I considered staying on the floor and taking a nap.

I could tell Frank later that I was sorry. I just wasn't the type of person who went on dates, or who went on outings in the evening. I thought about saying that, how much easier that seemed, but then I thought about Frank waiting for me at the restaurant, and I realized that if I didn't show I might not be able to go back to the coffee shop. I couldn't have that.

THE RESTAURANT WAS nice. There were white tablecloths on the table and wine bottles lining the walls. When I peeked through the window, I saw plates being served with neatly arranged vegetables and flowers placed along the rims. Was I fancy enough?

And then I saw Frank at a corner table, waving at me. There was no going back.

"Are you okay?" he said when he saw me.

"Yeah, why? Am I late? I'm sorry."

"Your leg."

The toilet paper had fallen off and I was bleeding. A red streak had trickled to my ankle.

"Oh this?" I reached down to touch the wound with the first napkin I saw. "It's fine, see? The napkin's dry. It looks worse than it is."

He didn't say anything for a minute, until he made a move to sit down.

"Is this table okay?" he said.

He was wearing a blue blazer, and his hair was slicked back and combed to the side, bar mitzvah–style. "It's the one my parents always choose."

It was the same as all of the other tables.

"It's great," I said. "Do you come here a lot?"

"Sometimes, with them. You look nice."

"Really?"

I didn't hear those kinds of compliments very often. I had been told about the potential with my looks, from the woman who did my makeup that time, and from random people who trimmed my hair, once in a heart-to-heart with Robby. But more often the compliments I got were "you're funny," or "artistic," or "quirky," if you could count that. One time someone told me that I seemed nice, but not that I looked nice, especially not when I was bleeding.

"I mean thanks," I said. "I appreciate that. Because I kind of tried. What do you like on the menu?"

"I always get the house salad and spaghetti with meatballs. It's delicious, but everything is rated highly."

I told him I hadn't gone out to dinner in a while, and then I began to ramble about my adjustment, or lack of adjustment, to the city.

"It's hard when you're not on the numbered streets. Thanks for picking an easy one. And close to me, so I didn't have to get on the subway. Do you have any siblings?"

"No."

Since that was all he said, I prattled on. The whole time I talked, a long time, he never shifted his eyes. It made me feel like I could go on for hours, that maybe I should since he didn't react one way or the other. At first, his stare made me uncomfortable, but I got used to it after a while.

"I think he might be allergic to Harry—Nate, I mean. Harry's my cat. I didn't always think I'd have a cat, but he practically followed me home one day, like a dog might. Dogs are followers; cats forge their own paths. I'm not a cat person, really, but with Harry, it was like he knew he was supposed to be with me. Sometimes I think he hides a journal where he keeps tabs on things, so he can pull it out and remind me later. I wouldn't be surprised if he wrote. He has the soul of a poet. Have you ever connected to an animal?"

"I've never had pets," Frank said. "Once I had a fish."

"It's harder with animals that aren't furry. They don't have as many facial cues. Dogs are extremely expressive. Cats can be occasionally, too. Fish essentially have one look."

"I like cats," he said.

I waited for more. Lettuce fell from his fork.

"I noticed your shop doesn't carry shade-grown beans," I said.

"Is that a problem?" he said. "I can tell my father."

"You should. It costs a little more, or a lot more, I don't know. That's probably why you don't have it, but it's worth it, not just because it tastes better, but because it's better for you. And environmentally sound. I've done a lot of reading on this. Do you have any idea how many trees have to be cut down for each pound of coffee beans? Fair-trade is important too, for the treatment of the laborers."

When I spoke, he crinkled his eyes like he was processing every sentence and storing it away. With other conversations, it seemed people were only fulfilling an obligation, waiting for something more substantial, or for the opportunity to excuse themselves. Or they smiled, as if mildly amused, without taking anything I said seriously. Robby did that sometimes. Nate could be that way too. But Frank just took it in.

He made a noise with his throat.

"Are you okay?"

"Do you think that, um—I was thinking."

"Do I have something in my teeth?" I checked my reflection in my knife. There was a crumb on my bottom lip. "You should have told me."

"I was going to say something else."

"On my dress?"

"It would be helpful if you could sample our different blends to help me learn about the difference between them," he said. "If you wouldn't mind. One day."

"You want me to try your coffee?"

"For free. And not all at once, if you don't want. Unless that sounds like a bad idea."

"No! I mean, I can taste. I'm pretty good at tasting things. Especially coffee."

By dessert, a cappuccino and chocolate-dipped biscotti for me, and a Lipton for him, my throat was raw from all of the talking, and it occurred to me that he hadn't said much the entire night. I'd forgotten that I was probably supposed to ask some things about him—how he was doing, how his week had been, what his life was like. I had read articles about that, conversation etiquette.

"So what do you do outside the coffee shop?" I said.

He didn't answer until I finished half of my drink and had nearly forgotten what I'd asked.

"Not too much," he said finally. I could tell he was going to say more by the line in his forehead. "I like video games. And cards. Sometimes I play online."

"Gambling?"

"No, just for fun."

"Interesting," I said. "Do you read at all?"

"Not really," he said.

"I get that. Sometimes I need to just zone out. Do you have any favorite shows?"

"I don't watch much TV," he said. "I don't like to piece together different stories."

"Oh."

The bottom of my cup had some grounds in it, lukewarm and a little bitter. I must have grimaced as I gulped it down.

"Did you like your food?" he said.

"I did. Thank you for choosing a vegetarian-friendly place. I try to avoid eating animals with faces."

"Oh no," he said. "I didn't know. I shouldn't have ordered meatballs."

"No, I shouldn't have said anything. I didn't say it because of that. I just said it to explain, you know, because you asked. What kind of cards?"

"What?"

"You said you played cards?"

"Solitaire." He spoke slowly, in considered segments. "And Gin. When I was young, I was in bed a lot, and my father didn't like to talk much, so we played. That was what we did."

"That's nice," I said. "My dad and I used to play, too. For M&M's."

In earlier years, I dominated Nate and Dad in hands of Gin and 21, almost always claiming the prized pot. We should take you to Vegas, Dad would joke, patting my head, and they'd laugh. But it was more than luck, I'd say, and then Nate would call me Rain Man, and I'd leave the room without sharing my winnings.

I won because I didn't think the way they did. I wasn't averse to risks or attuned to caution. I didn't care about stakes or probability. They felt hesitations and second-guesses that never crossed my mind. I supposed it was possible to have positive fortune in certain areas to make up for a serious deficit in others. My luck had always been in cards.

"Where's your luck?" I said.

"I'm sorry?"

"Are you good at cards?"

"I can be," he said. "But I'm better when I don't have to think. That's why I like video games. And the coffee shop when it's busy. When I get so focused that I tune everything else out. That's when I'm at my best."

"Flow," I said. "I get there when I'm drawing animals sometimes."

He nodded. "We talked about it in family therapy once. I got to play more video games after that."

"I'm terrible at video games," I said.

Frank looked defeated.

"But it's great that you're so good," I said. "And it's really impressive that you work every day, too. And that you live on your own. Wait, do you live on your own?"

"For the past twelve years."

"That's a long time," I said. I examined his face. It was so smooth. No deep lines or signs of facial hair. "How old are you?"

"Thirty-seven."

"You don't look that old," I said. "Not that that's old. I just would've guessed younger."

"Because I'm small," he said, looking down.

"No, because you don't have any wrinkles. People never know how old I am either. They think I'm younger."

"You seem very mature to me," he said, blushing a little.

"Do I? I don't always feel that way. Do you like being on your own?"

"Yes." He took a sip of his tea, as if in deep concentration. "Except that it gets—quiet. Especially at night."

"I can imagine," I said, picturing him sitting in the corner of a dark room. No books, no shows, just the glow of a game to keep him company.

"I like going to work," he said. "When I'm at work, other people count on me, and I have clear goals. I never liked school, but I always liked having a job."

"That must feel nice," I said. "To have that kind of purpose."

His stare was different now—not so much blank as captivated. I had seen this look directed at other people before: Nate, from the faces of girls he had brought home after school; and Mom, from Dad when they were all dressed up to go somewhere fancy. But it was something else to experience it for myself.

"I knew you would understand me," he said. "I knew it when I first saw you."

I finished my dessert, and the last bite crumbled into my lap.

"It was rude not to offer you any," I said. "Did you want some?"

He eyed my empty plate. "No, my tea was good. How was your coffee?"

"It was okay," I said. "They're better at biscotti."

"Making coffee is an art. That's what my father says. That's why I want to know more."

"It is a beautiful thing," I said.

Then I suddenly remembered the mess I'd left at Nate's and made a motion to go. I could at least attempt to clean the sink before he got home.

"What time is it?"

"It's almost ten," he said. "Should I get the bill?"

"Yes," I said. "Oh, wait. I have cash, I think. A twenty?"

"No," he said. He lunged across the table to touch my hand, but he couldn't reach. "I can pay."

He placed a few bills from his pocket in the fold. "We can leave faster because I only use cash."

"You don't like credit cards?"

"Cash is simpler."

"I guess," I said. "If you don't lose it."

I stood up quickly to make a break for the apartment.

"Can I walk you home?" he said. "It's dark."

"Um—" I wasn't interested in a leisurely stroll. We had to move fast.

"Unless you don't want me to."

"No, it's not that," I said. "It's Nate, his place I mean, the mess I left, but—no, you know, he's never home by ten anyway. You said it was ten? So, okay, you can walk with me—if we walk fast."

On our way out, he extended his arm slightly, as if he wanted to hold my hand, but my palms were sweaty, so I put them in my pockets. I didn't like holding hands. I liked my hands free, for balance.

We walked a few feet apart, mostly silent.

"Thank you," I said, when we reached the building. "For dinner. It was great. And for walking with me."

He studied the entrance.

"I know it's not that nice, but Nate says it's safe."

Then he stared at me so intently that I had to turn away.

"I should probably go in," I said.

I thought about giving him a hug, though I didn't know how to do it without it seeming forced.

His face was suddenly in mine, glasses scraping my cheek, the bridge of his nose crashing into the tip of my nostril.

But then, after a second, my lips sank into his, softer than they appeared, his tongue grazed my mouth, a slow tease, and for a moment I forgot where we were. So this was a real kiss. It was warm and soft, and a little bit slobbery. I considered that for a moment, and whether I might have liked to try again.

Then I thought of Nate, who was probably already home, putting in calls to the disabled home. I pulled away and told him good night.

Yet in the hallway, he lingered. His cologne, a faded musk; his cherry Chapstick, a trace of sweetness.

19

I raced to open the door, but there was only Harry and darkness. Nate wasn't back yet, which meant I had time to relax a little first, which was perfect—until I heard him.

"I think we have some beer left in the fridge," he called from the doorway.

I wanted to make a break for the bathroom, but the trunk got in the way of my foot.

His friend Byron caught me rubbing my toe. His hair was slick, his shirt fitted, and his jeans fancy; they hung loosely from his waist and draped over his shoes at the perfect angle. Every piece of him was in place.

"You okay?" he said.

I examined my toes. No blood. Did they notice the blood on the cushions? It didn't seem like they did. I wondered when they'd realize the lamp was destroyed.

"I hope we didn't wake you," Byron said as Nate entered with beer.

"No, I wasn't sleeping."

"Then you should hang out," he said.

He cracked open a can and handed it to me. It was cold and light in my hand.

I watched the lamp and made a move for it while they were talking about some "asshole bartender." If I could just somehow hide it—

But I wasn't subtle enough.

"What happened here?" Nate said, eyeing the pieces on the floor.

"Nothing. It's just a little— it was an accident. I'm sorry. I'll fix it."

He sighed. "With what? Your tool kit?"

"I have an extra one at my place," Byron said. "You guys can have it."

We thanked him, and then it was quiet for a minute.

"Damn," Byron said to me as I chugged.

This reminded me that I was still visible to them, and that you weren't supposed to drink alcohol as fast as soda.

"Rough night?" he said. "I'll get you another one if you promise not to pound it."

"Sure," I said. "Why not?"

Nate glared at him. Maybe the beer was expensive, or he was worried I'd get drunk. There was that one time in Mexico. That was last summer, our last trip together, the only time we'd left the country. At first Dad had wanted to take us to Israel, somewhere with spiritual significance, but Mexico was closer and cheaper, and ancient civilizations all had something in common, he told us, before he promised that we'd end up seeing the rest of the world eventually, that we'd start by making a bigger trip the following year, which would have been this year, which probably wouldn't have happened since we didn't have any money for trips. But we didn't know that then, which made all of the stories about the Aztecs and the pyramids and the iguanas and jalapenos all the more exciting.

On the boat ride to Isla Mujeres, Dad and Nate sipped cervezas while a man in a cheap Superman costume came around to our table and insisted on squirting shots of 7 Up and tequila into each person's mouth.

Superman stayed with me for a while because I kept closing my mouth too soon, and the shots kept dribbling down my chin and onto my shirt.

Since everyone thought this was so funny, he kept trying. I didn't mind because the tequila tasted sweet, and I was laughing too, maybe because the effects of the alcohol started seeping in. I refused to shut my mouth to more pours after that, and I was so nauseous by the end of the boat ride that it wasn't clear whether my heaving was because of the alcohol or the motion sickness.

But before I got sick, I had experienced what I imagined was the perfect buzz. And for a moment, as the satisfying mixture trickled past my lips, everything seemed perfect.

I was thinking about that while Byron was saying something about the hipsters ruining another perfectly good dive bar. When he noticed I was looking at him, he stopped talking to address me.

"We're being jerks," Byron said. "Why don't you tell us what you did today."

"Me?"

I considered telling them about the date, but what would

Byron think? There wasn't enough to tell. And what did he know?

I'd met Bryon briefly a couple of times before. Once was at the funeral. But the first time was about a year before that; Nate brought him to the house for dinner on a long weekend. When he told me it was nice to meet me like it really was nice and shook Dad's hand with a firm grip, I assumed it was all for show. Another one of Nate's superficial friends. Maybe this one was studying theatre, I had thought, or sales.

But then Byron let Dad fix him a scotch the same way Dad liked it—with tons of ice and sloppy lemon. And then when Dad offered him a second, and Nate suggested they couldn't because they were heading back to the city, Byron had said sure, he'd love another round. He had said they'd always have the city, but how often did they get to hang out in a warm house with a cool dad?

So they stayed, the three of them up late playing cards and watching baseball.

That kind of night meant everything to Dad.

But how much had Nate told Byron about me? Really told him. I wondered what people could tell just by looking at me. Maybe one night when they were out drinking—maybe even that night—Nate had said something like, "Just so you know, she's fucked up. In the head. Be nice."

Or maybe he hadn't said anything. Maybe just, "My sister will be there," like I was a regular sister.

"She's in a transition period," Nate said in response to Byron's question.

"Like all of us," Byron said. He gave me a little wink then, which would have seemed cheesy if he wasn't one of those instinctive winkers; you could tell he didn't have to think before he did it.

"I tried to get temp work in an office, but it was weird, you know, for me," I said.

"For anybody. Office work sucks. That's why I like to dip my hands in a bunch of projects at once—so I don't get sucked in. Diversify the options, keep things fresh."

He locked my eyes like I was the most important person he knew, so much so that I had to look down. He probably didn't even realize he was doing that. I was feeling the alcohol and wanted to say his name.

"Byron." I had said it out loud, apparently.

"I know," he said. "It sounds like I'm bullshitting. People sometimes mistake my enthusiasm for bullshit. But work shouldn't feel like work all the time. That's all I'm really saying."

"Sometimes I can talk to animals," I said. "Think there's a job in that?"

"Could be," Byron said.

"According to a survey I took a few years ago, my shamanistic spirit animal is a horse, which is known for having interspecies communication skills."

"Very cool," Byron said.

"The other day, I went to the zoo, and there's this polar bear, Gus, who smiled at me," I said.

"No. Shit."

"And Harry. Have you met him? He's shy around new people, but when it's just us, we have these conversations where he listens. Like, he'll give me this look, and I'll know what he's thinking. That he wants to be left alone, or that he wants to play, or that he needs a treat. And sometimes he'll read my mind, in a similar kind of way. Have you ever seen a cat do that?"

"I'm not big on pets," Byron said. "But if I could talk to them, I'd keep them all around me, like build an ark or something. Nate, did you know Lucy was Dr. Fuckin' What's-His-Name?"

"Doolittle," I said. "I'd love that, being surrounded by animals all day. I've thought about how great that would be, like if I could work in the zoo or something. That definitely wouldn't feel like work."

"Well, you should do it then."

"What?"

"Work in a zoo."

"Yeah right."

"Why not? We all have dreams, right? Why shouldn't yours come true?"

I had never really thought about it that way before. I'd just sort of existed for so long, fighting against Dad's impractical job talk. But I guess I had sort of dreamed of Gus, the first dream I'd had since my fleeting fantasy of an art gallery. Maybe that meant something.

"Nathaniel," Byron said. "You might be able to make some money off of that. Talking to animals. We could set up a pet psychic line."

Nate laughed. "Right after my first album drops."

"You know you guys have the same face," Byron said. "You're just inside out."

I panicked as I gazed down at my dress. The tags were in place.

"Nate, he's kind of like glass when you think about it, all clean and polished," Byron said.

I checked myself for stains. Nothing glaring.

"The guy can bench press like a machine, but put enough weight on there, and watch out for shattered pieces."

"What are you talking about?" Nate said.

"Look at your sister, man," Byron said. "She's like rubber or something. Put the weight on, and she'll bounce it away so it won't touch her."

"I am? Thanks, I think. Is that a compliment?"

"Of course it is. Your aura's all strength. I can see that in people."

"Actually, the horse is also known for power, stamina, and endurance," I said.

Nate rolled his eyes.

"I know Nate doesn't buy it, but whatever," Byron said. "I've been able to see it for years. You see animals. I see auras. Your sister's got it, Nathaniel. You're the one I worry about."

"Interesting," Nate said. "Since you're the one who can't get a date."

Byron smiled. "Only the suckers get locked down."

It took me a second. I looked at Nate, who wasn't looking at me.

"Wait, you have a girlfriend?" I said. "I mean, of course you do. You always do."

"It's nothing serious, Luce. Don't worry," Nate said.

"Why would I worry? I mean, good for you. People in relationships are supposed to be happier, right?"

Byron laughed. "Doubtful."

Nate didn't say anything.

"So this has been going on a while?" I said.

"Not that long," he said.

"She wasn't at the funeral."

"She was in Thailand."

"Is that where she's from?"

"She's from Vermont."

"It's just weird that you never mentioned her."

"I'm mentioning her now."

"By accident."

He sighed.

"Who's up for some poker?" Byron said.

I wondered what else Nate was hiding, if he spent his nights underground, or his weekends on an apple farm, raising chickens and growing a beard.

"Are you keeping secrets?" I said.

Nate sighed again.

"Deal," he said to Byron.

"Fine," I said, retreating to my sofa. "I guess the beer made me tired. Good night is what I should say. See you."

I flipped off the light and left them in darkness.

"Luce," Nate said, turning on the kitchen light. "What the hell?"

"Come on," Byron said. "Play cards with us."

I thought about it. I knew I could win, but I didn't feel like playing games.

"I'm going to bed," I said.

"We'll try to keep it down," Byron said.

"Luce," Nate said.

"Yeah?"

He paused for a second. "Why don't you take the alcove tonight?"

"Your bed? Are you sure?"

"You won't be able to sleep otherwise."

I retreated behind the wall, but I didn't sleep. We had tested the sound level when I first moved in. If I had the TV on by the couch, Nate couldn't hear it below a certain level when he was on the bed. With earplugs, he couldn't hear anything. But I didn't like the feel of things in my ears, and I had abnormally good hearing, so I took the opportunity to listen to their hushed tones.

"You okay?" Byron said when it was quiet.

"What?" Nate said.

"It's your move. It's been your move."

"No shit," he said. "I'm just thinking."

"About what? Your hot girlfriend?"

He laughed. "That's all I should be thinking about."

"So what's the issue?"

"I don't know. She's basically perfect. She's so nice to everyone, and earthy and grounded, and smart."

"So what's she doing with you?"

"That's the thing. We have this crazy chemistry, but sometimes I think—I feel like I wasn't supposed to meet her yet. Like what if I met my soul mate prematurely?"

"You worry about the stupidest shit," Byron said.

"It's a real concern."

"You really believe in that? One soul mate for life?"

"Maybe."

"You're just overthinking the best thing you have right now."

"Yeah, but I mean come on. We didn't meet too long before all this crap went down. That's pretty shitty timing, when you think about it. What am I supposed to say now when she says she needs more of me, when she says I need to let my guard down, when she says there's no point in being in a relationship with me? What do I offer her right now?"

"Does she say that?"

"She doesn't have to. And the thing is, I have no defense. She's right."

"You can't worry about something that hasn't happened yet."

Nate was quiet.

"You're falling asleep on me, man," Byron said after a while. "You have to sleep more. It's essential to maintaining the body's balance."

"Who has time to sleep?" Nate said.

"That's like saying who has time to eat. It's stupid. If you don't eat, you starve."

"You don't get it, By. I can't sleep."

"You can take something for that."

"There's nothing I haven't tried."

"Have you tried natural remedies? Herbal teas? Because that's a lot healthier than the poison you're taking."

"It's not like before. It's not like if I fail this test, I can make it up on the next one. This is real life. There is no security blanket, nobody to bail me out, so I have to keep going. Hell of a way to begin my twenties, huh? Running a household."

"Who's to say your twenties are supposed to be easy?" Byron said. "Maybe your easy comes in a few years, a little out of order. You just need to relax, man. Want to jam a little before I go?"

Nate didn't say anything, so Byron grabbed his guitar and started playing. *Don't worry about a thing. 'Cause every little thing gonna be all right.*

"You don't even know how to play," Nate said.

"So you play. Have you been playing at all?"

"I haven't had time."

"Bullshit. You have time now. C'mon, man. This is supposed to be your dream. Save the world from corporate evil by day and play in a band by night."

"I can't believe I ever dreamed that."

"Why?" Byron said. "You can't give up on everything."

Nate didn't respond, but after a minute, he started playing so softly I could swear his guitar was singing. I hadn't heard him sing in years. He was good—melodic, soulful, a little sad.

Then Nate's voice began to tremble the tiniest bit, and he stopped.

"This is dumb," he said. "I need to go to bed."

MUCH LATER THAT NIGHT, when I got up for the bathroom, I found Nate whistling the same tune as he was scrubbing at the makeup in the sink.

"Did a clown explode in here?" he said.

"Shoot! I was going to clean when I got back, but then you

guys were here, and—I'll clean it up tomorrow. I promise. I don't want you to have to do everything."

He stopped for a second and looked at me through the mirror. "How was it?"

"What?"

"Was it a date, or what?" he said.

"Frank? I don't know. Actually, yeah, I think so. He kissed me."

"What?" He turned around. "Who is this guy?"

"He's nice."

"What's he look like?"

"I don't know. He's cute I guess. Small, like my height, I mean. Five feet? But much thinner than me. And pale."

I found a dishrag, and I tried my best to help clean up. I wasn't strong enough to scrape the way he did, but at least I didn't make things worse.

"And he's nice?"

"Yeah, he is. He's really nice."

"But . . ."

"He's damaged."

"What kind of damage?" Nate said. "He has a job, right?"

It was stifling in that bathroom. The heat was bubbling from my pores, and Nate was hogging the sink.

"Yeah, he has a job."

"And you didn't sit in silence the whole night?"

"No, I talked. A lot."

"So what else do you want?" he said. "We all have our baggage."

"Right," I said. "Does your girlfriend have baggage?"

Nate acted as though he didn't hear me as he washed the sweat from his forehead.

"Are you going to use all the water?" I said.

"Yep." He boxed me out from the faucet as I tried to get near.

"Nate, come on! Does she even know you have a sister?"

"Sabine?" He got out of the way then. "Of course she does. Actually, she suggested a brunch next weekend. I told her that probably wasn't your favorite meal, but—"

"I can do brunch," I said. "I like brunch."

"Great," he said. "Bring Frank if you want."

20

BRUNCH WAS THE FIRST THING I MENTIONED WHEN I SAW
Frank the next day.

"Are you interested in that meal?" I said through a line of
people.

The customers in front of me turned around.

"I'll wait my turn," I said.

When I got to the counter, I told him it was okay if he didn't
want to go. "I still want a cup of the Ethiopian, and I can pay."

"No," he said. "I don't want you to pay. You're supposed to
try all the different brews. Didn't you say you would?"

"Did I?"

"I told my dad about shade-grown beans. He wasn't interested. But I'll keep trying."

"Great, so you don't want to go to brunch?"

"I can't right now. I have to work."

"No, I meant Sunday. Isn't that a thing? Sunday brunch?
We'd be going with Nate and his girlfriend, Sabine. Not that
we're supposed to be equal to that. I know we've only been on
one date, assuming it was a date, but we don't have to address
that now. I'd like you to come. If you want to. On Sunday."

"I'd be honored to meet your brother."

"Is that a big deal?" I guessed it was. I hadn't thought of it that way. "I mean it shouldn't be a big deal. It's not, really."

"Oh," he said.

I searched for Enid, but there were no signs that she was anywhere near, and so I wondered: What if she had already located a superior artist, someone who could communicate with Belle from the dead, with cards and tea leaves, who could bring her back to life, someone who could reclaim lost souls? If only I could do that.

"I'm ready to taste the coffee anytime," I said. "If the offer still stands."

I got to about five pours from Frank before my legs began to tingle, and I could feel the caffeine swishing through me in hot bursts. My hand was trembling when Enid poked me to say hello.

"Hi!" What time was it? I needed to remember this. "Do you always come to the shop now?"

"I come whenever I feel like it," she said.

"I'll take the ginger green," she said to Frank. "Nature's youth elixir." She stuck her thumbs in her belt loops.

"You want to know something?" She leaned in to whisper. "When I get a real yen for a cup of joe, I go to the shop four blocks down. You have to walk up three steps to get there, but it's half the price! You should tell that boyfriend of yours."

"Who, Frank? He's not my boyfriend."

"Well, it might help if you powdered your face and batted your lashes once in a while."

She pushed open a gold lipstick container to reveal a fuchsia tip. I was worried she was going to press it on me, and that traces of her saliva would propel me into the aging process, or old people's ailments like shingles or liver spots. But she slid a coat onto her own lips.

"It's your job to be the garden," she said.

"What garden?"

"You're obviously the one who needs the tending, but you have to plant some flowers."

"This isn't about sex, is it? Because I don't think I feel comfortable discussing that with you."

"Don't be disgusting," she said. "This is about looking like a proper lady. That's all."

"I wore some makeup when we went out."

"And today?"

"Makeup is not an everyday thing."

I touched my eye, still traumatized by the memory of the mascara attempt the night before.

"Do you have a boyfriend?" I asked. "Or a husband? I'm sure you do, the way you always look so put together. Is that a stupid question?"

"It is a stupid question," she said. "Because I don't look this way for anyone but myself."

"Were you ever married?"

She inspected her fingers. "In my day, you hit a certain age, you found a fella you didn't hate, and you got hitched. But everyone I knew was getting married, and they all seemed so miserable. So I waited. I thought I had it all figured out."

"Then what?"

"Then nothing. All the good prospects went away, and I got stuck with Herb, years later than everyone else."

"But you were happy?"

"Things aren't always so black and white."

She looked down, into her cup.

"He was a handsome devil. Don't get me wrong. Jellyroll hair and a soft leather jacket. And such a charmer. When he told me he wasn't the monogamous type, I thought, finally an honest man! But I was a fool. I didn't know men always tell you who they are. They tell you from the first moment you meet them. I was just too stubborn to listen. And what did I know anyway? I thought we were the same. Neither of us wanted the traditional stuff. We both liked our freedom. But then—out of nowhere, one day he started painting this picture of a family. A little girl with curls, a little boy with a wagon, a big dog in the yard. Before long, he was bringing home these tiny booties and building a crib. Who wouldn't get swept up in that?"

I thought about it. "I'm not sure I would."

"Well, you're smarter than me then," she said. "Because it was just an image. None of it was real."

"So you never had kids?"

Enid took a heavy breath. "It was too late. I was nearly forty by that time, and in those days—" She took a sip and grew quieter. "It just wasn't what the universe had in mind."

She seemed a little sad. I didn't want to push further, so we sat there for a good while just sipping until I realized she was probably waiting for me to say something.

"I'm sorry," I said.

"It wasn't in the cards."

"What happened to Herb?"

"He had a baby with someone else, he moved out, and that was that."

"What an asshole."

"He hardly ever pretended to be anything else."

I peeked over at Frank, who was busy at the counter organizing stacks of napkins.

"He's a kind one," Enid said, following my eyes. "Always with good intentions."

I watched him wipe away a few spills.

"Just pretty up that face and get him to lower the price on the java," she added. "I don't like climbing the steps."

THE REST OF THE AFTERNOON, Enid talked about Belle, about the paws again, and the waves of fur, the way she loved to roll in the grass, how she hated wearing sweaters. It was like she hadn't talked to anyone for so long that she needed to get it all out. Belle's food dish was lime green, and she owned the porch for sunbathing, as well as a marked pachysandra bush, and a spot on the living-room couch from which she could view the entire neighborhood—the same spot where she made her bed most nights, though she was never supposed to be on that couch in the first place.

I listened as best as I could, trying to contain my quickening heartbeat, and twitching eyelids, but it was hard when there was no promise of an end. Would she ever stop? Would I ever feel inspired enough to draw her? By this point, I had a number of false starts, little sketches of Belle's imagined world, but nothing meaningful enough to keep.

"You know I don't do regular portraits, right?" I finally said. "If I do this, it won't be Belle really. It will just be me projecting

Belle onto what I think could somehow happen in my alternate universe, which is probably just a variation on your interpretation of her, since I never knew Belle."

"I don't care about formalities. I just want something to remember her by."

"You don't have any photos?" I said.

"Didn't we already go through this?"

"I wish I had more photos." I wanted more than the few scattered shots of random days, rare moments outside, loose reproductions that had fallen away with our old house. "I guess I like concrete images."

"Why?" Enid said. "They're fake impressions of moments that never happened."

She took a big gulp of her tea, which must have been cold by that point.

"Film captures real life," I said.

"In posed form." She tapped my page again. "Is that all you've got?"

There was very little.

"For now."

"Oh well. My hip's killing me anyway."

I was relieved to see her get up.

"I'm done too," I said. "I'll go with you."

When he saw us at the exit, Frank scampered out from behind his register.

"Is it okay if I call you?" he said.

This was what people did. They talked on the phone to the people they met before and after dates. I could do that. Maybe I could even have a boyfriend.

"Okay," I said. "I'll try to pick up."

———

ONCE FRANK BEGAN CALLING, he called a lot. Up to three times a day. While I appreciated the gesture, it was clear neither of us were phone people.

If something mildly entertaining was on, or if Harry was making a noise, or if I thought I heard Nate jiggling the lock, I'd get distracted. Since his responses were so often muted, he'd have to remind me he was there by asking random questions.

I imagined Frank jotting down possible topics on his steno pad before he called—categories on one side, examples on the other, like a late-night host who only asked what was on the card. Do you like scary movies? No. When did your parents meet? A summer in college I think? What's your favorite ice cream flavor? Chocolate brownie. This is the way I sketched him a few times when I was bored. Inquisition Man—full of questions without answers.

"How did Harry get his name?" he said.

"I don't know," I said, actually stopping my sketch to engage. "I guess he just looked like a Harry. But it's true; I could have done better."

"I like his name."

"I could have thought of something Egyptian, you know? Because the Egyptians worshipped cat gods, something more regal."

He took a minute. "But Harry's not from Egypt."

"Of course not—directly, but it would be best to find a name to represent the traditions of his lineage. Like Nefertiti or something."

"Isn't Harry a male?"

It sometimes felt like we were having separate conversations.

Yet, a week later, it was almost like we were a couple.

21

ON THE DAY OF THE BRUNCH, WE WERE STUCK IN THE BACK
of a line that stretched around the block of a French bistro.
Why were we waiting to pay for a made-up meal?

"Are they giving away free food today?" I said.

Sabine smiled. "You're going to love it here," she said,
squeezing my arm.

Sabine didn't extend her hand when the introductions were
going around; she went in for a hug. Frank wasn't expecting
that. He winced when she lunged toward him, but it was over
before he had to think about where to put his hands. She was,
as I'd expected, beautiful, but in an uncomplicated, natural
sort of way.

"The omelets are incredible," she said to us.

They looked like standard omelets to me, judging by the
plates crammed around tiny tables I could make out in the
distance. "Do they use special eggs?"

"Farm fresh," she said.

When we moved a few steps, Frank positioned himself in
front of Nate and Sabine and cleared his throat. "How did you
two meet?"

He had rehearsed enough to make it sound spontaneous, except his shoulders were stiff, and his speech stilted.

Sabine held Frank's gaze as though it were the most insightful question she'd ever heard. "Isn't that always the thing you want to know?"

She looked at Nate then.

He was watching her as though she were draped in light. It almost looked like she was, the way the sun was bouncing off of her hair. "We were at a party. Well, I was. He was crashing."

"It was a beer garden," Nate said. "We didn't know about the party."

"He tried to buy me a drink, but it was an open bar."

"I wanted to save her from standing in line," Nate said.

"It was very sweet," she said, kissing him on the cheek. "I ended up missing most of the event because we talked the whole night. I thought, if nothing else, I have just made a new friend in this city."

"A friend, huh?" Nate said.

"Yes, a friend," she said. "Of course, once he began serenading me with that guitar, I was smitten."

He blushed a little, something I hadn't seen in a while. Was that lust or love?

"Is that what you do for all the girls?" I said.

"Of course not," he said. "There are no other girls."

"Aw," Sabine said, holding Nate's hand. "There's the romantic I fell for. You know he used to write me songs all the time? Poems from his soul. I've missed that guy."

"I'm still here," Nate said. "I haven't gone anywhere."

She looked at Nate for a second before turning her attention toward Frank.

"So, tell us." Sabine gave Frank a playful jab with her elbow, which made him stiffen further. "How did the stars align for you two?"

Frank coughed and took a minute to gather some thoughts. "She was looking for a job, and we didn't have one, but she drew this dog, and I asked her to dinner."

"He gave me free coffee," I said.

Frank nodded. "I got lucky working in a coffee shop."

"I wish I did that," Sabine said. "Can you imagine, sweetie?" She said "sweetie" as though it were Nate's name. I couldn't imagine Frank as anything other than Frank. "You must meet the most interesting people."

"Yeah, but he doesn't drink coffee," I said. "Which must be easy for him now, since we don't have any. Do you think we'll have some soon? Not like it's urgent, but I didn't have any this morning because I knew we'd have some with the meal. Will we have to wait much longer?"

Nate was tapping his foot, looking a little more fidgety than usual. It seemed as though he was stuck in one of two modes lately: restless and antsy or exhausted and half-asleep.

"This is standard procedure," he said.

My legs were wobbling, and I was getting flushed from the heat. Plus, the line was so crowded. Baby carriages kept brushing up against my feet, and people's newspapers were encroaching on my personal space. "Is there a place to sit?"

"We could go somewhere else," Sabine said. "If we had to."

"Maybe we should," Nate said. "What's the point of standing here all day?"

"The point is to get to know each other," Sabine said. "And

to enjoy a delicious meal. But I don't mind leaving if that's what everyone else wants."

"I just meant maybe we could find another spot," Nate said.

"As good as this one?" Sabine said. "Where?"

"No, I can wait," I said. "I just wanted an approximation, so I could mentally prepare. I could go somewhere to get a place-holder cup."

"I have a better idea," Sabine said.

We watched her prance across the street to a newsstand—she must have been a dancer with that stride—and return armed with a copy of the *Times* and the *Daily News*.

"Pick your sections," she said.

Normally I would have taken the *Times*, but the *News* had the comics, so Frank and I split up that paper, while Sabine and Nate took chunks of the other one, and by the time we got through our pages, it was our turn to be seated.

THE TABLE WAS SMALLER than it had looked through the window. Other tables surrounded us on all sides. I knocked over a woman's fork and rammed into a waiter trying to squeeze into place. The waiter looked at me and shook his head, as if it were my fault that this place was over capacity.

The seats were so close together that I was practically on Frank's lap. I wanted to leave until I caught a whiff of the coffee from the table next to us.

Nate smelled it too, and looked at me. "We'll put in the order as soon as we can," he said.

"How long do you think that will take?"

Not too long, apparently, because they wanted us out as soon as we got in. But the cups were child-size, and by the time the waiter finished serving everyone's first round, and tea for Frank, I was ready for my second. I motioned to him and my cup to let him know, but he didn't seem to appreciate that.

"You'll have to give me a minute, please."

I wanted to leave again. Why was brunch a thing? I looked around the table and grabbed a corn muffin from a basket, stuffing a large piece into my mouth.

"Aren't those amazing?" Sabine said.

I nodded, hoping I wouldn't choke.

When we placed our orders, we were allowed to pick one item from the six listed. NO SUBSTITUTIONS! it said on the bottom of the menu.

"Does that mean no mushrooms for onions?" I said.

"Yes," Nate said.

Still, when the waiter came, Frank didn't seem to get it.

"Could I have extra potatoes instead of salad?" he said.

"No substitutions," the waiter said.

Frank was ruffled by his rudeness, which made me a little sad, but also a little irritated because hadn't he read the menu.

Nobody else in the restaurant seemed to have any trouble with the setup. Least of all Sabine, who found enough room somehow to cross her legs and touch each hand multiple times, to talk so that we could all hear, to make her way through her plate delicately enough not to lose control of the conversation. How did she do that?

It seemed she talked the whole meal, first about her current internship at some fancy consulting firm with a long name.

"You crunch numbers?" I imagined a giant Pac-Man board, a digital version of Sabine swallowing complex decimals and fractions before spitting them out and rearranging them for the next player.

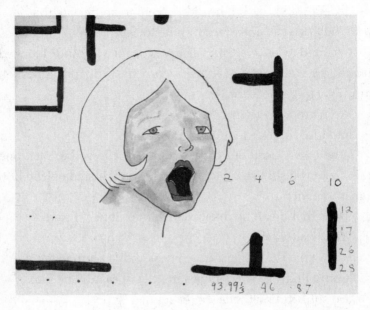

"In a way," she said.

And then she went on about some future internship in data analysis that lost me as soon as she began.

"I do some consulting, sort of," I said. I looked at Frank. "I mean, I kind of did the other day. With coffee tasting?"

"That sounds much more interesting," she said.

"She's an expert," Frank said.

"No," I said. "I just really like coffee. Do you think we could get more?"

I was hungry, and there wasn't enough on the plate. It looked more like a snack than a meal, though the fruit was arranged so skillfully I was hesitant to eat it.

"So," Sabine said. "Are you two planning on getting away this summer at all?"

"Away from here?" I said. "Why, are you?"

"Not really," Nate said.

"Well, we do have this wedding in a couple of weeks," she said. "My cousin."

Nate looked at her. "I didn't know I was invited to that."

"I reminded you about it the other day," Sabine said.

"Yeah, but you didn't tell me I was going."

"That was the reason I brought it up," Sabine said. "But that's fine. You don't have to go. Are you saying you don't want to go?"

"No," Nate said. "I'm not saying that. But I was planning on working full weekends this month."

"That's okay," Sabine said. "If you have to work, I'm sure I can find another date."

"Don't be ridiculous," Nate said. "I'll go. I'll just have to pull a couple extra-late nights this week."

"Again?" she said.

"So we can pay for things like brunch," Nate said.

Sabine didn't respond directly to Nate. She gave it a second and then went on about what a great match her cousin and her cousin's fiancé were with their musical theatre backgrounds, how they were so perfect for each other. I didn't care about her cousin, but I wondered what it would be like to attend a wedding with a date. I imagined Nate and Sabine dancing close, the ideal proportions for her to lean her cheek against his when the bass softened, for his hand to rest on her lower back. After a fight, they probably danced closer.

I bet Sabine knew how to dance the moment she stepped onto the floor. She seemed like someone who had been dancing her whole life. And Nate was a quick study, so he would know how to adapt to her style.

Listen to the music, he had said in Mexico, when I was too buzzed to worry about how out of sync I was with the mariachi band. Watch what they do. I tried. In my head I could see it, but my feet couldn't keep up.

Frank said he didn't like to dance, but that he'd take me one day if I wanted. I didn't want to go dancing; that wasn't the point. I only wanted to know how.

I wondered if I might have wanted to go with someone else. That man waiting outside the bathroom, for example. He was tall, and graceful-looking, kind of like Byron. What if I just walked up to him and started talking? I'd have to maneuver through narrow aisles to get to him, so I'd probably trip over a fallen spoon or an outstretched foot, and the creamer would fly, and all of us would have to leave with our heads down. And what would I say anyway? He wouldn't want to respond to someone like me. It was the shuffling that caused my problems.

"You think they make anti-shuffle shoes?" I said.

"What?" Nate said.

"You know, for people who shuffle?"

"Where did that come from?"

"I was trying to make a connection. You ever do that?"

"Between what?"

"Two things."

———

AFTER BRUNCH, as we stood in the foyer to say our goodbyes, it started pouring. Nate and Sabine grabbed newspapers as rain shields and ran off, leaving us standing on the welcome mat staring into the storm.

"Here," Frank said, handing me a compact umbrella wrapped inside the sweatshirt he'd brought.

"How did you know?"

"I always check the weather before I leave home," he said. "Take it."

When he suggested he could come over to our apartment for a while after the meal, I thought of the day-old coffee sitting in the pot, my clothes hanging over the arms of each chair, the litter box, Nate's disappointment.

"He's going to kill me if I don't straighten up before he gets back."

"I don't care if it's messy," Frank said.

Anyone else, that guy standing by the bathroom, or Sabine or Nate, would have cared, a lot probably. Still, I told him no thanks because I didn't want him to see it.

We said goodbye as I held up Frank's umbrella and watched his glasses fog. I supposed I was starting to get used to it, the image of him listening to me ramble, his forehead crinkling to absorb whatever confusion I unloaded, the look of enchantment that sometimes crossed his face. Yet I wondered if I'd ever register a look for him like the one Nate had given Sabine that day.

22

FRANK DECIDED THAT OUR NEXT OFFICIAL MEETING SHOULD be a real date, just the two of us. We chose a movie: shared fodder for conversation, and a shared armrest in the dark. Since the best theaters were within a ten-block radius of his place, it made the most sense to meet outside of his lobby.

I made sure I had clean clothes ahead of time, and my hat, and despite Enid's urging, I didn't bother with any eye makeup. Though I did use lipstick, red, which I figured was better than nothing. I asked Nate to write out how to get to Frank's place exactly—one train, and three blocks—and I packed my purse ahead of time with my wallet and a full MetroCard. Still, I was fifteen minutes behind schedule. I knew we'd have to rush to make it to a movie on time.

He wasn't standing outside his building when I got there, and when I peeked through the door, I saw he wasn't inside the foyer either. Had he left without me? That didn't seem like him. I found his name on the directory on the wall, and he buzzed me in.

When I got to his apartment, I found that it was open.

"Did I get the time wrong?" I called out.

He was sitting at his computer in a white T-shirt.

"Or the day?"

"No, I'll be ready in a minute."

As I made my way toward the couch, I noticed a pile of neatly folded laundry in his open closet tagged with a Post-it. *Love you* ☺, it said. I assumed that came from his mother, who was featured in the only picture he had on his desk—a snapshot of his parents at some buttoned-up event—he in a gray suit to match his gray hair, and she in a blue dress with pearls and permed hair.

Everywhere things were neat and ordered—a single bookshelf lined with classics that appeared as though they had never been opened. Bare, white walls.

He was focused on his computer screen.

"Just finishing up."

I moved to see what he was seeing. It was some kind of video game. It didn't seem like a sufficient excuse for missing the movie.

I waited for his character to die or for his fuel to run out, but he kept going. It had to be at least five to ten minutes. It felt like longer.

"We won't get seats if we don't get there soon. Do you know what time it is? I think it's late."

He was concentrating his cursor on a robot in the center of the screen.

"Frank?"

I would've rather seen a movie by myself than stand there any longer.

"I guess I can try to save you a seat or something," I said.

I walked toward the door. He didn't seem to see me until I was at the threshold.

"Wait! I'm not good at multitasking. That's what Mom says. Hyperfocus. I get too preoccupied. We can go now."

"It's too late for our movie."

He mumbled something. "What?"

"Sorry," he said.

I looked at the computer. "Can we turn this off now?"

He did, and then he excused himself. I heard the water running, and when he came back, his hair was slick, and he was wearing a plaid shirt.

"I don't know what to do now," he said. "I understand if you want to go home."

"It's okay."

"I ruined our plan," he said. "The movie already started."

"I guess we can pick something to watch here."

"That's a good idea." His face lit up. "You always have really good ideas."

But it wasn't easy to pick something. He wanted action movies, slapstick humor, manipulative characters, storylines that catered to the masses. He was the masses. He enjoyed simple plots and spectacles; I appreciated nuance—in my films anyway.

"I've never heard of those movies," he said of the few selections I'd suggested.

"That's because you have bad taste," I said.

He didn't respond, but I knew it was mean, so I reached for his hand across the couch.

At first he pulled back—startled, it seemed—but then he let me take it. I didn't know what I was supposed to do with it, really, so I just held it for a minute, limply, and then let it go.

He didn't know how to select a movie either, because he hardly ever used his TV. It took us a long time to figure out how to make it work. He sat there while I fiddled with the controls.

"You don't have any idea?"

"No," he said. "But you can pick whatever you want."

In the end, I made an awkward choice, *The Decalogue*; it was overly serious, and long, and full of symbolism and opaque language. Plus, it had ten parts.

"Aren't movies supposed to be fun?" he said after we watched the first section.

"Thinking is fun for me. Art. Beauty. Did you not get those things?"

"Did you follow what was happening? I can't follow that closely."

"Well, were you paying attention?"

"I was trying, but I don't think it's fun to think so hard while you're watching a movie."

I got what he was saying, but I didn't like it, so I told him that I would finish watching the other parts on my own.

THE NEXT NIGHT when Frank called, I told him I wanted to watch part two (although I hadn't yet found a way to get it), and he offered to come over and sit with me; he didn't have to watch, he said. He could do something else.

"Like what?"

He said he didn't know, but he wanted to spend time with me. That was his main priority. He'd even bring popcorn. The popcorn was tempting, but the idea was ridiculous. I didn't want to watch a movie with someone who wasn't watching, I said.

I needed my space, and my time alone, and I would've been happy not to have seen him for a few days. But he called me the next night and said he really needed to talk.

"About what?" I said.

"Can I come over?"

I didn't want him to. It was late. I was in my pajamas, ready for bed.

"Please," he said.

When he arrived, he looked slighter than usual, worn down and hunched over in his extra-small hoodie.

He said he'd gotten in trouble at work. One of the distributors had yelled at him for some kind of miscalculation and had told him he would have been fired by now, many times over, if not for his father. Instead of standing up for himself, he said, thinking of a strong comeback or even walking out, he had panicked and crumbled.

It was hard to think of the right response. I was supposed to comfort him; I got that, but I wasn't sure how. I would have made an ugly scene of it, called the distributor profanities and spilled some coffee on him. But I had hoped that somehow Frank wasn't as vulnerable to ridicule, or that if he was, that he would be able to handle it in a more manly way. It was difficult to see him this small. And to see me in him.

"Did you tell your dad about it?"

"I don't want him to know what happened, and I don't want anyone to get in trouble."

When I noticed his tears resurfacing, I had to turn away.

"Tea?" I said.

"What?"

"We have some. Nate bought it because Sabine said it was healthy. I can make hot water."

When I brought him a mug of chamomile, I noticed he was looking at me in his strange way: half daze, half grin.

"What is that look?" I said.

"I was just wondering what your dream for the future is. What do you see?"

"I don't know." I didn't see anything. That was the problem. "Gus maybe? The zoo? What do you see?"

"I see a wedding," he said. "A soul mate."

"Huh," I said. "Interesting."

"Do you—or have you—ever thought about marriage?"

I was fixated on the skin peeling off his lips.

"I found this cocoa-flavored lip balm the other day," I said. "It tastes like candy. Try it."

"Did you hear what I asked?"

"Marriage?" I handed him the stick. "Why? Do you know someone getting married?"

He put too much on his lips.

"A little goes a long way," I said.

"I love you," he said.

"What?"

"I said—"

"Why?"

When I thought of love, I thought of camping by a fire, warm flannel, wintergreen Life Savers in the dark—biting into sparks, crackly and raw. But maybe that was just something I'd seen in a commercial.

"What do you mean?" he said.

"Why do you love me?"

"I don't know."

"You probably just love the idea of me, of having someone to be with you. I've heard about that kind of thing."

"No, that's not it," he said. "I don't take away your feelings and correct them."

"That's stupid. I'm not—" I stopped when I noticed he was frowning. "You're not stupid. I didn't mean that."

"I know I don't have your education, and I don't read like you. But I like that you do. You make me want to know more things. I like being with you. You give me something to look forward to every day, so for me—I think that means I love you."

For the first time in a long time, I had nothing to say.

After a minute, he asked me if I needed him to go.

"No." I wanted him to stay. I knew Nate was at Sabine's that night.

I had previously explained to him that I couldn't imagine sleeping with another body stifling my movement, affecting my temperature, restricting my freedom. But also, I hadn't been ready to do anything more than kiss him. I didn't have any experience. I wondered if he did.

That night we did more than kiss.

His toes were like ice cubes, so I asked him to wear his socks and then asked him to move them away from me because they were scratchy.

I let him warm me in his grip. And for a little while, neither of us was wearing anything besides our skin, and I wasn't thinking about whether I was putting my hands where they were supposed to go, or about the fact that I couldn't see what I was kissing because it was dark, or about whether it was going to feel okay, or whether what we were about to do would constitute sex. Whatever it was, it was something I needed to try. It was what ninety percent of the world's jokes and stories and songs were about. I let him take the lead. It wasn't comfortable, really, and it wasn't fun or even pleasurable. But for a little while, I let go of my thoughts, and of myself. And for a little while, everything felt okay.

After, as I lay there listening to him sleep, feeling the heat from his chamomile breath and soft, clammy hands, I thought it was kind of nice to have him there.

But after another little while, I moved to the far side of the sofa and put on my clothes.

I couldn't sleep. I tried willing my eyes closed, and when that didn't work, I tried focusing my attention on the ceiling cracks until it was too dark to make them out.

I took a shower, and as I was getting out, I heard Nate turn the lock on the front door.

I'd seen him leaving earlier and earlier in the mornings, coming back later and later.

"You're home?" I said. "I thought you went to Sabine's on Wednesdays."

"She had an event. I went for a run."

"It's really late, isn't it?"

"I don't know," he said. "Is it?"

He extended his knee and winced, and I noticed that one leg was a lot bigger than the other.

"What happened?"

"Nothing. Not enough stretching. Old sneakers."

"Maybe you should see a doctor."

"No point in that." He limped to the kitchen. "I know what I need."

He grabbed a beer from the fridge first, and then he rifled through the freezer until he found an old bag of peas to squeeze into a wrap around his knee.

"Do you think you should rest more?"

"Probably," he said.

I followed him into his alcove; we walked past Frank, but he didn't seem to notice.

"Frank's here, by the way. He's asleep. I thought you should know that in case you see him in the morning, not that he has to stay."

He looked at me and then looked at Frank, who was in his boxer shorts and undershirt.

"Uch, are you kidding me?" he said. "Fine. Whatever, I guess. As long as he stays clothed."

"Very funny," I said.

"I'm not kidding, Luce. Remember I'm right here."

He popped a pill and lay down on his bed, making a show of putting in his earplugs.

"Are you sure you don't need anything?" I said.

He turned away and folded the pillow over his head.

I returned to Frank and watched him sleep. I wished in a way that he would leave so I could have the bed to myself, but I didn't have the energy to worry about it.

I lay next to him and let my head rest on his shoulder. It didn't sit well on the bone. But he shifted enough to allow my hair to ease over him without pulling, for my ear to find the soft spot between his collar and the crook beside his neck. I rested inside that spot until I could sleep, and I didn't move again until morning.

23

When the weekend arrived, Nate packed a bag and said he and Sabine were going to the Catskills to the wedding she had mentioned. I assumed he would spend a couple of days away; he had said as much before he left, so I invited Frank over to stay.

But Nate came back the night he left, charging in as Frank and I were watching cartoons.

"I thought you were getting a hotel," I said.

"Me too," he said.

"How was it?"

"Miserable." I could smell alcohol, whiskey maybe. "What are you watching?"

When Nate cut off the cable, we lost Animal Planet and the National Geographic Channel, any chance for watching a decent movie, and pretty much all signs of reception. But Frank had done his research and figured out how to access just about anything online, cartoons included.

"*Fantastic Four*? I was just telling Frank how much you used to like it."

He stuck his head in the refrigerator. "Wasn't there beer in here?"

"There was only one left," I said.

"And you drank it?"

"It's my fault," Frank said.

"No," I said. "We didn't think you'd be home, so we split it, for a change of pace, but we were planning to replace it. We only drank it because we didn't think you'd need it."

"I don't need it," he said.

What had Sabine done to him? I pictured her throwing drinks in his face, or slipping him something that caused him to lose more strength and power with each sip.

"I can go out and get more," Frank said.

"Forget it," Nate said, a little loudly. "Which one is this?"

"Something about Super-Skrull?" Frank said.

"No way," Nate said. "Top ten cartoon episodes of all time."

He loosened his tie, but when he looked for space to sit, he couldn't find any.

"We'll move over," I said, though there was nowhere to move.

He stood for a minute watching over us, swaying a little, before slipping away and collapsing in his corner.

NATE STAYED IN BED for most of Sunday, and on Monday morning when I didn't see him, I guessed it was because he had left early.

But when I came home from the coffee shop later that afternoon, I found him splayed out on the cushions, cartoons bouncing off of his undershirt, a beer bottle on the floor, and an ashtray packed with butts. He looked off.

"You went to work this morning, didn't you? Do I have the time wrong?"

He didn't answer. He just sat there looking bleary-eyed and messy.

I checked his watch. It was only four. I checked again and noticed there was dried blood along his fingernails, tiny wounds from biting his nails.

"Are you sick?"

"Yep."

"Did you call in today?"

He closed his eyes.

"Did you break up with Sabine?" I said.

He surveyed his hands and began chewing at the cuticles again.

"Because if you did, maybe it's for the best? She didn't seem that great. You can do better. Unless you didn't break up."

He didn't answer. He locked himself in the bathroom for a while and then went back to sleep.

NATE WAS SUPPOSED to leave before eight most days, eight thirty after a big night. But after the wedding, that whole week, he was late.

"Don't you have to go to work?" I said on Wednesday.

"I'm on a personal morning."

"Again?"

"Yep."

He looked thin to me, gaunt around his jawline. He hadn't shaved in a couple of days, and his hair, which seemed to need a wash, was sticking out on the left side.

"Are you still sick?"

"Did you see her last night?" he said.

"Sabine? Did she come by?"

"Mom."

I must have misheard him. I checked the coffee machine. He hadn't made any yet. Despite all his time in bed, he seemed to be sleeping even less than usual. The puffs beneath his eyes were colored as if he'd been punched a few times.

"She smelled like vanilla," he said.

I looked at him. I didn't remember telling him that. He was so small when she died, Velcro shoes.

"I wanted to talk to her," he said. "But she wouldn't answer."

Would she even have recognized him? I needed caffeine, but there weren't enough beans for a pot, a couple of cups at most, if I made it weak.

"I thought you wanted to hospitalize me the last time I said that."

He looked away, somewhere beyond the window. I couldn't track his gaze.

"But then I guess you did allow for the possibility, that time with the Lucky Charms. So this is kind of huge, isn't it? You actually think you saw her? What happened?"

"It was only half a second," he said. "Less than that. But the air felt strange. Did she speak to you at all?"

It would have been a fitting time for her to appear to both of us, to whisper something profound that could set Nate back on track, but all we could hear was the churning of the machine.

"Never," I said.

"I'm not sure it was her," he said. "How can you be sure of anything these days?"

He was drifting around the room like a deflating balloon, like all the life were leaking out of him.

"We know what we feel, right?" I said. "We can trust the vibration."

"I never felt her before last night," he said. "Not even when I tried."

"You tried?"

"After Dad told us she wasn't coming back."

"You remember that?"

"You don't forget shit like that. I prayed every night. She never came."

"Maybe you just weren't ready to see her before."

"Why now then? Why here?"

"Comfort maybe. Knowing that we're not alone without Dad?"

"That's some bullshit," he said, returning to his area. "It has to be more than that."

"She worried a lot, like you do. Maybe she was just checking in."

He didn't answer. I wished I had something more insightful to say, but I didn't, so I left him alone. I couldn't decide if his seeing her was a good or bad sign.

WHEN I HEARD A creaking noise in the living room much later that night, the hardwood floor moving, I hoped it was Mom. But when I realized it wasn't, I assumed it was Harry chasing after something.

"Harry?" I called.

"He's under the bed," Nate said.

Nate was on his back, his feet tucked beneath the TV stand. He was dripping with sweat, his shirt soaked through to his ribs, pressing against his chest as he finished what looked like an eight hundredth sit-up.

I watched him for a minute, the veins in his arms protruding.

"Did I wake you?" he said.

"Not really."

He pulled out some free weights from the corner and started lifting with the left arm, slow and steady pulls. Could veins burst? He was sweating, and reddening—a lot.

"Nate?" He had the bigger weight in his arm. "Are you okay?"

"Yeah, just give me a sec—actually, no, come here. Can you hold this for me?"

I tried to help him lift it from his chest. It worked for a second, but then he started giving it up entirely, and I couldn't take it, so it slammed to the floor.

He was out of breath, consumed. I looked at him, the bones of him, and remembered how he used to be so solid.

THE NEXT THREE DAYS in a row, he called in sick.

I attempted talking to him, he answered in short utterances; offering him food, he wasn't hungry; bringing him his guitar, he wasn't in the mood, not for anything. It was growing unbearable—watching him laze away the days, his underarms yellowing, his face peeling from the ashy undertones of his skin. I offered him moisturizer; he wouldn't take it. And then he wouldn't leave his bed.

I knew what this was. I had been here before when I was depressed. Those days when forming simple sentences felt like work, when the thought of getting dressed was too grueling, when the specter of hopelessness clouded every muddled thought. When I was convinced I would never feel any better. Those days were excruciating.

But those days had nothing to do with Nate.

It occurred to me that maybe the real Nate had swooped in earlier and left this pod in his place so he could go off and fulfill some greater mission. How could we know we weren't living as brains in vats somewhere else anyway? How could I know this person in his bed wasn't Nate's vat come undone?

"Do you believe in the Matrix?" I said.

He didn't answer.

He wouldn't pick up his phone either, no matter how many times it rang.

"Do you want me to get it?" I said. "I can tell them to stop calling."

He didn't say no.

It was Sabine.

"I need help," I said. "I mean he needs help, but I'm not sure how. He seems broken. Did you do this? It's okay if you did, but can you fix him? He's not acting like himself."

She was quiet on the other end.

"Are you there?" I said.

"He hasn't been himself for a long time," she finally said. "I was just calling to make sure he's okay."

"Well, he's not, actually. That's what I'm trying to say."

"I'm sorry," she said.

"For what? Did you guys have a fight? I think you should talk. Do you want to come over? I'm sure he'd like to see you. I could make brownies. Or you could, if you wanted. I could make tea."

"Lucy," she said, "this isn't about one fight."

"What is it about then?"

"This is about a fundamental shift in his being. When I

first met him, he was so sweet and fun and thoughtful. But he was also so focused. You don't understand. He was full of all of these plans and ideas. Goals."

"He'll have those again. You can't blame him for having to change course."

"No," she said. "You're right. I can't blame him for any of it."

"So help him. Please! Make him right again."

"He needs more help than I can give him."

"What do you mean?"

"I know it seems like this is my fault, but—this is bigger than me. He knows that. And I have my own issues to deal with."

She was sniffling on the other end. I could hear her.

"So that's it?"

She took a minute.

"I just wanted to know that he was okay," she said. "Can you tell him that?"

"But he's not okay!"

I could hear her breathing.

"He's stronger than he thinks," she said. "When he's ready, he'll know what to do."

"What does that mean?"

"I have to go."

I had a vision of Nate and me together then, two shrunken corpses on the couch, our bodies sticking to the fabric, sparse hair falling from our head, Harry squished between us. We wouldn't make it like this.

"Sabine called," I said.

I heard him rustle in his bed, but he didn't get up.

"She said she's sorry, and that she hopes you're okay. Do you want me to call someone else? Byron?"

"No," he said. "I didn't tell you to answer my phone."

He got up from bed abruptly then and got in my face. "I can't have you touching my stuff. Do you understand that?"

I backed away. This wasn't the brother I knew.

"I was trying to help you," I said.

"You want to help me?"

"Yes! I do."

"Fine. Then how about you leave me the fuck alone and give me my space."

I knew I couldn't keep my voice calm if I wanted to stave off the tears, so I grabbed my keys, and I started walking.

He didn't try to stop me.

For some reason, I couldn't get Mexico out of my head. My mind kept returning to the story of these two trees that were everywhere in that country, the Chechen and the Chaca—one with a poison, one with the remedy. We must have heard the same story seven times, but the way I liked it told best was by an animated tour guide in a forest. He was a natural storyteller who wasn't afraid to whisper or to shout to please the crowd. He told us that the Mayan legend posited that the trees were once brothers. One of them, a guy who had been scorned, was evil, and the other one, a guy who had everything, was noble. When the evil one was spurned by the woman he loved, he decided to kill himself and cast some spell so he could become a poisonous tree and hurt people for eternity the way he'd been hurt by his lover. But then the moral brother got wind of this and decided that he should kill himself too, and cast a spell so that he could become a tree that would act as a remedy to his brother's poison.

They were reincarnated in all of these forests, all over the place. And they could always be found within a few feet of each other, so one would always be around to ensure the other one wasn't doing too much damage.

If we were trees, I wondered which was which.

24

When I stepped into the coffee shop, Nate slipped my mind for a moment. I'd been thinking about him so much that I forgot about everything else.

After I had my first taste of the house blend, I noticed the way my seat in the back seemed curved the way I'd left it, how the light bounced off the front leg, and the music sailed past. I was beginning to get used to the song rotation there—Jazz Legends Volumes I through IV—and I recognized a couple of the people who came in for to-go cups. It was comfortable, and I felt a little better.

When Enid arrived, I was thrilled to see her.

"You ready to work on Belle?" she said as she pulled up a chair to my table.

"Yes!"

Belle was exactly what I needed then, though I was pretty sure the vague drawings I'd done when she first mentioned the dog were in the sketchbook I'd left in the apartment.

"I'll tell you something," she said, drumming the table. "The best things in life always leave before you're ready."

I waited for her to say more, but she only sipped her tea.

"You mean the dog?"

She nodded. "That's why we need to do this today."

I examined her face. No muscles were drooping, no signs of tremors in her limbs, no yellowing in the eyes. Still, her lips appeared especially wrinkled that day, as though they wished to hide inside her mouth. Too wrinkled to kiss or sip or whistle. I wondered if she used to smoke, or sing, or blow bubbles in her chewing gum. Was she a good dancer? If only I could've reached inside her mouth to extract her history.

She looked so shriveled as she sat there, washed out as though her face were going to fade into the white of her hair. I wanted to take a paintbrush to her skin and fill in her crevices with putty. I'd color her hair platinum blond, or black, or fuchsia, to match her lips. She must have been pretty. She'd said that once. A knockout.

"You're not dying are you, because I don't think I could handle that right now."

"Don't be ridiculous," she said. "I'm healthier than you are. I told you to start drinking that tea."

"You're probably right. Actually, do you have any more advice for me? Because I could really use some of that today."

She took a minute.

"Enid?"

"I'm thinking. I'm not a knowledge dispensary."

"Fine," I said.

"What's the matter with you?" she said.

"I wouldn't want to bother you with my troubles."

She went to the counter for more hot water, and when she came back, she handed me a napkin for a spill I hadn't noticed.

"You have something on your mind, say it," she said.

"I'm worried," I said.

She looked at Frank.

"Not about him, about Nate. My brother. He's not himself lately, and I'm scared he's getting worse. Do you have any brothers?"

"I had a sister," she said. "As girls, we were inseparable. We shared everything."

She took some time to finish steeping her tea bag before carefully placing it on her saucer.

"Then she married Howard, a buffoon, and moved to California. We wrote letters at first, tried visits on holidays. But our priorities changed, and one of us, or it could have been both of us—who knows—ran out of things to say."

Nate and I were different from each other from the start, different from other siblings. Maybe that was better.

"Do you ever see her now?" I said.

"She's gone." She looked into her cup. "They all are. That's what I was saying before. That's why you have to learn to take care of yourself."

"How do you do that if you've never done it before?"

"You just do," she said. She tapped her finger on the table and adjusted her posture. "The people who get on in this world are the people who get up and look for the circumstances they want, and, if they can't find them, make them."

"Is that another famous quote?"

"George Bernard Shaw. *Mrs. Warren's Profession.*"

"I should read more plays," I said. "How do you know so many plays?"

"Running lines helps," she said. "I auditioned for that one twice."

"I knew you were an actress."

"I wanted to be Ethel Merman when I first got here. But I didn't have the voice, the chops, or the right look. I wasn't good enough, plain and simple. Though I didn't want to accept that."

"So you persevered and became great in spite of yourself?"

"Of course not. I wasted my time failing. But then one day, I was sitting for an audition when a girl came in crying. Her dress was ripped. I pulled out a sewing kit (I carried that little pouch everywhere), fixed the hem, pinched in the waist, and pushed up the bust—did a hell of a job all around. She got the part because of me, and all the other girls in the room knew it. Could I help them with their dresses next, where did I get what I was wearing, had I altered my look myself? Before too long I had my own business."

"A costume designer?"

"A seamstress. The best in the neighborhood."

"I can't sew," I said. "The needles are too small."

She rolled her eyes. "The story isn't about sewing. The story is about life."

"I know," I said. "Finding your strengths in the face of adversity. Going through windows when doors close, all that stuff Dad loved saying."

"Sounds like a smart man."

"He was," I said. "And he always took care of me."

She looked outside.

"When you have no choice, you find a way to get things done," she said.

"Yeah, but—"

"But nothing. You don't dwell, you just do. And when you do, you realize lots of things take care of themselves. You'd be surprised. You spend too much time thinking about what could have been and what might be, and before you know it, you've missed what is."

"I think I need more coffee," I said.

I looked at Frank again, and this time he noticed, taking it as a cue for refills.

"Thank you, Franklin," Enid said. She took a sip. "You know, I've been meaning to ask you something."

"A special discount?" he said.

"When are you going to spotlight your girl's art on the wall?"

For a second I worried this was an ambush. Was this Enid's idea of forcing open a window?

Frank was rapidly flushing, and increasingly uncomfortable.

"Oh, I don't know," he said.

"What don't you know?" I said. "You don't think I'm good enough?"

"No, but . . . I thought that was just a hobby."

"A hobby?"

"You never really work on it, so . . ."

"So what?"

"So, I'd have to ask my father first."

Enid looked at me. "Show him what you've done so far on Belle! He'll think differently when he sees it."

I didn't have Belle. I wasn't even sure what I'd done with her.

"Well?" she said.

"It's not done."

"I don't believe it," she said. Her eyes were closing in. "You lost it?"

"No! I'm sure it's at home. I'll finish next time."

She didn't respond.

"Enid?"

"You know what your problem is?" she said eventually. "You don't even know what you want."

"That's not true, I don't think. I want to work at the zoo one day, I hope, if it's at all possible, and I want to finish that portrait of Belle, and have the old Nate back. It's just—with my frontal lobe—I have trouble prioritizing sometimes, and—it's not that simple for me."

She enclosed my hand with her own wrinkled grip, free from jewelry, chilled and soft. Inside those hands, there was power—balled-up bits of strength. I tried not to move.

"What if it is?" she said. "What if you and your excuses make everything too complicated?"

I gave it a second. "Was that a rhetorical question?"

"When you're ready to work, you can let me know," she said.

She turned quickly and headed for the door, her square heels clomping against the floor.

"But I am ready!" I called out.

I hurried to meet her at the threshold. "Why do you always have to go somewhere?"

I wondered where she went when she left the shop. She never mentioned having any close friends, hadn't replaced Belle with any new animals, hadn't said she had any particular activities to attend to, like bridge or mahjong, or swimming at the Y. I wondered if she sewed when she went home, blankets and mittens, patterns on pillows.

How did she fill all of those hours all alone, all of that time? It must have been quiet in her place. She must have gone whole days without speaking to anyone.

"What about the rest of our conversation?" I said.

She looked me up and down. "You're not the only one in this world with problems."

"I didn't know you had any problems."

"I'm talking about your brother."

"Nate?"

"You asked my advice, so I'll give it to you," she said. "Give him a break. We all have moments when we need extra space."

Was she saying she needed space? What if this was it? If Enid never came back, I wouldn't know where to find her. I didn't know her last name or have her phone number. What if she ended up in a hospital, in a gown that swallowed her, her makeup stripped away, hair on end?

I wanted to follow her home, but she was a fast walker, and the farther she went, the smaller she shrank.

I THOUGHT ABOUT heading back to the apartment, annoyed at Frank's earlier dismissal of my work, but I decided an irritating Frank was better than a hostile Nate.

It was the right choice, clearly, as Frank greeted me at the door with a hot cup of cappuccino.

"You have to try this," he said.

It was exactly what I needed then, warm milk, cinnamon, but I wasn't going to tell him that.

"Wait," he said, before I took my first sip. "Look first."

There was a heart shape in the foam.

"Did you do that on purpose?" I said.

"I watched a tutorial online," Frank said. "Dad says it could be a value-added for the customers."

"Can you do cats, or dogs, or bears?"

"No." He looked at the floor. "I'm sorry. About before—this is all I can do."

I examined the foam again.

"It's okay," I said. "The heart is nice."

I stayed at the shop until closing and waited with Frank to lock down. Before he was finished, he mentioned a chocolate cake his dad had mistakenly ordered that would go to waste unless I wanted it.

"Perfect," I said. "Let's crack it open."

"It's in my freezer at home."

"Oh," I said. "Then I guess—"

I had never slept the whole night at Frank's before. If I stayed there, in his real, queen-sized bed free from brothers and cats tonight, did that mean we would start sleeping in the same bed every night? Long enough that we would eventually stop noticing the feel of an extra hand, or foot, or elbow? Enough so that if they were suddenly taken away it would feel like we were missing something? Did people evolve or degenerate when they were stuck to someone else?

And what about Harry, and my contacts and contact solution? They wouldn't be there when I woke up in Frank's sheets. But then, neither would Nate, which was a benefit.

I left a rambling message. *Hope you feel better, or are feeling better. This is Lucy—in case you didn't know. I'm not coming home tonight. I'm with Frank. So you can have the place to yourself, or have a party if you want. But, oh, can you feed Harry? I mean if his bowl is empty, and water. Can you check to make sure he has enough? I'll be back in the morn*—In the morning, is what I would have said if the beep hadn't cut me off.

In the morning, Nate was gone.

25

I CAME HOME TO AN EMPTY APARTMENT. THAT HAD TO MEAN he was back to work.

Harry was well fed and happy to see me, it seemed, as he curled against my leg. Everything appeared to be in order. Except there was a note on the television. That's where he left his messages, the piece of tape hanging in the inch above the screen so it would obstruct the view if I didn't remove it, telling me to "clear dishes" or "scrub counter" or to let me know about "pizza in fridge" or "mail on table." No wit or whimsy, doodles or color, but a prescription, in chicken scratch.

This wasn't the usual scrap of used envelope. It was his special ivory stationery that he'd been using since his bar mitzvah for thank-you notes—NME in royal-blue script across the top.

L—

Had to go. Don't worry. Will call soon—

—N

There were a few words blacked out above those. I guessed he didn't want to waste a fresh note. Maybe it said "This is a test" in Sanskrit or Latin, or it was some type of puzzle. It must have been something like that because even the moody, mean version of Nate wouldn't just go without an explanation. Would he?

Had to go. Go where exactly? To do what? I guessed I needed to determine that first. Maybe he would be back in a few hours, or tomorrow. It would be okay if he were gone for a day. I got that, if he were on some sort of journey. I had seen a copy of Thoreau in the bathroom a couple of weeks earlier.

Had he left the book behind with highlighted clues? I searched the place—the bathroom, the closets, the hallway, under the couch. I couldn't find it, but lots of his other stuff was still around as far as I could tell. So maybe he was still there. He had left some laundry detergent and some change on the shelf, which he would have needed if he were going somewhere far.

I read it over again. What was I missing?

Don't worry. Why would I worry? I wouldn't. I needed to think it through first, what this was. It could have been nothing.

Why the note then? Notes were formal. They led to postcards, months away, years on the road, running from something. I needed to talk to him.

His phone went straight to voicemail.

What if he never picked up? There wasn't any cash. How would I handle the bills? Would he send checks? I could go to a different temp agency, but I didn't know where my black skirt was—probably on the floor, covered in dust and Harry, and I had no money for dry cleaning, and I'd never actually been to the dry cleaner. Plus, I didn't want to wear a skirt again. Ever, really. And they'd never hire me anyway. We'd gone through that. Maybe I could start gambling professionally, poker tournaments in Vegas.

But no, there was no need. Nate would be back. Any minute. He'd return in his old form, and all would be in balance again.

Extra space, Enid had said. Fine. I could give him that.

I waited hours before I allowed the panic to set in. I couldn't think of how to get in touch with Marty, or anyone else who might have seemed helpful—Byron, Sabine? I didn't have any numbers, so I turned my attention to Nate's corner behind the square of wall. That seemed like the best place to try to channel his energy. It still smelled like him, a musky deodorant mixed with traces of marijuana. I hunkered down in the middle of the bed, inside the darkness with no distractions. Only far-off honks, the hum of the empty refrigerator, bits of loneliness.

The space was so small, and spare—no decorations really, or color. I read somewhere that colors of bedrooms could affect your mood: red was harmful, yellow was helpful, mostly what you'd guess, but here it was dirty white. Did it even count when you had only a section of a room? I touched his wall. It was cool, and left a trace of dirt on my fingertips.

Next to his bed I noticed a brown box with a small stack of books he'd kept from his classes: Sophocles, Euripides, Plato, a course reader with Descartes, Nietzsche, Kant.

He should have been in school. If I were in that home,

maybe he could have found a way to go part-time. Maybe he could have stayed with Sabine and played his music in his band and gone back to the way things were. Maybe I could tell him that was still possible.

I picked up one of the T-shirts he had ripped sleeveless for his runs, and I wondered how he had kept it so clean. It was still soft. As I held it, I tried to imagine where he might be, psychic vibes. Twins had that, supposedly, telekinetic power; we had it too, in suppressed form. I was sure of it. If I lost my other pinky in the door, he would know. So if I cut my wrist, would he feel the pain? If he cut his, would I?

I let my mind go. I listened for Dad's laugh, sniffed around for Mom's perfume, tried calling out Nate's name.

I imagined we were a close-knit unit, all of us intact, injury-free, able to read one another's minds before the thoughts arose—to summon one another for aid at any hour. The Supersensory Squadron: never a moment alone.

But none of them heard me.

That night, I didn't sleep. Every time I heard a car outside, or a floorboard above, or a footstep in the hallway, I caught my breath and waited for him to appear.

At dawn, I sat by the window and searched for a sign, a light like they'd shine for Batman. But there was nothing. Bats symbolized long lives and good fortune. That's why they were on those rum bottles. For luck. We should have spent more time in bat caves.

I knew there were bats at the zoo, inside the tropical jungle zone. If I wasn't going to stay in the apartment all day waiting, it was the only logical place I could think to go.

———

AT THE ZOO, the lighting in the cave was adjusted to trick the bats into thinking it was nighttime. As I watched them from a distance, they hypnotized me with their frantic movement, gliding and flapping their wings rapid-fire, nearly missing collisions at every turn. But when I moved closer to the glass, I could spot a few of them resting in the front of the cave, hanging upside down. With their wings draped behind them, it was easier to focus on their furry faces. From that angle, they almost looked like kittens.

If I stared for long enough, maybe their good fortune could seep into my consciousness and spread to Nate. I stood before them for a long time, observing them, drawing them, hoping to absorb some of their energy.

Since Gus was sleeping at the Polar Circle and hiding from the crowds, and since I wasn't quite ready to leave, I decided to stop by the home of the macaques, otherwise known as snow monkeys. They had a sprawling residence in the temperate zone featuring a gigantic pond with a hot tub. For whatever reason, I didn't think to visit them very often. Maybe it was because they seemed angry, with their red faces and red behinds, or maybe it was because when I looked at primates I saw too much raw human in them—in their shifting facial expressions and different pitches used to communicate, and in the way they washed their food the same way we did. Watching them almost felt like an invasion.

I wondered what they did at night, after the zoo was dark and all of the people went home. Did they laugh about ending up here, in this controlled environment, when they were actually built to survive extreme conditions? Did they sit in a circle telling stories about their days—they could supposedly pass down information from one generation to the next—recounting tales of the strangest visitors?

Whatever else happened, I knew they stuck together. No matter how often they chased after each other and argued over rankings within, at the end of the day they relied on the family the zoo had created. In the winter, you could find them bundled together as one, literally leaning on one another for warmth.

The more time I spent watching them, the more I thought of Nate, and the more anxious I grew for his return.

I had only been gone for a couple of hours, but I needed to get back to check for him.

_____

I OPENED THE APARTMENT DOOR SLOWLY, reasoning an extra level of care would somehow help conjure him. But it didn't work.

When I found he wasn't there, I sat by the window and looked outside the ledge.

A pigeon was there. It seemed to set up shop right when Nate left, or maybe it had been there before and I hadn't noticed, but either way, once I spotted that bird, it didn't budge. When I looked closer, I noticed it was sitting on a nest, which meant maybe it was sitting on eggs, which meant actually that it could have been a male or a female because they both sit on the eggs. But there was only one. Pigeons mate for life, so what had happened to its partner? It might have died in a tragic window crash, or eaten some rotten food, or been the victim of an act of random violence.

Of all the ledges in the city, what made this pigeon choose this one? Was it because it sensed it would be safe here?

Pigeons might be able to sense that. They were kind of smart, supposedly, as smart as toddlers I read somewhere once. That seemed reasonable to me, considering they could be trained to carry messages, to be relied upon to find their way back home. Maybe I could train this pigeon to send Nate a note, if only I knew where to send it.

I fell asleep watching the nest, all of the hours of restlessness hitting me at once, and when I woke up the next day I saw five messages on my phone. They were all from Frank.

Where was I?

He didn't want to bother me, but—

I wanted to talk back, to share what was going on, but I didn't have the energy. Not for anything.

He knew I'd be mad at him for coming over unannounced—unless there was something wrong with me.

If there was something wrong with me, I should tell him so he didn't come over and make me angry.

He was going to come over just to make sure.

If I didn't answer soon, then he knew he should come over.

Should he bring the police with him?

Or a doctor?

"Frank," I said, picking up after the sixth or seventh or eighth call.

"Thank God."

I sighed.

"Where have you been? What happened?"

So much, and yet so little that I couldn't respond.

"Lucy—"

"I can't talk right now. I'm sorry."

He wasn't hanging up.

"Frank?"

"What should I do?" he said.

"There's nothing you can do. I have to go now, okay?"

I hung up before he could answer, but as it turned out, it didn't matter. Within a minute, there was knocking at my door.

I could see him through the peephole. "You were here the whole time?"

"I wanted to call first," he said.

"Don't you have to be at work?"

"I told my father I needed time to check on you."

"I'm not fully dressed."

I was wearing Nate's running shirt, which I liked to think he had left for me, but it was too hot for pants.

"I'm not changing," I said.

"That's fine with me."

When I opened the door, I noticed he was wearing his regular khakis and plaid, but his face looked redder than usual, as though he'd been out in the sun for too long. There were stains beneath his armpits. It was an especially humid day.

I moved some clothes out of the way, so he could sit, but he looked pained.

"It's okay," I said. "It was nice of you to try, but you can go now. I'm a waste of your time."

"I don't want to." He opened his mouth, but he didn't speak. "I want to know—are you breaking up with me?"

"No," I said. I was annoyed for a second. How could he make this all about him? But then I realized he didn't know what was going on. "You're out of the loop."

"What loop?"

"Nate left. He's gone."

"Where?"

"I have no idea. Now you know as much as I do. He left a note, but he hasn't called."

Frank looked at the floor. "What are you going to do?"

"I don't know."

We were both still for a minute.

"I don't know what to say," he said finally.

"It's okay," I said. "Me either."

"Is there anything I can do?"

"I don't think so," I said. "I probably just need to be alone."

He nodded and slowly stood up, but the processing was on his face.

"Will you come to the shop tomorrow?" he said.

"I don't know. Maybe."

"It would mean a lot to me if you did."

"Why?"

I could tell he was still thinking. "There's some new coffee I'd like you to taste."

"I guess I am almost out of coffee."

WHEN FRANK SAW ME the next day at the counter, he looked away as though he hadn't. His face was more pallid than usual.

I was showered and dressed. There was no reason for this treatment.

"Can I have a muffin?" I said.

"I wasn't expecting you until later this afternoon," Frank said.

"I was ready earlier," I said. "Do you want me to leave?"

"No." He seemed nervous. "Can you wait a minute?"

He finished serving the couple of people in line, looked around for more customers, and then put a sign on the register saying BACK IN FIVE.

"Where are you going?" I said.

He disappeared into the back room, made some noise, and reached his head around.

"Will you please come here?" he said.

I had never been in the back room. I liked to imagine it was an enchanted coffee forest: tea leaves carpeting the ground, biscotti hanging from the ceiling, beans lining the walls, an espresso stream running through the center.

Of course, it was a regular room filled with boxes and a small wooden table in the corner. He pointed me toward the chair, and I noticed a large latte with my name on it, Frank's handwriting, a tower of sugar and artificial sweetener packets by its side.

"This is cute," I said, sitting down to help myself. "Why here, though?"

He was still standing. "You don't need any sweeteners?"

"Not in a latte. It's diluted enough with milk and cinnamon. I wouldn't want to corrupt the flavor any more than I had to."

"Oh." He sounded hurt.

"But that shows how well you made it, actually, the fact that

I don't need to add anything. It's excellent. And the heart is perfect. It looks almost like a cutout from a picture or something. The chocolate raspberry drizzle around the edge? Genius."

"But aren't you going to look at the pile?"

He nudged it toward me.

"No, Frank. I like it this way; it's pure, you know? Especially with the chocolate."

He was staring at the stack so intently that I gave in and followed his eyes. "I don't understand why we're looking at this; I mean the tower is cool, I guess, but I've seen you do stuff like this before, so—"

I stopped when I caught a glimpse of a corner of a box, black velvet. It was too late to pretend I didn't see it.

He had seen me see it. My stomach began to swirl around the heat of the caffeine. Was it our anniversary? Not unless you counted random weeks. It had only been five, maybe six. I wasn't counting. Valentine's Day? Not in the summer. It wasn't a birthday or commencement day or an observation day of any kind. I knew what it was. I knew before I started searching.

It was too much. What was he thinking? Had he been thinking at all? He was trembling, dripping through a napkin he was holding against his forehead. Tears were caught in the corners of his eyes. *No, Frank, no*, I wanted to say. *Not now.* But I couldn't shove the words out. It was happening too fast.

"Frank—"

"Don't you want to open it? C'mon!" He tapped my arm, an attempt at playfulness that didn't land.

I did want to. I wasn't capable of holding back surprises. What shape was it? What color? These were the questions I knew I was supposed to be asking, but what was the difference? I had only seen a few rings up close in my life, on more delicate hands. On screens. My mother. Enid didn't wear one. Did he have any idea how small my hands were?

It was probably gaudy gold, ugly, whatever constituted inappropriate according to whoever cared. It could only have been that, except—it was perfect.

An opal in a wavy plane. It was silver, which meant platinum probably. Mom's was platinum, with tiny diamonds surrounding one big one in the center. That was too flashy; that was what I thought of when I thought of rings. I didn't know I could want one until this one. But I had no business owning valuable jewelry. I'd lose it and the gesture would be worthless. And I wasn't marriage material, and I wasn't sure Frank was either.

"It was hard to find," he said. "Actually, my mom helped. We went yesterday. When I thought you were breaking up, I knew how much you mattered. When I found out about Nate, I knew it was the right time. So—"

He extracted a piece of crumpled paper from his back pocket and started to kneel.

"Frank, this is—incredible," I said, before he made it all the way down. "The ring, and you. You're amazing. I just—I need—I don't know what I need. I can't talk, form thoughts? It's unexpected. You caught me off guard. And—"

I was worried he'd drown in his perspiration, begin choking on the saltiness and stop breathing altogether. I couldn't have that.

"I can't do this now," I said, and I darted out, banging my knee against the chair.

26

When I reached the apartment door, before I turned the lock, I imagined Nate sitting there. He'd say hey, and I'd scream at him until he begged for forgiveness. Then I'd say welcome back and initiate the perfect hug, without a trace of unease, and he'd offer a sensible reason for going, and for coming back, after which he'd tell me what to say to Frank.

He wasn't there, though. And there was too much space. Could my key have opened someone else's door? I had read of drunk or otherwise disoriented people doing that. I was surprised it hadn't happened before.

But no, there was Harry. It was just that things looked different. The clutter was more spread out, still messy, but not quite as bad as I'd remembered.

I opened the refrigerator and closed it, and then opened it again when I realized there was food inside: peanut butter, jelly, bread, cheese. Had that been there before? Maybe he had bought the groceries before he left? Or maybe it was a miracle and the food would last until he got back.

I wasn't hungry, so I returned to my living space, where I collapsed amidst a folded clump of mismatched socks.

I stayed in that position until the phone startled me out of a daze.

"Did I wake you?"

"No!" It was Nate. Finally. "Where are you?"

"This is the first chance I've had to call."

"Are you here?" He sounded so close I checked to see if he was in the bathroom. It was empty. "What's happening?"

"Nothing serious," he said.

"What is it?"

He sighed. "How's Harry?"

He was napping on the far cushion. "He's mad at you."

"Tell him I'm sorry," he said.

"Are you okay?" I said. "Because if you're in trouble or something—"

"Don't worry about me," he said. "I'll be fine. How are you?"

"You'll be fine?"

"What's going on over there? Any news?"

"No, not really. Oh, wait. Yeah, kind of, actually. I think Frank proposed today."

"What? Are you serious?"

"That is news, huh?"

"I've only been gone a few days."

"It feels like longer."

I waited for him to fight me, but when he didn't, I thought maybe it was because he was at the door, like Frank had been. I looked through the peephole, but there was only the hallway.

"Are you still there?" I said.

"I'm here."

"What do you think I should tell him?"

"Did he give you a ring?"

"It's really nice. An opal. It was because you left I think. He did this thing, with sugar packets and—it was—I don't know. I guess you had to be there."

"What did you say?"

"This is one of those times when you could say something like that, that you had to be there, because it was really strange."

"Did you say yes?"

"To who, Frank? I've told him I don't want to get married, I think. I hinted—in other conversations. He knows I'm not wifely. Is that a word, wifely? It sounds like one. Except when I think about the ring—"

"Lucy," he said. "Is this what you want?"

I examined my hands. "The left one?"

"What?"

"I should have tried it on."

"Did you hear what I asked?" he said.

I examined my fingers. Which one was left?

"Frank is serious about this."

"I know that!" My hand clenched into a fist. "You think I don't know that? I think I know Frank a little better than you do. I know what it means when a person commits."

He took a breath. "Okay."

"I'm sorry," I said. "That was loud. I didn't mean to yell."

"It's okay."

"Don't go, okay?"

"I'm not going."

"Can you tell me where you are?"

I could hear him on the other end exhaling through his nose.

"Or is that against the rules? Are you a spy or something? That would make me feel better if you were."

I knew he wasn't going to answer.

"Would you come home if I married Frank?"

He sighed, heavily. "Do you love him?"

"I don't know. I mean, yeah. I guess."

"You guess?" he said.

I thought about how much Frank was sweating when I noticed the ring, how important this whole thing seemed to him.

"How do you know?" I said.

"Nobody really knows," he said. "But most people say you just do."

"Like in your gut? Because in my gut—I mean, he's such a great guy, but in my gut, when I think about the future—I don't know."

"Then you shouldn't say yes."

"But it could be that I'll never know, you know? I mean, all those stupid movies about finding 'the one' and all that stuff, I don't connect to that."

"Because those movies suck," he said.

"Yeah, but it's more than that. It's like I never understood those characters. I never planned for any of that."

"You never planned for anything. Ever."

"That's true, but it's because I can't really. Executive—"

"Functioning. I know. That's what you say."

"So I should say no?"

"I can't tell you what to say."

"Can you tell me if you're on your way back?"

"I'm sorry," he said. "I'm not supposed to be on the phone for this long. I need to get going."

"Wait!" I said. "Why? Are you in jail?"

"No," he said. "But I have to go."

I took a second. "Is this because of me?"

"No," he said. "None of this is because of you."

"Can I do anything to help? If we need money, I can play poker."

"You don't have to worry about money. I've got all the bills electronically, and there's three hundred dollars underneath a stack of menus in the kitchen, far-left drawer."

"Isn't that your money?"

"It's ours. Mostly twenties. Don't use it all at once, but if you need more, you can ask Byron."

"Byron?"

"He has keys. Did you get the food?"

"That was you?"

"That was him, but you can ask for more."

"I don't have his number."

"He'll stop by again," he said. "You can always leave him a note."

"I don't like notes," I said.

He paused for a half a second. "His number's on top of one of the menus."

I checked. It was all there.

"You have enough pills in the cupboard to get you through the next thirty days, plus whatever you had left over from before. I'm sure you noticed that, but I wanted to make sure you knew you wouldn't run out."

"Because you'll be back before then?"

"Luce—"

"Yeah?"

"I'll call again later. I promise."

"When?" I said, but he'd already hung up.

WHEN I WAS SURE he was gone, I returned to the sill and searched again. Maybe that's what Harry did when he curled against the pane—watched for Nate, or when I wasn't there, for me. Or maybe he was thinking about getting out too.

It was real now. Before, I could sleep through it and imagine he'd return by the time I woke up. Now I couldn't close my eyes. I couldn't get Nate's voice out of my mind—the weight of each word, the stress on every syllable, the futility of what I'd expressed. I could have said more. Or less. I could have just listened.

I wondered when Byron would be back. Would he walk in the moment I had my spoon in the peanut butter, while I was in the bathroom, when I was asleep? If I timed it right, I could greet him at the door and ask him questions. I could stay up and wait for him—all day, if I had to.

Or I could call him.

I hovered over his number for a long time, contemplating what to say, how to say it, choosing my words, my tone, and then—

"Hi. Do you know who this is? You probably don't. It's Lucy, Nate's—"

"Lucy! Is everything okay?"

"Yeah, it's fine. It's just—will you come over? I mean, if you're in the neighborhood, if you were planning on coming back at some point anyway. I have some questions, and I thought if you weren't doing anything, then, you know?"

"Give me half an hour," he said.

WHEN HE WALKED IN, Byron smiled, his mouth a pearly landscape. He was very pretty, I noticed then. Not rugged like Nate, not boyish and nerdy like Frank, but pretty, like Captain America. His eyelashes were tangled and dark, his lips pink and wide. I wondered if his hands were as soft as they looked.

"I've been thinking," he said, surveying the space. "Would you be cool if I sent over this cleaning crew we work with sometimes?"

"Is it that bad?" I said.

I frantically tried to fluff a pillow, but I only ended up smooshing it.

"I can't clean. I'm sorry. I'm sure we can't afford a service."

"Don't worry about it," he said. "I can't clean either. But my uncle knows a guy."

"I'm trying harder to be neat. I really am."

"Forget it," he said. "It's a process."

"Right. So what did Nate say?"

Byron stopped inspecting and looked at me. "We only talked for a minute."

"Did he say what he's doing?

"He was more concerned about you." He nodded toward

the kitchen. "He told me about the money. Do you have enough food?"

"Yes!" I said. "Thank you. It's amazing. How did he sound to you? Is he ever coming back?"

"Of course he is."

"How do you know?"

"He promised he'd let me join his band when he starts one."

"But he took his guitar," I said, searching the room again. "I looked for it."

I started pacing, thinking about Byron going through everything, taking inventory.

He reached down to pick up Harry. Harry barely let me do that, let alone anyone else, but he was so calm in Byron's arms, so secure.

"I thought you didn't like pets."

"I don't, but they all seem to like me."

Harry was actually purring.

"What else do you know?" I said. "Has he ever done anything like this before?"

"Do you want to sit for a second?"

"I think I'd rather stand," I said. "I like the movement."

"I get that," he said. "You mind if I pace with you?"

"I guess not," I said.

He let Harry go.

"You know, when he first got here he didn't even drink. Total straight-edge. He said he was too focused to lose control. That's how he was: all or none."

I always thought he was more like Mom, but that sounded like Dad.

"First he was talking about being a doctor. Then he was

all about philosophy: freedom versus determinism and moral truth versus relativity and the value of religion. And then poli sci. And his guitar. He was on a good track, but—I think the stuff with your dad hit him pretty hard."

He stopped talking as if to gauge my reaction.

I looked at Harry. "You think he needed solitude?"

"I don't really know what he needed, to be honest. But my guess is that he wanted some space to figure out how to get focused again, to reprioritize. You're a big part of that. You know that, right? He wants to make sure you're taken care of."

"He doesn't have to worry about me."

"He's always going to worry about you. The key is that he worries about himself too. He's no good to anyone unless he's in the right state. I think he finally gets that."

"So is he okay now? Can you tell me that?"

"He's going to be fine. I'm sure of that. But look, you can't worry about him right now. Now you've got to worry about taking care of yourself. Do you have everything you need?"

No, I didn't. I didn't have my mother or my father or my brother, and I wasn't sure how to take care of myself. That was the whole point. But I couldn't let Byron know that, so I moved to the door.

"You don't have to worry about me anymore," I said. "I don't want to be anyone's burden."

"You're nobody's burden," he said. "You're your own person."

"Sure," I said. Whatever that means. "Thanks for coming."

He looked at the floor and held his gaze on a sketch of Gus.

"How's that zoo dream of yours?"

I hadn't thought about it in too long. I was ashamed of that.

And Belle. It had been a while since I'd seen Enid. I'd let her down too.

"Still just a dream," I said.

AFTER BYRON LEFT, I returned to the window and noticed the pigeon was still there. Pigeons were the rats of the sky, people liked to say. But I never understood why. They wouldn't give you rabies or eat your babies. They were just as good as other birds—common maybe, plain, sure, but they never hurt anyone. This pigeon looked perfectly nice, peaceful even, soothing if I stared into its nest for long enough.

WHEN FRANK CALLED the next day, I wasn't sure what time it was. It could have been dawn; it might have been dusk. It was all blurring together.

"Hi," I said.

"I hope it's not too early," he said.

"It's not. What time is it? I'm up. I've been up."

"I wanted you to know—I can take back the question."

When I looked around the apartment to think, I saw only the emptiness, and felt the quiet.

"No," I blurted, louder than I intended.

"What?"

The words poured out. "I don't want you to take it back."

He seemed to gasp. "Does that mean yes?"

"Was that what I said?"

I took a minute. Maybe this was the only responsible choice left.

"I guess so?" I said.

"When I didn't hear from you, I didn't think—I can't believe this. We need to celebrate. I'll come over."

"Now? I don't know," I said, but he was already on his way.

There was no going back.

He took a cab, so he arrived in twenty minutes, armed with a goofy smile and a gold box of chocolate. He said it was his mom's idea to add that, her favorite kind, "to sweeten the deal."

"She wants to meet you," Frank said. "She's been wanting to meet you since I told her about seeing you in the shop that first day, but now she can't wait. I always knew it was you. Tonight. Will you have dinner with us?"

"Tonight?"

I had no sense of where I was, how swiftly this was moving, where we were going. It was as if I were watching someone else's life.

I opened the chocolate box and ate three. At first, I was

just eating them to keep my mouth occupied, comfort. But on the third, the taste hit me. Dark-chocolate ganache in a darker chocolate shell covered in dusted cocoa powder. I let the filling melt on my tongue, brushed it along the roof of my mouth. They might have been the best chocolates I'd ever had. I imagined these boxes lining the walls in every room of his parents' house, me making my way through them row by row.

27

FRANK'S PARENTS' HOUSE WAS IN A DIFFERENT SUBURB AND IN a different direction from our old house, but it turned out Bergen County looked pretty similar to Westchester County. You could take a train there, and you could get picked up at the station the same way you could at home. In this case it was Frank's father, Stu, who was waiting for us.

Stu was solidly built, like a piece of granite with a chiseled face, a nose that was too long for his chin, a simple-to-sketch cartoon character. He didn't look anything like Frank.

When he saw us, he gave Frank a firm handshake and me a sort of half hug.

"Very nice to meet you," he said.

He had a good poker face; I couldn't tell what he really thought.

"Trip in okay?" he said to Frank.

"It was fine," Frank said.

"Good," Stu said.

That was all he said until we got to the house. The rest of the ride we listened to the radio in what seemed like a routine kind of hush.

Their home looked something like the one I'd known: two floors, a backyard. Except theirs was updated and maintained—the walkway, the flowers, the driveway—all of the things that began crumbling for us after Mom's funeral.

When we arrived, Frank's mom, Myrna, was in the kitchen. From the back, she resembled a Bartlett pear in dark pants, but we didn't see her from the front until later because she was humming along to the stereo and hadn't heard us over the music and the grind of the disposal. So Frank decided we'd say hi to her later.

We went to his room, which appeared preserved from boyhood—blue plastic bookshelves stocked with airplane-modeling kits, a miniature microscope, Operation, a railroad track still assembled to run along the perimeter of his room. I realized then that Frank would never see my childhood room, which was a good thing, probably, except that it was sort of strange to think that I didn't have a room left to visit. Some other family had probably transformed it into a nursery or home office. I envisioned a treadmill in place of my bed. I hoped Dad's ghost wasn't stuck there.

"You want to see the train run?" Frank said.

I did, actually. He said some things about saving up enough money for it for years, how it was a perfect replica of some-thing or other, and there were only so many produced in the world. I wasn't really listening to that part. I just wanted to see it go.

He fiddled with some controls until he got the track work-ing, and as soon as he did, I was transfixed. I thought about how much Harry would have liked it as we watched the train chug around the toy chest and chest of drawers, under the twin bed, extra-long.

"When I was little, the pediatrician told my mom there was room in my bones," Frank said. "That's why it's extra-long. I had the potential to be tall. What if I ended up that way?"

I imagined him stretched out, wondered if that would change his posture, demeanor, level of confidence. But he would still have the same skin, same face, same brain.

"You'd still be you," I said.

"You're here!" Frank's mother made her entrance by stopping the train with her toe. The sound of the railroad had apparently beckoned her.

His mother had a rosy, round face, with soft, appealing features, and she squeezed Frank in a way that seemed like it could break him. Dad had a hug like that, as though it were meant to leave an imprint.

"We were about to say hi," Frank said.

"Welcome, welcome!" Myrna said to me, granting me the same embrace. "Come. Let me look at you!"

She brushed a stray hair behind my ear. I realized it was probably a mess, but she didn't say anything about that. She didn't say anything for a minute as she took me in, as though she were assessing a raw space to weigh the possibilities.

"Well," she said finally. "I'll show you to the guest room. You're staying the night, I'm assuming?"

Frank had warned me she would make it so that there was no alternative.

"No funny business, Frankie."

"Mom."

"Frankie says you get headaches sometimes. This room is the darkest in the house, so if you need to lie down—whenever. We don't judge. You know, I used to get migraines myself. But then one day—" She sprung her hands open and let them stay that way, framing her face. "Poof. Just like that. It should only happen to you."

She locked my arm and led me into the living room, which was decorated with more of her amateur paintings. There was a flowerpot, a bowl of fruit, a piano in the sunset. These were worse than the ones in the shop. I had to look away.

"Sit," she said. "We'll get you something cold to drink. Sparkling cider? Perrier? Oh no, we don't have any more Perrier. I'm so embarrassed. What must you think of me?"

What must she have thought of me? When was the last time I'd showered? I touched my head and thought of all the days without enough sleep, too much stress, my mind roving into space.

"Water?" I said.

"That's it? Just water? How about juice? Pomegranate."

She brought me a glass before I could answer and moved to the bottom of the staircase.

"Stu!" she yelled.

"Just a minute," I could hear Frank's father say.

She shrugged when she returned to the sitting room. "Oh well. True love is acceptance."

She winked then, as though I had any idea what she was talking about. "The best marriages aren't built on true love anyway."

There was something in the way she beamed, how her

eyes beamed too—same eyes as Frank—how she held her hand over mine for the extra second, that put me at ease. If she noticed how ridiculous I looked, she wasn't going to talk about it. She was going to treat me like I was in the right place.

OVER DINNER, spaghetti with "wheat balls," Frank's favorite recipe modified for my benefit, Myrna discussed her ailments: acid reflux, arthritis, kidney stones, chronic sinus infections.

"Oh, and remember that time, Stu, when you had to rush me to the emergency room because I was so sick? Turned out the IUD was infected!"

"Myrna," he said, without much heart. He had been ensconced in his study in the hour before dinner, working, I guessed, or maybe hiding. "Our guest doesn't have to hear about everything all at once."

Myrna seemed like the type who treasured the days when dire things happened. The more unfortunate incidents that could pile up, the more opportunity she'd have to share her woe, the better the chance for her to save the day. More drama meant more fodder for stories. You could tell she lived for the stories.

"I apologize for the rantings," Myrna said. "I'm cursed with a vivid memory and a big mouth."

"I don't mind," I said.

The more she talked, the less I had to, the slighter the opportunity for probing about my intentions, my past, my plans, my own medical history. The more stories about her issues, or Stu's, or Frank's, the more accepted I felt. They weren't talking about me, weren't scoffing or exchanging looks of disapproval, at least in plain sight, and that felt like an accomplishment.

"Oh, Frankie was just miserable at baseball," she said, giggling. "We had to spare him the pain. 'Don't you want to try something else, sweetheart?' we told him."

Frank's face was as pink as I'd seen it, bordering on cherry. "Mom."

"What?" Myrna said. "It's not for everyone. That's what we said. But then you joined that robot club, and ooh, you got so involved, and after you were sick for so long, to see you were so interested in that was such a blessing. I was proud of you, so much pride. Who cared about the dyslexia then, or the other learning disabilities? The hyperactivity seemed to melt away as soon as you got some focus. And look at you now."

"You think he was compensating?" I said.

Myrna seemed to have forgotten I was there. "What?"

"For being deficient. I mean in a good way. Like he had a gap in one area and made up for it in another? I guess we all kind of do that, right?"

"Yes," Myrna said, examining me closely. "I suppose we do." She got up to wrap her arms around Frank's neck.

"But he doesn't have to compensate for much these days," she said. "He's perfect. So accomplished and handsome and put together, don't you think?"

I cleared my throat. "Definitely."

"You want to know what he always said when we asked him what he wanted for birthdays? Well, first he wanted a little brother, and then there was a snake phase, but when he gave up on that, he always said, 'I want to meet a girl.'"

She stared at me.

"Huh," I said.

"It's true, every year he said it: 'I want to find love.' And I always said, 'You will, Frankie. You will.' When he told us about you, I told him, 'If it's meant to be, it will be.' He said, 'It is meant to be.' He said, 'She was in the group! We're the same!'"

"I don't think I said it like that," Frank said.

"Sure you did, Frankie," Myrna said. "And he was right too. When I look at you two together, I think there really is some-one for everyone. You're like peas in a pod."

"Well, maybe not the same pod," I said. "Since I didn't have surgery directly on my brain. Maybe more like an adjacent pod?"

She wiped her mouth and took a slow sip of water. Then she looked at me, as though she were sizing me up, perhaps noticing all of the hair out of place for the first time, the food in my teeth, the spots on my shirt.

I took my own sip of water.

"I'm glad you're not exactly the same," she said. "How bor-ing would that be? I mean, let's be real here: Frankie has a job, Frankie lives by himself, Frankie has a supportive family with lots of resources. You're completely different! But at your core, you are two people in this world who are not meant to be apart. That's what Frankie says, isn't it, Frankie?"

He nodded, still pink in his cheeks.

My heartbeat was quickening. Did I need to defend myself? It was hard to tell. Her tone was so friendly, and yet—did she think he was too good for me, that I was lucky to have him, that I was using him for his resources? Was that true? I didn't think so. But how could I say that? Should I say that? I didn't want to make things worse. Things were going fine when I wasn't saying anything.

"When he asked for help with the ring, I was hesitant, of course," she said. "'It's only been a month,' I said."

"Five and a half weeks," Frank said.

"But he said, 'Trust me.' He said, 'I know.' He said, 'I've been waiting my whole life for this.' 'Okay,' I said. What else could I say? He's never asked for anything. Except for this! He's such a good boy. So, 'Fine,' I said. 'We'll help however we can. We'll make sure you can be a good provider.' And he is a provider. You better believe that. He cares so deeply, such love in his heart. A boy like that deserves love, I always said. We all do."

She looked at me. "Wouldn't you agree?"

I nodded, but I could tell she was waiting for more.

I pointed at my plate. "This wheat is delicious," I added, though all I could taste was the tomato sauce, which was pretty bland.

"Don't you just love that ring?" she said.

"Yes!" I reached for it, relieved to feel the stone. I hadn't lost it yet, probably because it was too tight.

"When he told me he met you, I nearly had a conniption," she said. "A girl, I said. I would have accepted a man, as long as he was happy. A monkey, for all I cared. His happiness is the most important thing."

"Mom."

"What? I've always told you that, haven't I? You're a wonderful boy. I just didn't know if you were ever going to—"

"Dad, can you—say something?" he said.

I didn't think Stu was listening. He was chomping away, focused on his food, but he raised his head and took the cue.

"Who's ready for dessert?" he said, clearing our plates. "I met with a cake man today. Can I interest you in a piece of the coffee crumble, Lucy? Best served with a cappuccino."

It was the most he'd said all night, but he'd come through when we needed him. He could take care of people. They all could. I could let them.

THAT NIGHT I found a glass of water with a cucumber slice by the bed, and lavender hand lotion in the bathroom. The cucumber was dried up, and the purple bottle was crusted at the end, but the thought of creating a comforting environment was touching. If only I could have let my mind rest.

I couldn't. I needed to get back. Harry would think I'd abandoned him, and what if Nate decided to show?

In the morning, I took a quick shower, got dressed, and made my way into the kitchen before I realized it wasn't light yet. It was only five. I sat at the table and waited, and I fell asleep until Myrna came in to make coffee.

"Well," she said, beginning to grind the beans. "You're up early."

"Is it early?" I said.

Frank came in soon after.

"Do you always get up this early?" I said.

"Do you?" he said.

"She must be excited about the wedding, Frankie," Myrna said. "Isn't that right?"

"Sure," I said.

"It's a big day for you two, the day after your engagement. Are you staying for lunch?"

Frank looked at me.

"I can't," I said. "I mean you could, if you want. But I have a cat, Harry, and he needs me. And I'm kind of waiting for my brother, too."

"Of course. Nate," Myrna said, examining me for a few extra moments. "I'm sure that's taken a toll on you."

I realized then that there wouldn't be any secrets.

"Do you have enough money for the train?" she said.

"I think so," I said.

"You think?"

"No, I do. Definitely," I said, though I wasn't sure that was true. I hoped I had stuffed a bill in my tote. "I just need to get back."

"I think I'll go back too," Frank said. "With my fiancée."

It took me a second to realize that the word referred to me.

"Are you sure, Frankie?" Myrna said, glancing at me.

"Yes," he said.

He reached for my arm, but I wasn't expecting it, so I flinched, and he only grazed the side of it.

ON THE TRAIN back to the city, it was so crowded that almost as soon as we started moving, I felt sick. I hadn't thought to bring my pills. Now my stomach was flipping and my head was pounding.

"Do you want to get off?" Frank said.

"No," I said. "I just need to shut my eyes until we get there."

"We should talk about the wedding," Frank said, placing his hand on my head. "We need to start planning."

I turned my head away from him. "I thought your mom was going to take care of that."

"She is, but she wants us to have a say in picking a date. And a place. And the food, the venue, the guest list—"

"I can't talk about this now, Frank." I bumped my head against the window. "I don't feel well, and I don't have any guests anyway. Nate I guess. If he comes. Robby, if I could track him down. Marty. Nate would know how to get to him. Enid. I'd invite her, though I don't have her address. But we could tell her. She probably has a dress. I'll need a dress."

I didn't want to squeeze into a fancy gown, or get my hair and makeup done, or be the center of attention in a group of people who didn't know me, with no parents and no brother.

"Maybe we could elope," I said.

He took a minute. "Mom would hate that."

"Why?"

"She wants to help you find a dress."

I closed my eyes. I didn't want her in my dressing room. What was all this for again?

I looked at him. His button nose was cute, those gold-rimmed glasses that were always so clean. But why was it so hard to find a comfortable spot to lay on him? He needed to let his body relax.

"We should also plan a move-in day," he said.

I hadn't considered that before, the after-the-wedding part. I tried to imagine Frank's train running through the living room.

"What's wrong with Nate's place?" I said.

He looked at me. "It's not very big."

"You think we need more space?"

My head began to pound.

"I feel sick," I said.

"You should rest now," he said.

"Now I can't. I have too much to think about."

"Do you want to talk about it?"

"No." I willfully shut my eyes, but I could sense he was still looking at me.

"I'm glad you met my parents," he said.

"Oh yeah," I said. "Me too."

I could have given him more than that, maybe, something about the day we'd have a home like theirs. But I couldn't see past the end of the day, us sitting before the clearing sky, looking out, wondering about things.

"Are you okay?" he said.

"I will be."

I slid farther down the seat, slouching my way toward the floor, and the more I slunk down, the more I imagined sinking further into myself, bending backward and over until I became small, smaller than Frank and Enid and Harry, until I folded into the gap between the seats and found a spot to sleep.

28

HARRY WAS WAITING FOR ME AT THE DOOR WHEN I OPENED THE apartment, clingier than usual, then vocal. He mewed at me once, and when I didn't respond, he did it again, louder.

"I know," I said. "I come and go as I please, manipulate your environment, play God—feast or famine, heat or A/C, light or dark."

First I'd told him he would have to live inside for the rest of his life, then to grow accustomed to a dirty room in a big house, then to adjust to a clean apartment, and now he was stuck with something in between. Once, he was free to sprawl out in his kingdom, then he had to make room for one more— until he grew used to an extra body, until that body left. Until he was left with me.

When I was gone, I imagined he might have circled around the apartment a few times, searching; slept in my bed—there was evidence of his shedding; lay his head on the pillow and dreamt, his paws batting at my image. He might have imagined that he'd have to fend for himself.

He mewed until he saw I had no answers, and then he recoiled into the closet.

I followed him, picked him up, and squeezed him until he squirmed from my arms.

"I'm sorry," I said.

As we sat in the dark, I contemplated hibernation. It made a lot of sense actually, to shut away the world for months at a time—no thoughts, only sleep, only self. I could be a bear.

If only I could sleep. I missed Nate. And Dad. And Mom. If I didn't have Nate, maybe I could have them back—in spirit at least. The two parents could come together and form a protective circle around me, shielding me from every harm. Ghost-rents. I took out my sketchbook and began to draw.

———

I HAD MOMENTARILY FORGOTTEN about the headache I'd woken up with, but now it was an 8 on a scale from 1 to 10, and I rarely slid past 6. The slightest move intensified the pressure, like someone was sitting inside my face, playing the drums against my temples and nasal passages, against the back of my head, adding more weight and tension with each beat.

I tried imagining myself in the pool with Gus, or in Mexico with Nate, but I kept ending up back where I started, on the couch, spinning around the center of the room, floating around the fringes, alone.

If I was going to be alone, I had to take care of myself. That was what Enid had said, and Byron. So I could take care of my pills. I could find things in my home. This was my home now.

I began rustling around the cabinets, and sure enough, after going through each drawer, I found my refills. I swallowed the pills dry, and then I noticed another baggie full of other pills I didn't immediately recognize.

Up close, I could see what they were: Ritalin and Dexedrine. I used to take those, for greater focus, and metabolism, but they had to keep upping the dosage until it was too high, and then my doctor weaned me off. There was still a bottle of that stuff somewhere. I hadn't thrown it away. I guessed I had wanted it just in case—

It dawned on me all at once.

Nate.

Those were the pills he had been popping. Those were the

refills he was getting for himself. Just a couple at first, to keep himself going, and then . . .

I threw the bag at the trash. Of course I missed. They scattered everywhere. Asshole!

How could this have happened? Sure, he smoked a little pot, drank a little too much. But this? Who did this? Who was he?

I envisioned him in a hotel room then, a terrycloth robe, with piles of my old pills encircling him. He was hollow in his cheeks, sickly, and he had constructed a wall of capsules around him to block out human touch, to repel telepathic energy.

I had never imagined the day when Nate was as messed up as I was.

Was it my fault? Probably. I wished I could push him back in time, to his life before my invasion of it. It wasn't fair that this was who he was now.

What if he was getting worse out there? I wished I could call him to check in.

I looked to Harry for consolation and found him at the window. I sat with him for a while and looked for my pigeon. Every day that pigeon had parked itself and waited, predictably, beautifully almost. I could count on that.

But now the pigeon was gone.

Almost as soon as I realized it, Frank called.

"Hi," I said. I wasn't in the mood to talk to him. I was distraught about the pigeon, and about Nate and his drugs. But I'd already missed his earlier call.

"I wanted to see how you were feeling," he said. "Do you need anything? I tried calling you earlier from the drugstore, but I guess you didn't hear."

"Oh, yeah. I had a really bad headache."

He didn't say anything. I could hear him rustling some papers.

"I took my pills, though, so I'm sure I'll be fine soon."

"Good," he said. "Should I get the wedding spreadsheet?"

"Now?"

"We need to talk about the wedding."

"Frank—"

It was a great idea, in theory, to pour myself into an event that could turn all of the darkness and doubts into sugar and

Champagne. Poofy dresses and makeup to hide the flaws, slow songs to conceal shuffling feet.

Maybe the ceremony could stop time for a night, and halt all the hoping and waiting and holding of my breath. Maybe brides could be declared invincible.

Maybe. But even if I'd somehow made it through the aisle and the first dances and cake unstained, what would happen when the party ended? It would just be Frank and me and Harry, alone. Maybe that was all I needed. But what if it wasn't?

I didn't want to think about it then, or talk about it. I wanted to go back to sleep.

"I'm a little preoccupied right now."

"Well, we can't move forward until you tell us what you'd like," he said. "That's what Mom says."

"Frank, what does that even mean?"

"You should know," he said.

"Well, I don't!" It was too loud. "Sorry, I didn't mean that. Frank?"

He hung up without saying goodbye.

29

THE NEXT DAY I DECIDED TO GO STRAIGHT TO THE SHOP. I HAD
to see Frank after the abrupt end to our conversation. Who
was he to be mad at me? That seemed unfair. I wanted to let
him know that. Plus, I was determined to see Enid again, to
tell her about everything that had happened, and to ask her for
her insights. I hadn't seen her since she had stomped off, and I
needed to make sure she was okay, that we were okay.

When I got to the counter, Frank barely acknowledged me,
but it was a busy day, so I ordered my coffee and took my spot
in the back, waiting for signs of Enid. I was armed with Belle,
and a few lines to impress her: "Would you say her coat was
more a caramel or cappuccino color?"

At first, I tried to refrain from doing any more work on the
dog before I saw her, but after a while I got bored. Frank was
ignoring me, the jazz rotation was all instrumental, and I had
already read even the driest sections of the paper.

So I went to work on the drawing, shading and coloring
and guessing all the way, convinced I was making things
worse with every stroke. By the end of the day, I knew I had

to trash it, but I didn't want to lose the evidence of my effort. I wanted Enid to see, so I waited for her until closing time.

She never showed.

"You didn't see Enid today, did you?" I said to Frank when everyone else had finally gone.

"No," he said. "But she wasn't my main focus."

"That makes sense. Are you hungry?"

I was starving, and in his brown shirt, his arms looked like pretzel sticks. I imagined him salted, knotted at the ends.

"Chinese?" I said. "Or you can pick the place if you want."

"I have an online game scheduled for tonight," he said.

I watched his back contract as he swept the surface with paper towels. I hadn't noticed those muscles before. They were so delicate, yet strong.

"Is it a pay tournament? I'm really good at poker."

"No," he said. "I told you I don't gamble."

"Sorry," I said. "I was only asking. What's with you today?"

He stopped cleaning and stood up straight.

"Do you really want to marry me?" he said.

I looked at the ring, which was still gleaming somehow.

He turned around to face me. "Did you hear me?"

"Frank, I'm really hungry right now."

"I asked a question."

He locked the door and turned out all but the front lights. We stood at the threshold, in the shadows.

"About the wedding," he said.

The only thing I'd had that day had been the coffee, and the milk that went in the coffee. How had I managed to sit for that long? All at once the wooziness hit, and I was missing a chair to lean on.

"Is there any food left in the back?" I said.

"No," he said, though I knew there was.

Why was he doing this? I was trying to read him, but he had that blank look about him. If only he were a dog or bear. Then I'd be able to feel him.

"Can we go somewhere else?"

I pushed on the door, but it didn't open.

He locked my eyes. "Mom says she worries you're not really in this."

"She said that?" I turned away, searching for crumbs. "The other day I told you I loved you, didn't I? I didn't just say it in my head. I said it to you."

"I tell you all the time."

"Well, maybe we're different in the way we say things, like it's some brain thing that isn't turned on in me that is in you, or maybe it's the opposite; I don't know. Can we talk about this over food?"

"I need to think about it," he said.

"I said I'd go anywhere."

"I don't like Chinese."

"We can go wherever you want."

"I want to get married," he said.

"I know!"

His eyes were glossy, almost beautiful in their translucent glow.

"I'm sorry," I said.

He loved me. That was probably more than what most people had. More reliable than Nate and Dad, more under-standing and admiring, so why couldn't I give him what he wanted?

"I just—why are we having this talk now, in the dark?"

His voice began to crack. "Can you imagine your life without me?"

I didn't know how to answer. My whole life had been imagined without him.

"Well?" he said, opening the door for me to leave.

"I don't want to blurt out the first thing that comes to mind because—"

Now there were tears at the creases.

"Please don't do that," I said. "You're crying? You're making too much of this. I don't even know what this is right now."

He looked down, locked up, and turned out the final light. When we got outside, he started walking, fast, rushing away from me.

"Frank!" He halted for a moment. "Where are you going?"

He let me catch up to him before he started moving again.

"You said you'd take back the question," I said. "Can we go back to that? Please?"

"No," he said. "It's too late for that."

"But why? It's not like I want to date anyone else."

"It's not enough," he said. "If we can't move forward, we're stuck."

"Is that what your mom said?"

"It's true," he said. "Isn't it?"

I wasn't sure what the right answer was, what I was supposed to say, what I was actually feeling, what was happening, so I just watched him leave.

But how could I let someone who would serve me heart-shaped coffee and pastries for eternity walk away?

I couldn't.

By the time I reached my door, the fog of confusion had transformed into irritation. Why did he get the final say? Was I even involved? How was that fair?

As I began to turn the key, I envisioned the cover of darkness, and I thought about how I'd grown accustomed to contact that summer, life beyond Harry. And I got it, kind of—the fuss about other people. Intimacy. I'd felt it, for a second, and I had appreciated it. Relationships. Romance. Companionship. What if I had pushed them all away?

I wasn't ready to lose everything.

Before I finished opening my door, I closed it again, and I took the train straight to Frank's.

As I knocked, I could hear game noises emerging from his computer, pings of people joining in and messaging each other. He had a community.

"Can I come in?"

He stepped aside, and I moved toward the loveseat, but he didn't join me.

"Am I interrupting? I could come back."

"No." He turned off his screen and sat at his desk, as far away from me as possible. "But I don't get why you're here. I didn't invite you."

"Am I a vampire?"

He was confused. "I never said you were a vampire."

"No, it's a thing—with vampire mythology? They can't come in unless . . . Forget it. You wouldn't know that."

"Why? Because I'm stupid?"

"No, because you don't watch TV, or movies, or read books. That's not necessarily a bad thing. It's just you."

"I don't know if you mean that as a compliment."

"Let's forget it," I said.

"Fine."

We sat in silence for a minute.

"So this is it?" I said, after what seemed like an hour.

"I guess," he said.

"We're breaking up?" I said.

"We have to," he said.

"Why?"

"You don't want to marry me."

"But it's not you—I don't think. It's marriage. In general. I don't think it's for me."

"What we have is not enough," he said.

"Why?"

"You don't love me enough."

"I've never loved anyone before. I don't know what enough is."

"It's not enough."

"According to who?"

"You're the first one I want to talk to when anything happens," he said.

"I know," I said. "I appreciate that."

"When Nate left, you didn't call."

"I didn't call anyone."

"Did you even think of calling me?"

I couldn't answer. I thought of Byron, Sabine, of Enid for a minute, of Nate of course. Nate was the one I wanted to call, but I didn't think of Frank until he showed up.

"It hurts too much," he said. "When you look at me like you don't want to be with me, like you're not excited to see me, like you want to kill me sometimes."

"Isn't that what marriage is?"

"No," he said. "That's not what it's supposed to be. It's not supposed to sting when you see someone, like you're not good enough."

"No, that's not what I mean for it to seem like, Frank. That's never what I wanted."

"Well, maybe you can't help it, but that's how it feels."

"I'm sorry," I said.

His face tensed, and he reached into the drawer inside his desk. For a moment I panicked: Was he going to pull a gun, or a rock to throw at my head?

It was a folded piece of paper, just like his proposal note, which I realized then that I would never have the chance to hear.

He cleared his throat and began to read.

"'Are you sorry for how much you hurt me? Or are you sorry for never giving us a chance?'"

"When did you write that?"

"'Are you sorry because it means you won't get more coffee?'"

"Was I supposed to say I was sorry again?"

It was starting to hit me—hard. I had gone in knowing this was inevitable, but I didn't know how it would feel. My eyes were filling. I couldn't contain them.

"'Are you sorry because I loved you every day, and you never loved me?'"

"Who wrote this? Did your mom say that?"

"'Are you sorry because you couldn't say no? Or are you sorry because you ever said yes?'"

"I'm sorry," I said, tears streaming out.

I hadn't cried in ages. Weepiness from the stints of depression, but not real tears of pain. Not at Dad's funeral. Not when Nate left. Not since Mom had died. But this time, I let it go—all of it—because I knew we were over.

"You can keep the ring," he said. "My mom wanted it back, but I told her I got it for you."

"I never asked for it," I said. "I don't want it."

He looked down.

"I don't know what else I'm supposed to say now," I said.

I took a deep breath and used the back of my sleeve to wipe my face. "I don't know why I can't force those feelings. But I know I don't want to say goodbye."

"The ring is yours," he said.

"No," I said. "Forget the ring!"

I wanted to throw it at him, but of course it wouldn't slide off.

I went into the bathroom and used the soap and water to loosen the grip. *Don't fall in the drain. Don't let this be tragic. Don't give his mom another reason to hate me. Just let this be painless and easy and*—it was off without a fight. That had to mean something.

I washed my face and inhaled deeply. Then I brought it to him wrapped in tissue.

"Here," I said, placing it on his desk.

When I gave it back, I had hoped to feel lighter, but I only felt sicker. This pain was physical. My stomach ached, and my throat was closing in.

I'd never had the chance to say goodbye to anyone who mattered.

"Can I sit down?" I said. "I can't stand right now."

"Okay," he said.

I was supposed to be hungry, but I didn't feel like eating anymore. I thought of the coffee, all the time we spent together, Enid, how all of it would be lost.

"Can I still visit the shop?" I said. "Sometimes?"

He looked away, his ears crimson. "I think that would be confusing."

There was a tightening in my chest, and then another wave of nausea. "I feel sick."

His eyes were red. I could see that, though he refused to make eye contact. He kept touching his nose, and when he turned his back on me to reach for the tissues, I could almost feel the hole inside me expanding, breaking through the seams, all the extra tears pooling in the void inside.

"I guess you want me to go," I said.

He opened the door for me. "I never wanted you to go."

I could tell he wanted to hug me, but leaving first was easier. As I made my way through the threshold, I almost bumped my elbow against the lock, but I pulled it back in time, managing to just skim it.

I decided to walk home.

The streets were so muted somehow. There was space all around me, but all around me, it was empty.

FOR A DAY, or two, or three, I stayed with Harry on the couch, staring into the darkness, drifting in and out of sleep. I ate a little bit, but I wasn't very hungry.

I couldn't move. Except from my bed to Nate's bed because he wasn't using it—he wasn't coming back, I was sure—and it allowed me to sleep for longer. I hid in the corner and faced the wall for hours upon hours. Stared and drifted in and out of consciousness.

Slowly, I felt myself slipping past the fringes of sanity, into the darkest reaches of impulses. I could drink some of that cleaner beneath the counter, or take too many pills. That would be easiest. If I could sleep for long enough, I'd be able to stop crying. I could find some relief, and possibly even find my parents. If I believed in that stuff. It was probably best for everyone.

I gathered enough strength to make my way to the kitchen.

I picked up the bottle and considered it, and then I heard a noise.

"Harry? Is that you?"

He didn't come out.

"Where are you? If that's a mouse, you're supposed to scare him away, your one household duty?"

Harry was next to me. I touched his back. "Harry, go get the mouse."

He didn't move.

I heard the noise again, closer this time. There was some creaking of the floor, rustling, shuffling, or shifting.

Who was there? A chill bristled past my skin. Every hair was on end.

"Byron?"

No answer. It had to be a mouse. Better a mouse than a roach. Or maybe it was just the furnace. In August. Or the neighbors making noise through the walls. Because there were no such things as monsters, or robbers. That only happened in the tabloids, and in my mind.

This was stupid anyway, all this guessing.

"Go ahead," I said. "Do what you will."

I looked up.

The pills spilled from the counter and scattered across the floor. Did I do that?

A faint shadow shifted past, and I smelled a slight whiff of perfume. I could feel her. Something big. A presence.

"Mom," I said. "Can you hear me?"

Nate hadn't been able to talk to her either; that's what he said. I needed to tell him, to let him know she was here. I thought she was. He needed to come back so he could see we weren't crazy.

"Nate?"

There was no response.

"Mom?"

For a second I almost thought I felt a warm spot on my shoulder. A whisper, a hiss so soft it could have been the wind. *"Thissss . . ."*

"This what?" I said.

And then she was gone.

This apartment, this situation, this life? Or—

A hackneyed phrase. A boring platitude. An important message. Maybe it was all the same.

This too shall pass. It was her go-to phrase when nothing else was working, when she was exhausted from comforting us, when there wasn't anything left to say.

Mom and Dad used it like a one-two punch—Mom with the phrase, Dad with the explanation—a rare synchronous effort.

So maybe this was synchronicity. Maybe both of them were there, in that moment, to force me off the pills and off the couch.

I began to draw.

Maybe. But probably, and like each time before, she hadn't actually said anything. If she had, I doubted she'd waste her word to start a cliché.

And yet one thing I was certain of: Something or someone or some presence had been there. I could still almost feel it. The phrase had worked its magic, and then the moment was gone. There was only silence after that, not even a squeak from the pipes.

30

IN THE MORNING, I FELT A CERTAIN LIGHTNESS—AS THOUGH I had been holding my breath for weeks, sucking in my stomach to make extra room, and now, suddenly, I was allowed to exhale.

I went into Nate's chest of drawers and began rifling through them. I hadn't done this before because I didn't want to invade his privacy, but I figured he had squandered his rights when he left. If there were more pills in there, I needed to get rid of them before he came back. I needed to start making this space my own.

I didn't find any more baggies, but in the third row of socks, I did find a small treasure chest: three rolls of quarters. Not only could I use the socks to buy more time before I'd have to do laundry, but with the detergent I had found earlier, I was equipped now to actually do laundry, assuming I could figure out how to do it. I also found two pens and a third of a bottle of cologne. And something else, too. A watch.

It wasn't his regular watch; that he must have been wearing. It was the watch Mom had given to me in my teens, the same one I had given to Nate after he begged me for it, when

I realized I'd lose it anyway. Apparently he had never lost it. It was Batman: the emblem on the face, watching over the numbers. And it was a symbol, a call to action. I strapped it on and made my way to the door.

OUTSIDE, I took a deep breath and braced myself for the sun. It was a little hot, but I appreciated the warmth on my shoulders and back, like a bear hug.

I had only one necessary appointment: the Polar Circle. When I found the front gate, I went straight to it. All I needed was a glimpse.

Gus must have been having another off day, though, one that made him shun the outside—sun was worse than gloom sometimes; and the people; and the eye contact; and me too, because he didn't feel like communicating. Or doing laps. This was a day when he didn't even feel up to his neuroses.

As a cloud cover drifted in, I wandered around the Children's Zoo and visited with the Alpaca (*"Alpaca my bags,"* I could hear Dad say); watched the kids play with the goats, sheep, cows, and pigs; and thought of our times at the Nature Center. I could feel Dad limping beside me as I remembered that once I had thought about working with kids. That had seemed so long ago, considering how loud they were here, how they kept hogging face time with the animals, the best spots in front of the fence, the crayons at the arts-and-crafts station. They could have their zoo. I only wanted Gus.

When I went back to look for him, it started to drizzle. And still, he was under cover somewhere, out of sight.

Then the rain came, and the burst of a storm. I was drenched, and he hadn't moved.

But just as I was about to leave, it was as if he could feel me. He emerged, swam close to me, and showed his gums. I took out my sketchbook and found a dry spot beneath a small overhang.

"He smiled at you!" a little girl said. She was about seven, I guessed, though I was bad with ages. Her hair was perfectly arranged in braids, and she was wearing a little white dress. For a second I was distracted by how white it was, how pristine.

But I didn't respond because I was too busy trying to capture Gus. He was pouring onto the page almost as fast as the rain.

The little girl had been watching, and when the showers stopped, and my sketch was done, she was giddy.

"Can I have that?" she said.

"What?" I said.

"That." She pointed at my page. "It's really cute."

"Thanks, but—"

Her eyes were actually sparkling. I couldn't tell if that was from the rain, or if it could have been more than that, something else.

"Are you real?" I said.

"Are you?"

"I don't know," I said. "I think so."

She giggled—a light, squealing flurry that was contagious. When I laughed, she laughed harder.

"How did you draw that?" she said.

"I can show you," I said. "If you want?"

"Yes!"

I tore out a piece of paper and gave her a pencil.

"You start with the shapes, see? Like big ovals and circles. That's basically what he is, when you look at him. And then you try to get inside his head, if you can, to see what's going on underneath."

She nodded and followed my lead. After a few minutes, a woman called out to her.

"There you are!"

It was her mother, a grown version of her child, also wearing white. I wondered how they managed to stay so clean.

"Bleach?" I said.

She didn't hear me.

"Don't run away like that again!" the girl's mother said.

"But Mom, I was just asking—"

"Leave her alone, honey."

She might have thought I was homeless, or crazy, which I probably was, on both counts, in large part, but it didn't matter. I was still absorbed in Gus's glow.

"Mommy, look at what we did!"

The woman glanced in my direction. She looked familiar. I was trying to place her when she caught sight of the sketch.

She gave the drawings a hard, close look.

"You did that?" she said to her daughter.

"Can I keep it?" the girl said to me.

"Sure," I said. "You did it."

"Yours," she said. "Can I have it?"

"That's someone else's work, sweetheart. Don't bother her."

"Motorcycle accident," I said.

"Excuse me?" the mother said.

"Are you the talk-show host?"

She smiled. "I've gotten that before."

It wasn't her. Her bottom teeth were crooked, and she had a few more wrinkles than the woman on TV.

Still, it was difficult not to see this as another sign.

"Here," I said to the little girl, handing her my Gus. "Take it."

"Say thank you, honey!"

"Thank you, honey!" the little girl said to me, giggling again.

And then she was gone, disappearing with her mother into the mist.

As I let the rain wash over me, something else came over me, this sudden flood of confidence. I was going to march over to the first zoo-attire-outfitted person I saw. He was a large man, so tall that I actually had to look up to him, but I didn't care. I was high off of Gus's vibrations. I was going to ask him how to work there—if he wasn't so scary-looking.

I would ask the second person I saw.

"Excuse me?" I said to a woman with her back to me.

When she turned around, I realized it was Sally, the same khaki-clad worker I'd seen the first day I visited Gus on my own.

"You did a great job with that little girl," she said.

"You saw that?"

"Her mother pointed you out. They come here two to three times a week."

"I hope I didn't scare them off."

She laughed. I liked her. Her glasses were round and thick, her stringy curls were in her face, and she didn't care how loud she was.

"I remember you," she said.

The first time I'd met her it was dusk, and she seemed tired, but now, in the daylight, bouncing among the people, between the cages, she seemed so much more alive.

"You knew all about the pigment in the bear coat," she said. "I never forget a face."

"Me either," I said. "But I'm not as good with names."

"What is your name?" she said.

"Oh, right. It's Lucy."

"Lucy," she said. "Have you ever considered volunteering?"

"Seriously?"

"I know. Working for free sounds ridiculous to some, but I'd pay any day for the pleasure of being around these animals."

"Me too," I said. "I already spend all my money here. You get to come here for free whenever you want?"

"All that and a free shirt!" she said. She laughed again. "There are different levels of commitment, depending on your interests and openness to education."

"I'm interested," I said. "And open."

She took out a piece of paper and wrote her full name on it, with a number of the volunteer line at the zoo and an email address.

"Send your application to my attention. Don't forget to mention both your knowledge and your artistic skill. If it's up to standard, you'll make it through the first round. Then you'll have to interview, and I can't guarantee anything, but this should give you a way in."

I thought of windows and doors and Mom and Dad and light.

"Is this a dream?" I said.

She examined me for a second. "You're funny," she said, without laughing. She was serious about volunteering.

The first person I wanted to tell was Enid, but I knew before we could have any kind of real conversation, I'd have to finish Belle.

WHEN I GOT BACK to the apartment and reexamined the work I'd done on Belle, all I could see was an incompetent version of a cartoon, a poor imitation of something that was artificial to begin with. It must have been the negative influence of the wall paintings, or the fact that I never had the chance to meet the dog. That showed in the eyes, which were vacant, and nowhere close to finished.

There was a chance the nose could be reclaimed, half a paw. The pad on one paw looked okay in one of the earlier sketches. I could layer in different kinds of paints to conceal the absence—everywhere. Or maybe I could try to start over.

Maybe then I could finish.

I found my pencils between the forks and knives in the kitchen. And once I located my sharpener in a bag under the bed, I began to peel away the dull edges. I had pulled an all-nighter once trying to finish a poster-board project in school. I could do it again.

In the morning, there was no time to waste.

It had been almost two weeks, and that was a lot when you were old. I hoped she was the same Enid, and that she wouldn't mind seeing me, that she might even be pleasantly surprised.

She had mentioned the coffee shop four blocks down, the one that served cheaper java. I had seen it once, so I knew I could find it again. I was prepared to camp out and wait there for her return—for hours, or days, or however long it took.

The other coffee shop was not as appealing as Frank's. It didn't have as much light, or space or warmth. The middle-aged woman working the old-fashioned register did not acknowledge me when I walked in. Her face was craggy, and her build was sturdy enough to match the hard linoleum counter. She was all business, taking money quickly, ringing up orders, and working on whatever tasks she was working on.

I was a little nervous to see Enid again. I wanted to make a good impression.

"Where's your bathroom?" I said to the woman at the register.

It was clear that she didn't want to answer.

I pulled out the roll of quarters I had found. "I'll have a coffee. And a pastry, too. One of those poppy-seed things?"

"Pirozhki," she said.

And then she pointed to the restroom in the back.

When I looked at myself in the mirror, I was grateful I had remembered a hat. At least I didn't have to worry about my hair. I washed the sweat off of my face and applied lipstick, hoping if nothing else that she would appreciate the gesture.

The seats here were scratchy and wobbly, and the walls were dull and stark. This establishment did not offer cappuccino heart-foam drinks or fancy blends from disparate regions around the world. There were only two choices: regular or decaf. And there was only one type of creamer and one choice for milk.

But the coffee itself was excellent—hot and strong.

I sat at a table, and I tried, and I tried, and I tried to look at that portrait of Enid's dog from every direction, to make sense of her, and bring her back to life based on all of the images of spaniel mutt mixes I'd ever collected, all of the speculating I'd done, all of the conversations with Enid. But without meeting Belle, the picture remained only a picture, a surface image of a being I could only imagine.

After a while, I tried instead to focus on her owner.

Superoldwoman, older than anyone cared to guess, impossible to pin down. Armed with the enduring spirit of her sidekick Belle, fistfuls of energy, and her green-tea elixir, she was capable of accomplishing any task, no matter how small.

Three cups later, I was on a roll. I was so immersed in the work I was doing I forgot I had been waiting for Enid, and when she finally appeared a couple of hours after I'd first entered, she nearly fell over.

"Well, well," she said. "What the hell are you doing here? Scoping out the competition?"

"I was looking for you," I said.

"What for?" she said, joining me at my table.

I swallowed my last sip of coffee.

"Oh," she said, glancing at my fingers. "You changed your mind."

"Kind of," I said. "Or he did. I'm still not really sure. Wait, how did you know? It happened so fast."

She shrugged. "It's a small coffee shop, and there's always a story. Are you ready to work now?"

It was the best thing she could have said.

"I've been working," I said. "Really hard. Though it's not exactly what you asked for."

"Just let me see," she said.

"It's not done yet," I said. "I can change it back if you want. But I got inspired in a different direction so—"

"Lucy," she said in her most serious voice.

She didn't have to say anything else. I handed it to her cautiously, to make sure it wouldn't tear.

She slapped it on the table and began to stare, grazing her fingers over the corners and edges, smudging pieces of sky as she went. She examined the whole thing, section by section, without revealing a single expression.

I couldn't take it. I got up and told her I had to go to the bathroom, which I did, and I stayed for too long, lingering over the sink, washing my inky hands.

When I mustered the nerve to return to the table, I took a heavy breath and confronted her: "I tried, okay? I'm sorry if it's not up to your standard, but—"

"Stop apologizing already," she said, finally looking up. "It's not what I asked for."

"I know."

"But it's not bad either."

"Really?"

"My nose is too big."

"It's for dramatic effect. Heightened senses?"

"And where's my hair?"

"It's not done yet."

She nodded and made eye contact. For a second it was like she was looking inside of me. "I'm sorry it didn't work out with Frank."

She had never held my gaze for this long.

"Thanks," I said. "I guess that's what I'm supposed to say."

"The good news is that now that the Frank business is over, you can get busy doing the important business. You finally got the portrait done. In your own way, but it still counts. Who knows what else you're capable of."

"Actually, I think I'm supposed to go back to the zoo," I said. "I think I might have dreamt it."

I told her how Dad had mentioned volunteering at the Nature Center, ages ago it had seemed, and then recounted the story of Gus and the girl in white. And the connection to the talk-show host who volunteered with the animals. And Sally. It all felt associated, but it still didn't feel real.

"Well, you're the one who's always talking about signs and spirits and all that other jazz," she said. "What more do you want?"

"Will you go with me?"

"To the zoo?"

"If you'd be willing. I want you to see. You can tell me if I'm crazy."

"I don't have to go to the zoo to tell you that," she said. "But I did always like the penguins. Do they still have penguins?"

"We can start with the penguins," I said.

"Fine," she said. "I'll be at the front gate at ten."

"Eleven?"

"Ten thirty, but I'm not waiting past ten thirty-five. No excuses."

31

"TEN THIRTY-TWO," ENID SAID WHEN I ARRIVED AT THE GATE. "Not bad."

"What, you didn't think I'd make it?" I said. "I set my alarm. Four times. I figured out how to do that. Aren't you proud of me?"

"I already got the tickets," she said. "Ten percent off when you buy online, and I bought two senior ones, so pretend you're old when you walk through."

"You bought my ticket?" I said.

"Just keep your head down," she said.

As promised, we started with the penguins, and as soon as we came within eye level, I started talking.

"Did you know they're black and white like that to camouflage themselves—above and below water? They can swim twenty miles per hour. They can actually see underwater. They have to be able to do that—to eat. They're hunters. I guess they don't have to hunt here, but they have it in their blood, the killer instinct."

"You have to work here," she said. "I hope you know that."

"Right. I'd like to, but they probably wouldn't take me."

She shook her head.

"What?" I said.

"You know every cockamamie story about every animal in here. Why the hell wouldn't they take you?"

"Maybe they would," I said.

"They'd be stupid not to," Enid said.

"You're right."

"Of course I am! So draw me a penguin, will you?"

"Here?" I said.

"Where else? What am I doing here if not here?"

"Now?"

"I'm not planning on staying all day," she said.

I took out my sketchbook, I took a seat at the back, and I took a serious approach. It was hard at first, because it was a little dark in there, and I didn't like the idea of her watching me. But then I found my penguin.

I tuned out everyone else as I tracked this one little waddler trying to find his way toward the group. They were social, these guys, always traveling in packs, but this one seemed a little outside the intimate circle; he kept trying to catch up and force his way back in.

"Now, that's something," Enid said before I was finished.

I tore out the paper and handed it to her.

"Take it," I said. "I mean, if you want it."

"Don't you want it?"

"I want you to have it. I think it will go well with Belle."

ENID AND I both noticed the coffee cart the moment we stepped outside. We ordered lattes, found spots on a bench, and took sips slowly, as if to savor the moment. I was expecting something sweet, like victory.

"It's terrible," Enid said before I could.

"I can't believe I wasted five dollars on this," I said. "Though if I volunteered here, I bet I'd get a discount."

"I bet you would," she said.

She pushed a big paper bag toward me.

"What is this?" I said. "You're not giving me your valuables, are you? Because I'll lose them."

"Just look inside."

It was a calendar sponsored by the Wildlife Conservation Society, and it was glossy, vivid, and beautiful.

"You said you used to have one on your icebox," she said. "I got it in the mail because I donated once a few years back. I thought you'd like the pictures."

She'd written a note on the bottom too. *Call if you need someone.* She scrawled out her number and address.

"It's perfect," I said. "I can put it up when I get home."

I examined the address. It was only a few blocks from Nate's place.

"You know, you live pretty close to me," I said. "I think it's probably like a ten-minute walk, maybe less?"

"Well, I assumed you lived in the neighborhood."

"You ever think I could see your home?"

"What for?" she said. "There's nothing to see."

"Right," I said, pretending to focus on a red panda. "It was a stupid thought."

She took a second.

"Oh, all right," she said finally. "Maybe one day."

"Like one day next week?"

"Maybe. I was thinking about getting a new companion. You could probably help me decide on a breed."

"Is that an invitation?"

"No, that's not an invitation. But you do have a calendar in front of you, and all of your days appear to be wide open. So when would you like to come?"

"How about Wednesday?"

"Fine."

"It looks like I have an opening at noon," I said.

"That's lunchtime," she said. "You expect me to feed you?"

"No, I'll bring coffee."

"I have perfectly good coffee at my place."

"Then I'll bring milk. Can I write it down? Our date, so I won't forget?"

She handed me a pen.

"Now." She took out a tiny leather address book embossed with silver. "I need your information."

I looked at her.

"Don't get sentimental," she said. "I need to know how to get a hold of you in case you stand me up."

On our way out, we stopped by to see Gus. I could never go to the zoo without at least trying to see him.

We waited for a few minutes, but as soon as we made it to the window I knew he wasn't going to come out that day. Somewhere in my bones, I could feel him retreating.

"Oh well," Enid said. "I guess he can't bear to see us."

I looked at her. "I've never heard you pun before."

"Must be something about this place," she said.

I HAD LEFT THE PARK that day feeling pretty good, but after I got home, that night, I felt sick. It wasn't the regular kind of nausea from too much coffee or chocolate or time on the subway or in the sun. It was something else, like something was wrong. I feared for Nate, convinced it was him calling out to me.

Slowly, cautiously, I turned on the news.

There was Gus, a vintage video of him doing his laps, the mass of white fur pushing against the wall, giant paw pads skimming the surface.

A beloved icon of Central Park was lost today.

No.

Inoperable tumor . . .

I was listening, but not really. I couldn't hear what the anchor was saying. I couldn't let myself.

Twenty-seven years old . . .

Lightheaded.

Euthanized.

I had to lie down.

There was just one bear left now, in the Bronx Zoo, but Gus, my Gus, was gone.

No.

The TV offered some comfort. I didn't dare turn it off. I watched without watching, trying to clear my mind of any thoughts.

Hours later, Enid called.

"I heard about the bear," she said.

I didn't feel like talking about it.

"You have to go back there," she said.

"I can't," I said.

"You have to," she said. "If you don't go now—"

"Maybe later" was all I could promise.

"You'll go tomorrow," she said.

I didn't answer.

"You can't give yourself a choice here," Enid said. "There is no choice."

"Tomorrow," I said eventually, because I knew she was right.

That night, I dreamt of Gus. He had battled through anxiety in the pool, had struggled through depression after the death of his companion, Ida, had beat the typical life expectancy of twenty years in captivity.

He had never given up.

THERE WAS NO NEED to go anywhere else the next day besides the Polar Circle. I wasn't sure what I was expecting to find, but it was like I was being summoned, a gravitational pull to a sacred citadel.

As soon as I reached my favorite bench, I noticed a portrait of Gus. I stared at it for a long time, the way it perfectly captured his eyes, his smile, his depth.

I took out my book, hoping to try to reproduce the magic of the image, but before I knew it, Gus was pouring onto my page. His face, his paws, his fur.

Gus was an angel at peace; he was a young cub playing in his pool; he was a shadow cast over the zoo.

He was a friend and companion.

He was in the trees, and the sky, in the clouds, in the sun, in the earth.

He was in the water, in the empty tank, in the ice.

He was in the sea lions, the red panda, the snow monkey, and the snow leopard.

He was in the birds and the bats, the penguins, and the snakes.

He was with the zookeepers and the visitors, inside their baseball caps and baby strollers.

He was everywhere.

I rolled up my sleeves and went at it. I must have done about fifteen sketches of him without ever leaving my spot. Page after page, I drew.

Maybe he was with Mom now, or Dad, or both.

Maybe he was Dad, or Nate, or me.

Maybe I was officially losing my mind, but all of it was good for the art.

I would finish a sketch, tear it out, and put it beside me. Then I'd go again.

It was like a cleansing, a purging of all the images I needed to empty from my brain.

When I was done, I left a few sketches on the bench, a tribute to all Gus had inspired, and said goodbye.

THAT NIGHT, I pulled up the volunteer application, and I stared at it for hours.

Why did I want to do this? The whole thing seemed futile. I had nothing to write.

But then I reviewed all of the sketches I had done, and all at once I could feel Gus coursing through me. I was destined for this position since that first day I met him. The zoo held magic and power. It was a sanctuary and a haven, not just for animals but also for people who needed animals. I needed this job. There were no other options.

I could envision myself in one of those shirts, interacting

with kids one-on-one, educating the masses with obscure facts. And I could see myself sketching on my favorite bench in all of my free time, channeling the wishes and dreams of the animals.

I was finally ready to work.

32

IT WAS THREE DAYS LATER THAT I HEARD THE DOOR.

I wasn't sure what time it was. I had passed out early the night before, so I figured it might still be nighttime when the lock rattled.

I braced myself for a burglar, and for a fleeting second, I wondered if I had given Frank a key, or Enid, and then—if Mom had learned to move objects. I had almost forgotten it could be anyone else.

But then he emerged, a shadowy figure standing in the doorway.

For a split second, I didn't recognize him.

"Byron?"

It was Nate.

Harry sprung to the door as I scrambled to find pants.

"Did I wake you?" he said.

"No, I was just—resting," I called as I stumbled toward the bathroom, where I splashed water on my face to force consciousness.

When I was standing before him, he went in for a hug.

We hadn't seen each other in about three weeks, so this was an understood expectation, what should have been a natural impulse.

Except we still weren't huggers, and it still didn't seem right. He didn't look sick anymore, but he was thin, rubbery almost, as though he could fit between the cracks in the floorboard if I compressed him hard enough. I didn't feel like hugging him.

"I can't believe it's you," I said. "It is you, right? You're here?"

Part of me was afraid to touch him again, concerned that if I did, my hand would move through him.

"Not just a pod, or a vision, or a spirit of you. This is you, you?"

Another part of me wanted to push him—hard. I stood beside him and poked him a little.

"Luce," he said. "It's me. I promise. How are you?"

"I'm not sure."

"It looks like you've been busy," he said.

He nodded at the coffee table. My sketchpad was out, stray fringes of paper creased over the edges.

My face warmed. I didn't have time to organize my things. He didn't have the context to appreciate what I had been doing.

"The place looks clean," he said. "Did you do this?"

"Byron got someone to do it, but I've tried to keep it neat the past few days. It's not bad, right?"

"Not at all," he said.

"Where were you? Or, wait. Are you not supposed to tell me anything? If I ask you things, will you run away again?"

"I never ran away," he said.

He walked over to the window and stayed there for a while, taking in the outside. Did it smother him to see these things again—the same construction, storefronts, street vendors, scuff in the bottom-left pane? Grimy with residue and weather changes, bird droppings that had appeared and gone and reappeared in his absence. Or was he relieved by the familiarity?

Home. Sort of.

"So that's it?" I said. "That's all you're going to say?"

"No, that's not it. But I can't say it all at once, so can we sit down first? Have some tea and hang out a little?"

His lips were chapped, the corners of his mouth white, an old man's mouth.

"I have water," I said.

I went to the kitchen and filled a mug from the sink.

"I know you like tea," I said. "If I had known you were coming, I could have saved you some. But of course you didn't tell me you were coming. Unless I missed a message, or my phone broke, but you don't leave messages. We used to have tea. Well, you did. I drank it all. Or Frank did."

I handed him the cleanest cup I could find. "It's chipped, but it shouldn't be toxic. It doesn't have that warning."

"Thanks," he said.

He shot a quick look at the alcove. He might have seen some of my stuff beyond the wall.

"You can have it back," I said.

"No," he said. "It's yours now."

He pulled a pack of cigarettes from his pocket and took back his spot by the window.

"You smoke?" I said.

"Just for today."

"That many in a day?"

"I'm quitting," he said. "After today."

"Good. They're disgusting."

"They are," he said, lighting up like he had been doing it his whole life.

Then he looked at me, closely, as though he were seeing me for the first time.

"You look good," he said. "Did you get a haircut?"

Enid had insisted I wash it each time I left the house. She said a hat was not the same as an excuse.

"I guess I've been wearing it a little differently lately. Enid said—"

"Who's Enid?"

He didn't even know who Enid was.

As I tucked the front strand behind my ear, he inspected my hand.

"No ring?"

"I didn't lose it," I said, flexing my fingers to find the right one. I could hardly remember what it felt like.

"So you said no."

"No, I said yes."

"Well, I didn't miss the wedding, did I? Or the divorce?"

"No."

"Then when is it?"

"There is no wedding." It was louder than I expected. "I have to make coffee now. My head hurts. It's weird that you're here and you don't know so much. I'm tired."

"Need a hand?" he said.

"No, I can do it. You want some?"

"No thanks," he said. "I'm off of it."

"That's depressing," I said. "That's the last thing I'd give up."

"So what happened with Frank?" he said, following me into the kitchen.

"Nothing really. I mean he's fine. Not like he died or something. He's just out—of my life. We're not together. I gave the ring back."

"Are you okay?" he said. "He didn't hurt you, did he?"

"No, nothing like that. Not intentionally anyway. He wouldn't know how to do that. I mean he's a great guy, but— I didn't want to marry him. That's all. He wasn't the right person—for me. For someone else, he'd be great. I'm fine now."

My stomach was tight even then as I listened for the crackle of the machine and waited for the warm notes of roasted nuts and cocoa. I wanted to dive inside the pot.

"You want to talk about it?" he said.

"Coffee?"

"Frank."

"Frank?" I said. "I'm over Frank."

I was tired of thinking about it, and I didn't appreciate all the questions all of a sudden, like I was the one who had things to explain.

I had to get away from him.

"I need to sit," I said.

I filled my mug and headed back to the couch.

"Are you ready to talk about you?" I said. "Because I am."

I gulped down my coffee and pills, and he resumed his place by the window.

It took him a minute before he started.

"I was never planning on going anywhere," he said.

He locked my gaze so I knew he was serious. I couldn't take his eyes. They were so dark, and pleading.

"Sure," I said, looking away.

"And I never really left you either."

"You didn't?"

Now he was looking out the window again.

"Because it definitely felt like you did. It definitely felt like just one phone call and one note and that was it. Everyone assumed you were gone."

"Who's everyone?"

"Everyone! Harry, Frank, Enid."

"Who?"

"Nate."

"I know," he said. "I should have called more. I just felt so much worse after I talked to you."

"Why'd you come back then? Do you want me to leave? I can go this time if you want."

I grabbed Harry, refilled my mug, and lurched toward the door.

I spilled a little as I went, but I didn't fall.

I was halfway down the hallway when he called after me.

"Please, Lucy."

I stopped walking and turned around, but I didn't move.

"You're the one who left!" I said.

Harry wriggled out of my arms and snuck back inside.

"But I'm back now."

"You didn't even try to stick me in a home."

"Because you didn't need a home," he said, in his irritating calm. "You never needed that. Come inside."

I didn't say anything for a minute. I didn't want to leave, but I didn't want to be near him either. I wanted to stay exactly where I was.

"I was an asshole," he said. "I felt like such an asshole that when I heard your voice, it was like—I couldn't breathe. Like my whole chest was caving in. And then I felt like a bigger asshole. So I couldn't do it. No matter how I approached it, or tried to rationalize it and reason my way out of it, I couldn't call. I picked up the phone so many times. So many times, but after a while—it just felt like too much."

"I was the one in the dark, Nate, and it was really dark here. Black sometimes."

He took a moment to compose his thoughts.

"It was only a few weeks," he said.

"It felt like more."

"I knew you had your pills and that the bills were paid. And I made sure Byron was around if you needed him. Plus, shit, Luce, I thought you were getting married!"

"You told me not to marry him."

"I didn't say that."

I sat down in the middle of the hallway and leaned against the concrete.

He squatted next to me, and I looked at him. He was genuine. I could see that, but—I turned away from him. "I want to sit here alone, okay?"

"Okay," he said. "I'll be inside."

I'm not sure how long I was out there. It could have been twenty minutes; it could have been two hours. It was confusing, all these emotions churning together—relief on some level to see him, excitement even, euphoria. I couldn't wait to tell him all that had happened. But there was also uncertainty, aching, maybe a little dread.

After some time passed, he came out holding an offering, a brown box.

"It's fudge. I met this guy who makes it custom, and of course I thought of you. I know it's not coffee, but . . ."

I appreciated that he didn't say anything else. He just left me with the box, and for a second I thought, I could go now. For a night or two nights. I could wander with this fudge.

But I was exhausted, and my back was starting to hurt, and it was so much easier to just go back inside.

"I'D REALLY LIKE TO KNOW what happened," I said.

I took a seat on the far end of the cushions, though there wasn't much room between us no matter how I positioned myself.

He took a deep breath and cracked his knuckles. "It started when I saw her."

"Who?"

"Mom."

He pointed toward the closet area.

"She was there, in the shadows."

"Like a flash in the corner of your eye?"

"You saw her again too."

"I'm pretty sure," I said. "It seemed like her. When was this?"

"I don't remember exactly. It was a rough night, really fuzzy, but it all kind of went downhill after that."

He finished his cigarette and lit another one.

"Before I saw her, I poured myself a scotch to help me sleep."

"I thought you drank beer."

"Beer wasn't strong enough," he said. "This went down so easy, Dad's drink. I could almost smell it on his breath. For a minute, I felt a calm, like the kind that comes after the snow, when it's just you and the crunching, and the wind across the powder. You know what I'm talking about?"

It was the peace Mom had given me.

"I think so," I said.

He took a drag.

"I couldn't sleep, so I kept promising one more shot. Just one more shot, and I'd pass out and be fine. But I was still awake, so I had another one and then another."

He was the one who kept all of his emotions inside, smothered them until they fed on his fat cells, his muscle, his hair. I imagined him standing in the middle of a shower, water washing over him, draining away all of the skin and bone and blood, his center, his spine, and I wished I could have been there to hold on to some of it, to stop it up and stuff it back into place.

"I was eating cake," I said. "I could have been here."

"It wouldn't have mattered," he said. "I was messed up way before that. I remember seeing the bottle, almost empty, and thinking, Shit, I shouldn't have had that much. Then, it was like as soon as I realized it, I looked up. And there she was. Of course she didn't talk, but I almost thought I heard her whisper. Something."

"Like a whistle," I said.

"Yes," he said, dragging out the s for an extra second.

"She was trying to save you," I said. "Without her you could've died of alcohol poisoning, or—I don't know, something else."

"Maybe, but I was pissed at her then for leaving so fast. "

"Maybe she didn't. Maybe she's here now."

We both paused to look around the room. He slowly made his way toward the closet and peeked inside. There was nothing.

"You see her all the time?" he said.

"I'm starting to think it's only we're really desperate, when she's afraid we're going to die."

"It's a nice thought," he said. "Though at the time it seemed like she was trying to kill me. When I reached out for her, I lost my balance and banged my head on the corner of the cabinet."

He gestured toward the front of his scalp. "Nine stitches."

"That happened when you were little too. I remember that."

"It was my chin that time," he said.

He ran his fingertips over the scruff to feel for the scar.

"I figured I'd go home and sleep it off. But when they asked how it happened, I couldn't explain."

He started walking around the room as if re-piecing the fragments of the night.

"I was confused and drunk, so they kept me around for observation, and along the way, they did some blood work and saw all the other toxins in my system."

"My old pills."

He sighed. "You figured it out."

"I know pills," I said. "I'm not dumb."

"No," he said. "But I was sneaky."

"I should have figured it out sooner."

"How? It's not like I planned it. I thought I was just using enough to get through each day. They wanted me to stay, but I didn't care. I was still going to go back to the apartment and crash, but when I thought about what I was going back to—"

"Me."

"No, not you," he said. "No Sabine, no money, no plan. A shitty job, a ghost, a dark apartment, cat hair. I couldn't do it. I was suffocating. All I could think about was getting out."

"Grieving," I said.

He stopped pacing.

"Just enough time to get back on track, and then I was supposed to get back to work, but I knew that if I did—I worried I'd end up in the same place."

"You could've called more."

He wiped his eye.

I looked outside.

It might have been a real tear.

I sort of wanted to hug him then, but he was too far away.

"But look at you now!" he said. "I mean, shit, Byron said you were stronger. He always said that, his stupid thing about glass, but—I see it now. You're different."

"Yeah, well thanks, I guess. I do feel kind of different, in a way. Older maybe. But it's not like I miraculously transformed. Don't expect me to go work on Wall Street or keep the place spotless or anything. I just kind of figured out what I was supposed to do—I think. But I'm still not like you."

"Thankfully."

———

A LITTLE LATER, I moved so we were sitting together on the cushions. At first it was strange to be so near to him, so I could almost feel his leg hairs, so little space, so few words. But I didn't shift from my spot, and neither did he.

I looked at his bag on the floor and back at him.

"So what now?" I said.

"Are you hungry?"

"I ate fudge," I said. "Are you staying?"

"If that works for you," he said. "I was thinking I could take some classes again, figure out a way to slow down. I talked to some people at school. There are scholarships out there, different loan options. We'll have to start over, but it looks like they're willing to work with me."

"That's great," I said. "You can fill up your cereal container."

"Exactly."

"And I won't cost as much," I said. "The zoo will be free, if I can get this position, which I think I will, and I'll be busy with Enid. And I'll have my disability checks and insurance. So you don't have to worry about me."

"You don't have to worry about me either."

He put out his last cigarette and put up his feet.

We stayed close, just staring in silence, almost like we were waiting for Mom to reappear.

After a while, when she didn't, I opened my sketchbook and started thumbing through it. There were sticky notes on a few of the loose pages.

"What are these?" I said. "Who did this?"

"I did, when you were in the hallway," he said. "I tagged the ones I thought would really pop."

I examined his face. No signs of ridicule or condescension.

"What?" he said. "Have you noticed there's nothing on the walls? We can't live in a home with nothing on the walls."

"I put a calendar on the fridge," I said. "You can feel free to put stuff on it if you want."

"Thanks," he said.

Then he turned on the TV, and somehow amid all of the fuzz, he landed on one of the old kitschy superhero shows, one we both knew by heart. He knew not to change the channel.

As long as we watched, there was no need to say anything else.

ACKNOWLEDGMENTS

MY GREATEST THANKS to everyone at W. W. Norton who helped bring this book into the world, especially my editor, Jill Bialosky, for thoughtful insights and invaluable feedback, for asking the most difficult questions at the right times, and for continually pushing the story in the right direction.

I am so grateful to my agent, Molly Friedrich, who guided me through this process with exceptional humor, wisdom, and honesty. Thanks, too, to Lucy Carson, who provided useful perspective when I needed it, and to the rest of the team at the Friedrich agency, for their tireless assistance along the way.

This novel might never have evolved beyond scattered thoughts had I not received guidance from outstanding teachers and peers at Columbia University. My thanks to Binnie Kirshenbaum (and the whole of our thesis workshop), Sam Lipsyte, Rene Steinke, Aaron Hamburger, Jennifer Epstein, and Joanna Hershon for providing especially perceptive comments. To Clare Beams, Helene Wecker, Kara Levy, and Ashley Murray for overall support, friendship, and kinship from the start. And to Ruth Galm, for always getting it, on every level.

I am indebted to Jessica Tuccelli for wonderful advice at a moment's notice. And to Jane Ratcliffe, one of the finest readers I know and the first teacher who ever made me think that I could do this. I'd also like to recognize my friends in San Diego (and elsewhere for that matter) for offering respite from book talk; my colleagues at Francis Parker, for emphasizing the importance of continually learning and growing; and my students, especially my Craft kids, who inspired me more than they realize.

I can't adequately express appreciation to my mother, an expert proofreader, for a lifetime of cheer, care, and compassion. To my dad, who dreamed this before I did. To Tevin, for unqualified friendship and for understanding the big picture. To Bill, because I always want to impress you, and to Sue and Jen, because you're always so encouraging. To Emily, Molly, Abby, Jake, and Dash, because you're all beautiful and amazing and you remind me what matters most. And to Jeremiah, because I am the lucky one—for your genuine love, support, patience, and faith in me.

This book would never have been conceived without my sister Caren, who sketched all of the pictures and whose brain helped inspire Lucy's. I am intrigued, entertained, and awed by you every single day.

ABOUT THE AUTHOR

MICHELLE ADELMAN HAS an MFA in writing from Columbia University and BS and MS degrees in journalism from Northwestern University. She has worked as a magazine writer and an editor, a university instructor, and a high school English teacher and dean. She grew up in Connecticut and has lived in New York, San Diego, and the Bay Area, where she currently resides. *Piece of Mind* is her first novel.

PIECE OF MIND

Michelle Adelman

ABOUT THE BOOK

Lucy, the protagonist of *Piece of Mind*, was initially inspired by my older sister, Caren, who, like Lucy, suffered from a traumatic brain injury at the age of three. Our family didn't specifically discuss the effects of a TBI, and while I had my catalogue of nonscientific observations, it wasn't until I started researching and writing this novel that I began to understand the profound physical and emotional repercussions of this kind of injury—not just on the person impacted, but on all who know her.

When I began the book, I realized I had never encountered anyone quite like Caren—with so much aptitude and intellectual intelligence, yet so many limitations in the organization of her daily life. I wanted to understand and explore this tension on a deeper level, and thus *Piece of Mind* started in many ways as a character study, with the idea of capturing the experiences of my main character through an outside lens. Lucy was a woman who could draw, read, and write with great skill and perception, who could connect to animals on an almost cosmic level, but who lacked simple interpersonal skills and major executive functions. She couldn't follow a schedule, filter her speech, or maintain the cleanliness of any given space. She also found the prospect of a job both daunting and insurmountable. Yet she was funny, compassionate, and richly layered.

As I delved further into her narrative, however, and as Lucy began to evolve on the page, I realized that this was not only the story of a unique individual. Nor was it a story solely for those who had been impacted by brain injury, or by other kinds of disabilities or disadvantages. In fact, all of the characters in this book are flawed and even unhinged by various limitations. This is a story, then, that transcends a singular experience by exploring the complex relationship between siblings, and parents, and different kinds of families; of adapting to new and unfamiliar circumstances; of coming of age and discovering one's identity and purpose; and of trying to fit in and act "normal" without sacrificing individuality.

The more I learned about Lucy's specific experience, the more I understood how relatable she was, and how universal her challenges could be.

DISCUSSION QUESTIONS

1. How is Lucy's relationship with her mother different from her relationship with her father? After their deaths, how do those relationships manifest themselves in Lucy's life?

2. Nate finds himself without parents, unable to afford to stay in school, and suddenly in the role of Lucy's primary caretaker. How does he handle these drastic changes? How does the relationship between Nate and Lucy evolve over the course of the book? What would you have done in his position?

3. Lucy describes her brain as "a pinball machine lit up with pockets of potential" (17). In what ways is this outlook reflected in her actions?

4. Lucy's father makes "to-do" lists for Lucy, but his death throws her into an unexpected situation with more independence and less support. Does this change her goals? How so?

5. Lucy and Frank first meet in a group for people with brain injuries, and later she goes with him to visit his parents. What are the differences between how Frank's parents treat him and how Lucy's parents treated her?

6. Love takes Lucy by surprise. What do you think draws her to Frank? And why does she decide to leave? Do you think Frank was ready to marry her?

7. At first, Nate does not believe that Lucy senses their mother's spirit, but later he has a change of heart. What do you think accounts for this change? What is the role of the supernatural/ extrasensory/religion in the book?

8. Lucy is drawn to Gus, the polar bear at the zoo. Why is she so interested in Gus? What does he represent to her? Why do you think Lucy has a special connection to animals?

9. Drawing a portrait of Enid's dog Belle is very important both to Lucy and to Enid. Why? What role does Enid serve in the story?

10. Holding down a steady job is a challenge for Lucy. At the end of the book, she begins to fill out a volunteer application to work at the zoo, and admits "I was finally ready to work" (297). Do you think her injury was the only thing that hindered her from keeping a job? What do you think will happen after Nate settles back into his life with Lucy?